"What are you suggesting? That we cut right to the divorce?"

Scott nodded. "One incision. Swift. Neat."

Like hammer blows his words penetrated Meg's consciousness. Her throat clogged with sudden tears, and she struggled to keep her voice even. "Is that what you want, Scott?"

Head down, he marched another thirty yards, then stopped and whirled to face her. *"Want?* I'll tell you what I want. I want the girl I married."

Anger replaced shock. "What's that supposed to mean? Am I so awful?"

"You're not awful." His shoulders sagged, and he ran a hand tiredly through his hair. "You're just... different. Meg, we started out with big dreams, and, hey, we've even achieved a lot of them."

"But apparently they didn't buy happiness."

"That doesn't mean they can't, does it?"

"That's up to you," she said.

Laying his hand on her shoulder, he sought her eyes with his. "No, Meg. It takes two of us. But is there any us left?"

Dear Reader,

In most of my previous books, setting has been an important element. I've enjoyed researching various areas of the country and discovering how my characters not only belong in their particular environments but are molded by them.

This story, however, could take place anywhere in suburban America. The landscape is not one made up of mountains and rivers or rolling farmland. Rather, it is the territory of family.

Often when we think of romance, we envision the thrill of attraction and courtship or dewy-eyed newlyweds walking dreamily into an everlasting sunset. Yet the most enduring love stories are not always pretty. Sometimes it is not until a relationship is tested in the crucible of real-life crises that a genuine, lasting understanding of love and commitment is forged. This, then, is a love story that unfolds in the most important place of all—within a marriage.

In *Second Honeymoon*, Meg and Scott Harper are not unlike many of us who face the challenges of work commitments, child rearing, social obligations, community involvement and responsibility for extended family. As life grows more complicated, Scott buries himself in work, Meg devotes herself to their children and, along the way, they forget that marriage is a lifelong effort and that love can never be taken for granted. Bur where there is a spark, there can be fire. I hope you'll enjoy discovering how Scott and Meg learn to tend the flame.

Laura Abbot

P.S. I enjoy hearing reader comments. You may write me at P.O. Box 373, Eureka Springs, AR 72632, or access the Superromance authors' Web site, www.SuperAuthors.com.

SECOND HONEYMOON
Laura Abbot

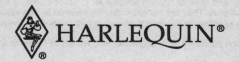

HARLEQUIN®

TORONTO • NEW YORK • LONDON
AMSTERDAM • PARIS • SYDNEY • HAMBURG
STOCKHOLM • ATHENS • TOKYO • MILAN • MADRID
PRAGUE • WARSAW • BUDAPEST • AUCKLAND

ISBN 0-373-78045-1

SECOND HONEYMOON

Books by Laura Abbot

HARLEQUIN SUPERROMANCE

639—MATING FOR LIFE
721—THIS CHRISTMAS
747—WHERE THERE'S SMOKE...
803—CLASS ACT
818—THE WEDDING VOW
843—TRIAL COURTSHIP
937—HOMECOMING
970—A COUNTRY PRACTICE
1059—YOU'RE MY BABY
1101—A SUMMER PLACE
1162—MY NAME IS NELL
1191—THE WRONG MAN

For my tolerant, accepting and loving
daughters-in-law, Lailan and Lynne. Thank you
for being such blessings to me and our family.

CHAPTER ONE

Tulsa, Oklahoma
Early September

WHEN THE AUDITORIUM LIGHTS flickered, Meg Harper twisted around in her seat, scanning the latecomers straggling in the door. Where was Scott? He'd promised her. Promised their son. She glanced at her watch. Two more minutes.

The seat beside her remained conspicuously empty, but what else was new? She watched other children's parents—other children's fathers—scurry to find seats before the program began. Meg faced the front again, her eyes darting to the stage where in a few moments Justin would lead the Pledge of Allegiance. Her manicured nails bit into the flesh of her palms. She didn't ask much of her husband, but Scott should be here supporting his son, and later accompanying her to the classrooms for the middle-school open house.

She craned her neck toward the door again. Her tennis partner, Jannie Farrell, and her lanky, absentminded husband, Ron, scuttled in just as the lights dimmed, leaving behind a deserted lobby. Meg's jaw tightened in anticipation of Scott's apology. *Sorry, babe, something came up at the last minute.* As if his son were a mere afterthought to some business deal. In all honesty, she hadn't expected Scott to show up. But that didn't make her disappointment any less painful or quell the childhood memories of all the times she'd searched the audience for the father she knew would never come, the father buried in the cemetery on the hill.

The balding principal stepped up to the podium, greeted the assembled parents and uttered the usual platitudes about the school year getting off to a great start. When he finished, he introduced Justin, who strutted with his athlete's swagger toward the microphone, his baggy khakis bunching at his ankles, pretty much obscuring the new Nikes he'd insisted on wearing. "Please stand and join me in the Pledge," he croaked into the mike.

As the crowd stood, Meg moved to the left for a clear view of her son, his spiked black hair, so like Scott's, gleaming in the spotlight; his tall, skinny body braced at attention. He looked angelic, a far cry from the mouthy thirteen-year-old who, only an hour ago, had resisted wearing the freshly-ironed dress shirt she'd laid out for him. He'd held it up as if it were some odious life-form. "This is nerdy! I suppose you think I'm wearing a tie, too." After a brief battle, they'd achieved a compromise. The shirt, yes. The tie, no.

Yet watching him now, seriously intoning the Pledge of Allegiance, she could almost believe that one day he'd grow into a responsible young adult.

As the audience sat back down, Meg felt a tap on her shoulder. Her neighbor Carrie Morrison leaned forward. "Justin did great," she whispered. Then came the infuriating question Meg had heard all too often in the past several months: "Where's Scott?"

WHEN SCOTT PULLED his SUV into the garage of their two-story Tudor-style house, he noted Meg's missing Lexus. He slumped over the wheel. Hell. The middle-school open house. He buried his head in his hands, as if that act would both absolve his oversight and wipe away the exhaustion riddling his nerves. It would be only a matter of minutes before

Meg returned and recited the litany of her complaints: his thoughtlessness, his forgetfulness, his self-absorption, his selfish disregard for her, his willingness to sacrifice his family on the altar of his ambition. He'd heard it all. And then some.

What was it about his goals she didn't understand? She had no concept of the pressure he was under at the agency or how responsible he felt for his employees. Beyond that, didn't she know that the reason he worked so hard was to support her and the kids in the lifestyle to which they'd grown all too accustomed?

Wearily, he picked up his briefcase and headed into the house, which was for once blessedly quiet. He set down the case and loosened his tie while he sorted through the mail—all of it bills, except for the monthly country-club newsletter and a cruise brochure from his university alumni association. It was no mystery why the brochure was prominently displayed instead of thrown in the trash. Meg's suggestions that he needed a break had become tiresome. She kept pointedly reminding him that the Farrells took annual trips, just the two of them.

He slung his suit jacket and tie over the kitchen bar stool, grabbed a beer from the fridge and plopped down on the family-room sofa, foraging under the cushions for the TV remote. Tuning into the replay of a golf tournament, he took a swig of beer and rested his head against the sofa back. He felt burdened by challenges on all sides. The Atkisson project had hit a huge snag, John Miller's sudden resignation had left the firm perilously shorthanded and there was the unsettlingly provocative behavior of his colleague Brenda Sampson. On the home front, he and Meg couldn't have a simple conversation without its deteriorating into an argument. The subject didn't matter. Child-rearing practices, social obligations, current events, the household budget. The list of triggers was never-ending.

Hoisting his beer, he watched Phil Mickelson sink a putt, then chugged half the can. As for sex? What was that? Either he was too tired, Meg was too tired or one of them was angry with the other. Would a cruise change that? Or would it just put a further dent in their savings? A romantic getaway was idle speculation, anyway, because he couldn't afford to take time off from the advertising agency he and his partner, Wes Williams, had built from small capital and big dreams.

Meg needed to get a grip. His eyes swept

across their expensive furnishings and decorative accessories. Did she think the good fairy made all of this possible? Just once he'd like a little appreciation.

Over the sound of the golf commentator, he heard a car door slam, followed by the front door opening. "I'm home," his fifteen-year-old daughter, Hayley, shouted.

"In here," Scott said.

"Where's Mom?" Hayley looked around the room.

Who was he? A giant dust bunny?

"She's at your brother's school open house."

"Ha! I can't wait to hear what the teachers said about dork boy."

"Is that any way to talk about your brother?"

She flopped in the armchair, her low-rise jeans revealing an expanse of bare flesh that caused him to gnash his teeth. She and all her friends made themselves fair game for every horny punk in the county. How often had he heard, *Chill out, Dad, it's the style?*

"He needs to get a clue. Sports are all he's got going for him. It's sure not his grades."

Scott tried to conceal his disappointment, but he had to acknowledge Hayley was right. His son wasn't much of a student.

Still, boys often lagged behind academically, or so he'd been told. "Hey, why don't you try looking on the bright side for a change?"

Tugging on her thick, dark French braid, she gave a wry grin. "There is one?"

Sibling rivalry. Some things never changed. "Of course. Without Justin, you'd be an only child."

"I wish!"

Scott decided to ignore that response. "Where have you been?"

"Cheerleading practice, then at Jill's for supper."

"Where's your homework?"

"I finished it at school."

He didn't know whether to believe her, but until her grades dropped, he'd have to trust her. Lately she'd become more uncommunicative. Typical teenager behavior? Or something more?

She stood, her navel exposed in all its questionable glory. "Gotta call Jill. See you later." She took the stairs to her room two at a time.

He shook his head. Why would she have to call Jill? She'd just been with her. A few seconds later, his tranquility was shattered by the reverberations of music—or what passed for it—blasting from Hayley's CD player.

The half hour chimed on the hallway grandfather clock. Nine-thirty. Meg should be home soon. Would she be accusatory or icily stony?

Did it matter? They'd already discussed the *S* word. *Separation.* He didn't know what had happened to the connection they used to have, the dreams they'd shared. They'd been so good together, once. There'd been a time when he couldn't wait to get home from work. Now? They were hardly more than a habit to each other. And not a particularly pleasant one, either.

He missed their old closeness, but couldn't begin to put his finger on when things had started to go south. The kids were the glue that kept them together. But at what cost?

Although he'd never imagined it would come to this, he had to admit the prospect of some time apart held a certain appeal.

But it was a big step. Maybe an irreversible one.

The whir of the garage-door opener soured his stomach. He knew that no apology, regardless of how sincere, would suffice. Meg would come in poised to take the offensive.

SCOTT IGNORED Meg's withering gaze and went straight to his son, clapping an arm around his shoulders. "Hey, buddy, sorry I couldn't be there tonight. How'd it go?"

Justin stiffened. "Good."

Scott winced. Increasingly, Justin limited his responses to monosyllables. "Were you nervous?"

"Come on, Dad, everybody knows the Pledge. It was no big deal."

Scott wanted to disagree. Justin needed as much affirmation as he could get. The big deal was being selected in the first place. "It was to me. I'm proud of you, son."

Justin wriggled out of his embrace and grabbed a bag of chips from the pantry. Scott strained to hear his muttered words, which sounded ominously like "If you're so proud, why weren't you there?"

Meg shot him a scathing look as if echoing their son's question, then picked up the phone and turned her back on him. Justin carried the chips into the family room, where he collapsed on the sofa, gangly legs splayed. Scott stood in the middle of the kitchen, abandoned. Persona non grata in his own home. Meg's falsely cheerful voice rang in his ears as she called a list of soccer parents to inform them of a change of playing field.

Scott's stomach growled, and he moved to the refrigerator, rummaging for cold cuts. He'd skipped dinner and was suddenly ravenous. He slathered two pieces of bread with honey mustard, unearthed a limp leaf of lettuce and a single slice of Swiss cheese and slapped the sandwich together. Meg glanced up, her brow furrowed, and mouthed, "I could've done that." Wonderful. Now, on top of everything else, he had to feel guilty for making his own dinner.

He grabbed another beer and took his meal into the family room where he settled in his recliner, aware of the jarring sounds of both his son's action movie and Hayley's stereo. Chewing the sandwich, he thought about asking whether Justin had any homework, but why add to his troubles? Justin would be resentful and Meg irritated that he didn't trust her to oversee their son.

Meg carried the phone with her as she paced back and forth in the kitchen, unloading the dishwasher. Between her chirpy voice and the clang of silverware, he longed for his earlier solitude.

He'd just finished his sandwich when Meg

entered the room, phone held between her chin and shoulder, and stood behind the sofa. "Justin, did you finish the notes for your oral book report?"

He stared at the TV. "Yeah."

She gave her son a you-better-be-telling-the-truth glance before strolling back to the kitchen. "I know, I know," she clucked, "that coach just seems to have it in for our boys."

Scott rolled his eyes. Women micromanaging sports. It didn't seem right. Scott faced Justin. "What book did you read?"

"Huh?"

"For your book report."

"I dunno. Everybody's reading different books. Mine's something about a dog."

Before he could inquire further, Hayley came pounding down the stairs. "Mo-om, you've gotta help me." She dashed past Scott holding a tiny piece of fabric. "Mo-om!" she repeated.

"She's on the phone," Scott said, to no effect.

"Look. The zipper on my cheerleader skirt broke. You've gotta fix it. It's our uniform for tomorrow night's game."

Scott heard Meg mumbling a hasty good-bye before hanging up the phone. "Oh, honey. I'm sorry."

"I've gotta have it." Hayley was wringing her hands. "It's required."

Scott ambled into the kitchen. "You could explain the problem to your sponsor."

"Oh, right, like that would do any good." Ignoring him, she appealed to her mom. "Can't you *do* something?"

Meg's shoulders slumped and Scott noticed the dark shadows beneath her eyes. For a fleeting second, he thought about reaching out to her.

"I'll run over to Wal-Mart and get a new zipper," Meg said.

"Can you finish it by morning?"

Meg's lips were set in a thin line. "I suppose I'll have to."

"Why?" Scott's one-word question had a stun-gun effect on his audience. "Your mother's tired. Not wearing your uniform for one day isn't the end of the world." Besides, Meg's constant catering to the children made him feel oddly jealous.

Hayley glared at him. "I knew you wouldn't understand. I'd rather stay home than wear something else."

"That could be an option."

Meg clasped her daughter around the waist, and the result was a solid line of defense against which he was powerless. "She needs her skirt. I'll take care of this."

Hayley gave her mom a quick hug and started from the room. "Just a minute, young lady." Scott felt adrenaline pumping. "Haven't you forgotten something?"

"What?"

"You could thank your mother."

"Oh. Sorry, Mom. Thanks." As she brushed past him, she muttered, "Satisfied?"

He wasn't. Not by a long shot. Not with Hayley, consumed by her own self-importance; not with Justin, a lazy, indifferent student; and not with Meg, who always put the children's needs above everything else.

And what about himself? He obviously wasn't doing so well in any aspect of his life except for his business. Little wonder that was where he invested his time and energy.

Meg scowled at him. "Do you have to be so hard on everybody? You hurt Justin tonight. Your absence sent a big signal. And Hayley *is* required to wear her uniform. If you spent a little time around here, you might actually begin to learn the lay of the land." She picked up her purse and fished out her car keys. "I'll be back in half an hour. Don't wait up. The sewing project will take a while." The door leading to the garage closed abruptly and she was gone.

If it wasn't the sewing project keeping her from their bed, it would be baking cookies for teacher-appreciation day or assigning the pairings for the ladies' golf event at the club. Any handy excuse.

When he passed through the family room on his way to their first-floor master-bedroom suite, he noticed Justin had already gone upstairs, leaving the television blaring. Scott turned it off, dimmed the lights and continued, head down, toward the bedroom. As sexual evasions went, wifely headaches were passé. Now Little League, PTA, the golf association and kowtowing to the kids served just as effectively.

He couldn't remember the last time he and Meg had made love.

Sadly, he wasn't sure he cared.

MEG LAY ON HER BACK coaxing sleep, yet unable to turn off her brain. She needed to quiz Justin on his spelling words at breakfast, call the upholstery shop about the fabric for the dining-room chairs, retrieve her cocktail dress from the cleaners before the country-club dance this coming Saturday, and then she had to find time to go to the supermarket. She closed her eyes, mentally composing a grocery list.

Beside her, Scott sprawled on his back, one knee drawn up, the sheet tangled around his legs. His gentle snoring used to comfort her. Now it punctuated her dissatisfaction. She glanced over at him—his dark hair against the white pillow, his strong chin, now lightly stubbled, his muscled chest tapering to a trim waist. One hand lay close to her hip. There was a time she would have picked it up and held it until she fell asleep. As she was often reminded by teasing friends, he was a handsome man. A charming, attractive man. She was so lucky, they told her. Earlier in their marriage she would've agreed. But now?

That train of thought led her not to Scott but to Jannie and Ron Farrell. Ron hadn't missed the school open house tonight. On the contrary, not only had he made it, but the way he'd ushered Jannie through the halls, one hand at the small of her back, his head tilted to smile at her as if she were the only person in the corridor, said all kinds of things about his dedication to her and to his kids. There was a special glow about the two of them that set them apart. Like her and Scott, the Farrells were coming up on their twentieth wedding anniversary. Yet they still acted like honeymooners.

In contrast, she and Scott could hardly say two words to each other without getting into an argument. He was always so sure he was right. If he had his way, the children would live in a domestic boot camp. So what if she was busy? Hadn't that been what Scott had wanted when he'd started his firm? It was primarily about contacts, he'd said. Well, she'd done *her* part, meeting all kinds of potential clients in the various organizations to which she belonged. And what thanks did she get? A husband who spent nearly every waking hour with business associates and couldn't be bothered to help out in domestic crises. She squeezed her eyes shut. *Good grief, I sound like the poster girl for self-pity.*

She didn't know who had been more hurt tonight by Scott's absence—her or Justin. Oh, Justin didn't want to let on. "No big deal," he'd said. But his downcast eyes and silence in the car on the drive home had spoken volumes. She knew how he felt. Even though it was years ago, she remembered with painful clarity her humiliation at the Girl Scout father-daughter banquet. She'd sat red-faced, the only girl without a father, wondering how he could have just up and died before she ever really knew him.

Scott's failure to come to the open house tonight was the final link in a long chain of disappointments. This was no marriage. The kids deserved better—and so did she.

Yet the prospect of separation terrified her. That was one step closer to divorce. What would that mean for the kids? For her? Was it what she really wanted?

But the reality was that she and Scott couldn't continue on as they were. Living in an armed camp was no kind of life for any of them.

She flipped her pillow over, then lay back down, forcing herself to remember the good times, those heady days long ago when the mere sight of Scott could stop her breath, and the many nights they'd spent wrapped in each other's arms, when they'd lose track of time, so insistent was their need for each other. That all seemed eons ago. Some other life.

A single tear moistened Meg's cheek, and unrelieved tension stiffened her body.

When had romance faded to familiarity? And familiarity to contempt?

Silently she wept for what used to be. And for the inevitability of what was to come.

FRIDAY MORNING Justin groaned, then rolled over, burrowing his head under his pillow and ignoring the patter of his favorite disc jockey on the clock radio. He didn't move, dreading his mother's customary "Justin, are you up?" and then he heard her calling up the stairs. Well, she could yell all she wanted. He wasn't moving. His stomach hurt. Big-time.

He didn't have a soccer game today, so what did it matter if he stayed home from school? Mom would be running all her errands and going to meetings and stuff, so he could hang out watching TV and trying to get to the next level in his Nintendo game. Those other suckers could go to class. Take the stupid math test. Present their stupid oral book reports.

His stomach tensed as he remembered his father questioning him about his book. Dad would kill him if he found out he hadn't read past the first two chapters.

"Justin?" His mother's footsteps sounded on the stairs. Then she was standing in his doorway. "Get up. You'll be late."

He moaned for effect. "I'm sick."

She approached the bed. "Oh, honey, what's wrong?"

"I have a stomachache."

"Is there a bug going around at school?"

Heck if he knew, but he glommed on to the excuse. "Uh, yeah. A bunch of kids went home yesterday." He didn't know if that was true, but it probably happened almost any day.

His mother placed a cool hand on his forehead. "You don't seem to have a fever. Are you nauseated?"

Crap. He didn't want to think about throwing up and the grotty taste afterward. "No, it's more like a pain."

His mother sat on his bed looking worried. "Is it on the right side?"

Jeez, he wasn't angling for an appendectomy. He just wanted to stay home.

"No, it's kinda all over." He scrunched up his face, hoping she'd figure he was in agony.

Just when he thought he had her convinced, she put on one of those mother looks, like she could see straight through him. "I'll tell you what. Get dressed and come downstairs. Try to eat something. Then we'll see."

He hated it when she said, "We'll see." That almost always meant no.

"You've worked so hard on your book report. I don't want you to miss school today."

"I'm not supposed to give my report until next week." She didn't look convinced. He tried one last ploy. "What if I go to school and puke?"

"I'll come get you."

Great. Now he'd have to take the dumb math test and worry about how to fake his book report in a few days. If his dad knew his current grade in English was a D, he'd flip.

But what else was new? Everything in his life was off track. The coach had moved him from goalie to center, his grades were in the toilet, his father was never around and when he was, all he did was criticize him. But Dad wasn't the Lone Ranger. Both his parents nagged all the time. And argued with each other. He was sick of it. Some days he wondered why they'd gotten married in the first place. If that's what love was like, no question about it—he'd stay a bachelor his whole life.

He closed his eyes. That might be okay. Yeah, he'd be a big-league pitcher or a pro soccer player and have lots of blond girl-friends with big boobs. But he wouldn't have to marry any of them. Ever.

"*Now*, young man. Up."

His mother ripped off the sheet, leaving him exposed. Thank God he didn't have an early-morning boner. But that was the only good thing about the day so far.

SATURDAY EVENING Meg sat at the linen-covered table, nursing a gin and tonic, listening to the Earl Hines Orchestra and trying to muster a smile for Ward Jordan seated to her right. He and his inane wife, Melody, were their guests for the country-club dance. More importantly, they were potential clients. Meg bent forward to hear the punch line of Ward's joke, finding it in questionable taste but managing to keep her mouth shut. Scott had come a long way. The chain of department stores the Jordans owned was well known locally. Now they were expanding throughout the Southwest, and Scott's firm was bidding for the ad campaign. Meg sighed. More work, more travel for Scott.

His success and their affluence were a mixed blessing. Growing up with her hard-working, widowed mother in a cramped house on the wrong side of town she could never have imagined all the luxuries her marriage provided—stylish clothes, exclusive memberships, a lovely decorator home. She should've been satisfied. But something was missing.

She glanced over Ward Jordan's head to see Scott steering Melody around the dance floor. The petite redhead had flung back her head to laugh up at Scott, who towered above her. They were flirting. Meg felt a pang of jealousy. Scott had that effect on women and he capitalized on his charm. Once, she'd been secure in his love and had found such innocent flirtation amusing. Not anymore.

Back then, there'd been no Brenda Sampson to worry about. Scott claimed his creative director maintained her professional distance, that her easy familiarity was simply a result of their working closely together. Brenda was a knockout—a big-boned Scandinavian blonde, comfortable with her own sexuality. Of course, she and Scott needed to stay late some evenings to work. Or... Meg shook her head impatiently. She didn't want to think about it. She had enough problems without the disturbing mental picture that had just popped into her head. She paused, considering her choice of words. *Disturbing* because it highlighted yet another flaw in their marriage? Or because the image left a sudden emptiness in her chest?

Around her she heard a smattering of applause for the band. Scott escorted Melody to the table and helped her into her chair. Then he put a hand on Meg's shoulder. "Dance?"

The band had segued into a slow number. Scott ushered her onto the floor and took her in his arms. He danced just as he did everything else—smoothly. He held her close, seemingly preoccupied. "How do you think it's going?" he asked, nodding in the direction of the table.

"I have no idea. I'm doing my part, though."

"You always do." He whirled her around, then leaned closer. "I appreciate it. You're a great asset."

Wonderful. Just the sweet nothing every woman hopes to hear. Didn't he understand she wanted to be his beloved, his everything? Not a business asset. Not just his housekeeper and the mother of his children. She ground her teeth in frustration. She ached for love and affirmation, knowing it was asking too much to expect romance. She longed to feel like an interesting, desirable woman again.

She stared, unseeing, over his shoulder at the kaleidoscope of moving colors. Twenty years. Simultaneously, it seemed like forever and a mere blip on the radar screen of her life.

When Scott nuzzled her cheek with his

chin, she could hardly hold back the tears. She used to feel special in his arms, used to snuggle closer, teasing him with the pressure of her breasts against his chest. Suddenly, he dropped his hands and moved past her. "Lloyd, you son of a gun, good to see you," he said, and he was off, schmoozing with a former client. Almost as an afterthought he turned to her and, encircling her waist, included her in the conversation.

Meg surreptitiously consulted the diamond watch Scott had given her last Christmas, a gift that had felt more like a payoff than a sentimental gesture. Another hour and a half to go. Somehow she would survive. But when they got home, it was time for a serious talk.

SCOTT ROLLED UP the sleeves of his dress shirt, fixed himself a brandy, then sat down in the family room, like the proverbial condemned prisoner awaiting his executioner. Meg had gone upstairs to change and check on the kids. On the way home from the country club she'd uttered the words no husband welcomed: *We need to talk.* He pinched the bridge of his nose and sighed. Why now, for God's sake? He was on the brink of exhaustion.

After midnight there was no one to interrupt them, no phone call to distract her, no reason for him to hurry back to the office. Reluctantly, he acknowledged that they needed to settle some things. They couldn't live in limbo indefinitely. Yet he couldn't ignore the fear in the pit of his stomach.

He braced himself when Meg came into the room, her feet bare, her thin nightgown covered by an old chenille bathrobe she'd had since she was pregnant with Hayley. *Her security blanket?*

He lifted his glass. "Can I get you something?"

She shook her head, then took a seat in the big armchair, tucking her feet under her. She wrapped her arms around her chest and peered around the room as if seeing it for the first time. Or the last. His heart plummeted.

That was exactly where they were in their relationship. "So?" he finally said. "Talk."

"What are we going to do? I don't know about you, but I can't go on like this, just coexisting in the same house. Wearing a phony smile in public."

"Are you that unhappy?"

She glanced up. "Aren't you?"

He thought about her question. About his

feelings of entrapment and the weight of overwhelming expectations. "What happened to us?"

She shrugged. "We've been over everything more times than I care to count. Is there any point in rehashing it?"

"Do you want us to go back to Dr. Jacobs?" Scott knew he was clutching at straws. The marriage counselor had identified some of their problems, but had been of little real help. Whose fault that was, Scott didn't want to think about. "Or find someone else?"

"We're far beyond that."

"Then what do you suggest?"

Her eyes held sadness. "A trial separation."

Before, he'd always sensed that their discussions about separating had been rhetorical. The brandy warming his stomach turned to acid. "You're serious?"

"I need some space."

She needed space? Terrific.

"I'd hate to move the kids. Maybe you could rent an apartment."

So he was supposed to pack his things and go merrily off into the night? Anger radiated through his body. Why him? Why not her? Oh, right, moving out was what spurned husbands did. One last measure of gallantry. He stood up and paced to the hearth, then turned to face her. "You expect me to make other living arrangements, just like that? And what are you proposing we tell the kids?"

"What we've already talked about. That we need some time to step back and figure out where we're going." She lifted her chin. "You don't imagine they're oblivious to the tension between us, do you?"

"No." His gut curled in on itself. "When?"

"As soon as your parents leave."

He groaned. He'd all but forgotten their upcoming visit, meant to coincide with his and Meg's twentieth anniversary the very next weekend. Tulsa was one of his parents' first stops on what they were calling their "big adventure." They'd sold their house in Nashville and bought a huge motor home and were embarking on a two-year odyssey across the country.

"Are you suggesting we put on the happy-family front while they're here?" He knew his parents better than that. They'd spot the act from a hundred feet away. His mother, who had been cool to Meg early in their relationship, might even utter the dreaded words *I told you so*.

"We could try. At least until we talk with

the kids. Then I guess we'll need to tell your folks, too."

Scott felt his control slipping. This conversation bordered on the surreal. "Why not cut to the chase? Do you want a divorce?"

Her cheeks reddened and she ducked her head. "I don't know."

Scott waved his hands helplessly. "Hell, Meg, I don't think you have a clue what you want. But I'll tell you one thing. I can't handle any more stress in my life. One way or the other, we need to decide this, once and for all. I'm not interested in putting the kids through any more suffering than necessary."

She frowned at him. "You think I am?"

Weariness overwhelmed him. "I'm tired of arguing. I'm tired of accusations. This hasn't been a marriage for quite a while."

"No, it's been a business arrangement."

He couldn't help raising his voice. "That's not fair."

"Isn't it?"

He felt them moving perilously close to words they might regret. "Okay. You win." He slumped back on the sofa. "After Mom and Pops leave, I'll find an apartment."

"Fine." She gathered her robe around her. "We can work out the details later. Right now, I'm going to bed." She started toward their bedroom, then turned back. "Maybe if you struggle really hard you can remember Justin's soccer game tomorrow. Five-thirty at the south fields."

He didn't even bother to reply. He might not win any Father of the Year Award, but he cared about his son. Last week, he'd entered the game in his Palm Pilot. After Meg was gone, he reached for the brandy, swirling it in the snifter as he stared into space.

Fear—and an overpowering sense of failure—slowly drove out his anger. He was facing the big unknown, financially and emotionally. Yet there was no denying he and Meg were both miserable.

But what good could come of a separation?

He downed the contents of the snifter, knowing the liquor couldn't begin to touch the emptiness growing inside.

CHAPTER TWO

"DO YOU THINK Meg and Scott will be surprised?"

Bud Harper took his eyes off the road momentarily to glance at his wife, who was dwarfed by the leather passenger seat of their new motor home. "They will be if our grandkids have kept their mouths shut."

"Oh, I don't think they'd spoil it for anything. I'm so excited." Marie practically squirmed with satisfaction. "Twenty years. Why, it seems like only yesterday that Scotty brought Meg home to meet us."

"Remember how you thought no one would ever be good enough for your baby?"

"Scott was—and is—pretty special. But so is Meg. Even if she did take some getting used to."

Bud let the remark pass. Over the years, the arrival of grandchildren—and geographic distance—had mellowed the relationship between the two women. "Scott works too hard," he said, remembering their last visit to Tulsa, when his son had been frantically trying to meet a client's unrealistic deadline.

Marie raised an eyebrow. "Hmm, I wonder where he learned that work ethic?"

"Guilty as charged," Bud admitted, recalling the strains in their marriage when he'd been putting in eighteen-hour days to get his plumbing business up and running. "But look here." He waved his arm expansively to indicate the interior of their rig and the open road before them. "If you wait long enough, there are compensations."

"There always were," his wife said, smiling fondly.

"Even as busy as I was, we had some good times. Maybe I'm an old fogy, but back then, families didn't have the added frustration of learning how to operate all these doodads. Computers, Palm Pilots, cell phones, DVD players—it's enough to boggle the mind." Simply figuring out all the intricacies of the motor home had been enough to tax his ingenuity and patience.

But now there were months of camping by rushing mountain streams to look forward to. No schedules. No obligations. Time for the two of them at last. He and Marie had dreamed of this trip for years. She had boxes filled with articles and photos she'd clipped from travel magazines. Lulled by the hum of the powerful engine, he mentally ticked off some of their destinations: Yellowstone Park, Bryce and Zion canyons, Crater Lake, Vancouver Island. And that was only the first leg of the journey.

Hearing the comforting click of Marie's knitting needles, he thought back to the first time he'd ever seen her at his marine buddy's wedding. A little bit of a thing in a picture hat and flouncy bridesmaid gown. Summer of 1957. He'd taken one look and made an instant decision. Sidling up to the groom, he'd asked Marie's name and then announced, "That's the girl I'm going to marry." And, by God, he had. From that day on, he'd never had a single regret.

They'd spent last night in Memphis and done the Graceland tour. He wasn't a big fan of the King, but he'd never let on. Marie still listened to Elvis CDs, and he had to admit the songs restored an era for him.

West of Little Rock, Highway 40 ran in gentle ups and downs along the Arkansas

River. Soon they'd roll into Oklahoma and catch the turnpike to Tulsa.

"Only two more days. I hope our little surprise works out," Marie said. "It's hard planning things long distance."

He patted her knee. "Everything will be fine. I've never known anything you organized to bomb."

She blushed. A seventy-two-year-old woman, still capable of enjoying a compliment and still as beautiful, wrinkles and all, as the first day he'd laid eyes on her.

He was a lucky man.

THURSDAY AFTERNOON Justin got off the school bus, flipped the bird at Sam Grider, then glared at the departing vehicle, choking on the noxious exhaust fumes. He'd had it with that guy's bullying. Sam had ragged on him unmercifully for his stupid oral book report in English. "Whatsa matter, Harper? Can't ya read? That's not how the story ends, dork."

Whether Mrs. Kelly, his English teacher, knew that or not, she sure did when Grider got finished. Even now, remembering the snickers and stares of his classmates, Justin reddened. Crap. He hated Grider, he hated books, he hated school. Actually, he hated his whole lousy life.

Which was about to get worse. Thrusting his hand in his pocket, he fingered the note that would probably get him grounded for a month. Mrs. Kelly had kept him after class, her steely gray eyes boring into him. "Justin, I'm extremely disappointed in you." Then she'd written the note informing his parents that not only had he not finished the book, he'd "prevaricated"—Jeez, who talked like that in real life?—a form of cheating she found a "serious breach of morality."

In other words, he'd screwed up royally.

He wondered briefly what would happen if he threw the note away. But Mrs. Kelly had asked him to have his parents sign it and return it to her. Ha! If he lived long enough after his father got through with him.

The only thing that might save his bacon was that his grandparents were coming that afternoon. Maybe his dad wouldn't make a big stink in front of them. Or maybe his grandfather would remember some ancient story about a time when the perfect Scott Harper had actually messed up. *Fat chance!*

Out of the blue, an idea came to him. Tomorrow was Friday. He could tell Mrs. Kelly his parents hadn't been home to sign the note, that he'd have it for her Monday. Lots of things could happen between now and then. Especially if his parents were pleased with the surprise.

He scuffed his toe against the curb, then started slowly for home. He had a feeling they wouldn't be pleased. Not when they barely even talked to each other. Mom was always rolling her eyes at Dad when he was late getting home from work, and he kept telling her how important every darn business deal was. They acted like they didn't even love each other, and it was enough to make Justin puke.

With a jolt, the familiar sick feeling punched him in the gut. He closed his eyes, holding back tears—and fear.

What if they *didn't* love each other?

He crossed his fingers. The surprise just had to work.

MEG HAULED THE LAST BAG out of the grocery cart and stuffed it into the back seat of her Lexus. She glanced at her watch and swore. The Harpers would be arriving any time within the next hour and she still had to pick up Hayley at cheerleading practice, unload the groceries, marinate the steak, toss the salad and set the table. No doubt Marie, in her day, would've finished most of her chores by noon. Easing from the parking lot into the flow of traffic, Meg grimaced. Her mother-in-law was a wonderful person, but she was a hard act to follow and always made her feel like a Martha Stewart dropout.

Halfway to the high school, her cell phone rang. One hand on the wheel, she groped around in her purse, finally coming up with it. The caller was Jannie reminding her of their scheduled Saturday tennis game. "I'm sorry, but Scott's parents will be here. I should've let you know."

"No problem. I'll find another game. Enjoy the in-laws."

"I'll try." Meg steeled herself, wondering how on earth she could hide the state of her marriage from Scott's parents. "They're really nice people."

"Right. That must explain why you get so uptight every time they come to Tulsa."

Meg raced through an intersection on the yellow light. "I like them. But…they dote on Scott. He can do no wrong." She could hardly restrain her sarcasm—or her sense of inadequacy.

"Ah, the golden-boy syndrome," Jannie said knowingly.

"That about sums it up."

"And you feel…what? Snubbed? Like you don't measure up?"

Waves of insecurity swept over Meg, dating back to the first time she'd met the Harpers and realized no one would ever be good enough for Scott, at least in his mother's mind. "Something like that."

"Join the crowd, honey. But what these mamas don't know is how happy we make their little boys, right?"

Happy? Meg controlled a snort. It was easier just to agree. Saying anything else would open the floodgates of her emotions. "Oh, yes. What Mrs. Harper doesn't know won't hurt her." The irony of her intentional double meaning brought her up short.

After setting another tennis date, Meg hung up, wondering what had happened to her sense of humor. "Mamas" and "little boys" once would've provoked a grin.

When she turned into the circular drive in front of the high-school gymnasium, she spotted Hayley and three other girls sitting on the concrete wall, their tanned legs swinging, talking to two young men wearing low-slung jeans and baggy shirts. Hayley hadn't dated much, to Meg's relief, but there was something in her expression, the high color in her cheeks, that made Meg suspect her daughter had more than a passing interest in one of these boys. Meg sighed. She wasn't ready for the angst of teenage love. Especially with a kid who looked like a wannabe rap star.

Recognizing the car, Hayley hopped off the wall, waved at her friends and climbed in the front seat. "Who were those boys?" Meg asked as she pulled out from the school.

"Oh, just Zach Simon and some other guy in my biology class."

"They looked like they were into you. What's up?"

Hayley shrugged her shoulders. "There's nothing to tell—"

Meg bought it until Hayley added, "Really."

Acknowledging that her daughter probably wouldn't welcome further inquiries, Meg dropped it. She glanced at the dash and realized she was speeding.

After several minutes of silence, Hayley turned to her. "When do Gramma and Grampa get here? I can't wait to see them."

"Not for about an hour." Meg prayed that

was true. She had too much to do in the meantime.

"Will Dad be home for dinner?"

Was Scott's presence at the evening meal so rare that Hayley had to ask? "I certainly hope so. After all, your grandparents would be disappointed if he wasn't."

Meg thought she heard a catch in her daughter's voice. "So would I." Hayley's mask of nonchalance slipped. In its place was—yearning?

Good Lord. How would Hayley react when she and Scott separated and she only saw her father on prearranged visits? *If* Scott took his role as a parent seriously.

Even as she formed that thought, she admitted it was unfair. Scott loved the kids. She'd never doubted that. But he loved his ad agency, too. And it was hard to compete with Harper Concepts. Especially when you were only fifteen.

"He'll be there," Meg said in a firm voice, as if emphasizing it would make it true. Hayley picked at the strap of her backpack but said nothing.

The sun was low in the sky when Meg turned onto their tree-lined street.

"What's that thing?" Hayley asked, her tone of disgust unmistakable.

Meg followed Hayley's gaze. There, parked in front of their third garage and taking up most of the length of their driveway, was a huge brown-and-beige motor home. Why, oh why, hadn't there been a tie-up on the freeway, a rainstorm, anything to slow the Harpers down? No one but Justin had been home to greet them, no cooking aromas wafted from a dinner simmering on the stove, no welcome flag flew from the pole. Once again, Meg had failed the domesticity challenge.

"That's your grandparents' new motor home."

"I didn't know it would be so big." Hayley stared incredulously. "It's gross. I'm so embarrassed."

"Why on earth would you say that?"

"The other kids'll laugh. Mom, it's total senior-citizen geekdom!"

Meg stifled a giggle. The motor home did scream AARP. "Get over it. You will be gracious and accepting of your grandparents."

Hayley gave her a mock salute. "Aye, aye, captain." Then, to Meg's surprise, she relented. "I'm sorry. It's just...so big. But I do love Gramma and Grampa."

"I know you do, honey." Meg decided to capitalize on Hayley's temporary good graces. "I could use your help with dinner."

"Ask Gramma. She loves to putter in the kitchen."

In one fell swoop, Hayley had removed herself from consideration and volunteered her grandmother—the very person whose help Meg had hoped to avoid.

But what did she deserve? Her marriage was falling apart, and now she couldn't even pull off being a gracious hostess. Easing past the behemoth and into the garage, she muttered a silent prayer, then told her daughter, "The least you can do is help carry in the groceries."

WHERE THE HELL was Scott? Meg's face was a mask of good cheer, but internally she was boiling. Did she have to entertain by herself? The Harpers were *his* parents, after all. Somehow she'd managed to light the gas grill, and Bud and Justin were presiding over the steaks. Marie, however, had not left her side during the rest of the food preparation, inserting culinary tips into the conversation like "You'll want to chill the salad bowls, Meg"—which necessitated rearranging the refrigerator. Hayley had willingly set the table under her grandmother's direction, but heaven forbid the salad forks went on the inside of the dinner forks.

Meg was within minutes of serving the meal, and still there was no sign of Scott. He hadn't even bothered to phone. Despite the awkwardness, Meg refused to make excuses for him, but Marie more than made up for that. "Scotty works so hard. I know he'll be here as soon as he finishes whatever business he has."

Meg bit her lip. Marie's very words got at the heart of the problem—Scott would be home when he'd addressed his more important obligations. Only then would he be ready to face priority number two—his family.

The sliding glass door to the patio opened. Beaming, Bud raised a platter toward the women. "Behold. Best darn steaks you'll ever put in your mouth."

Justin followed, rubbing a hand over his stomach. "I'm starving. Can we please eat?"

Well, why not? Meg thought to herself. *Let the Harpers experience what we do. Dinner without the lord and master.* "Call your sister," Meg said, and instructed Bud to set the meat on the table.

Marie readjusted the parsley around a plate of deviled eggs. Apparently Meg hadn't even done that satisfactorily. "Surely we're not going to eat without Scotty."

Meg clenched her fingers. "He should be here any minute. He wouldn't want us to let the food get cold."

"Those steaks are perfect now, sweetheart," Bud added, by way of support.

Marie stared wistfully out the kitchen window. "It doesn't seem right not to wait."

Hayley and Justin took their places at the table. "Come on, Gramma and Grampa," Justin pleaded. "Let's eat."

Reluctantly Marie picked up the plate of eggs. Meg gave one last desperate look down the street before following with the salad and baked potatoes.

Fortunately, the kids kept the conversation going and, to Meg's relief, displayed obvious pleasure in their grandparents' visit, asking them numerous questions about the great motor-home odyssey. Hayley, especially, seemed eager to make them feel at home. Meg toyed with her salad, resentment robbing her of an appetite. How could she and Scott maintain this charade of a marriage for even one more day, much less carry off an anniversary? And when would they have the opportunity to make the decisions so vital to their future? Find time to communicate those decisions to their children and the Harpers? First, though, before anything could happen, Scott had to appear.

As if her thoughts had conjured him up, she heard the garage door open, followed by the sound of a car pulling in.

"That must be Scotty." Marie nearly knocked her chair over, bounding up to greet her son. Bud rose, too, but the kids went right on eating.

From her seat, Meg watched Scott embrace his parents, then heard him apologize for being late. "...last-minute changes the creative director needed to go over." Meg flinched. Brenda Sampson. It figured.

"It's good to have you here," Scott said as he accompanied his parents back to the dining room, false heartiness apparent in his conciliatory gestures. "Sorry, honey," he mumbled, resting a hand on Meg's shoulder. "Kids, I'm glad you didn't wait. I'll bet you were hungry."

"Starving," Justin said, helping himself to a second steak.

Hayley pointed to her brother's plate. "Too much red meat isn't good for you."

"At least I'm not a picky eater, like you."

"Children," Meg admonished.

Somehow Meg endured the rest of the dinner, watching stoically as Marie and Bud hung on Scott's every word about the Jordan department-store account.

At one point, Marie leaned over, and, eyes glowing, asked Meg, "Aren't you proud of your husband?"

Even as Meg reluctantly murmured, "Yes," she had to admit that in some ways she *was* proud of his accomplishments. But why did she have to play second fiddle? Why couldn't she feel as important to him as his new accounts?

Between the main course and dessert, Bud tapped on his wineglass. "I have an announcement to make."

Hayley and Justin made eye contact as knowing grins formed on their faces. Meg went on alert. Her children were seldom in cahoots.

"Saturday, you two—" he nodded at Scott and Meg "—will celebrate a milestone twenty years of marriage, and if you don't have anything special planned…"

Meg was overcome with bitterness. *Anything special? Just a separation. Is that special enough?*

"...Marie, Hayley, Justin and I have arranged to take you to dinner at the country club to celebrate."

Scott caught Meg's eye briefly as if to say "Don't ruin this for them." Then he said, "Mom, Pops, that's really not necessary."

"Nonsense," Marie interrupted. "We are so proud of this wonderful family you've created. You're both busy, talented people who somehow manage to keep the spark alive. That needs to be celebrated."

Meg, cheeks flaming, nearly choked as she responded, "That's very generous of you."

What she was really thinking was that, unbelievably, she and Scott had his parents fooled. For the moment, anyway.

EXHAUSTED, SCOTT FINISHED brushing his teeth, turned out the bathroom light and made his way to bed where Meg was already sleeping—or pretending to—her back to him, one arm tucked under her pillow. There'd been no opportunity to talk with her, to apologize for being late. Not that he could have convincingly explained what had detained him. She wouldn't care. Especially if his reason involved Brenda. And it did.

He should've been home to greet his parents. He could have called. But cowardly as it was, he hadn't wanted to hear Meg's nagging accusations; he was harboring more than enough guilt himself. On the drive home, he'd second-guessed his motives. Could his conversation with Brenda have waited until tomorrow? Not if they wanted to get the logo redesign ready for Monday's pitch to the Jordans. Brenda had needed an immediate decision. They couldn't afford to blow this deal—it was the firm's big chance to nail a high-profile client.

He lay on his back, head cradled on his hands, willing sleep to come. Moonlight striped the far wall. He heard muffled movements above as his parents prepared for bed. He'd been glad to see them—and grateful for their presence, buffering him from Meg's hostility. Lately it seemed most of his conversations with her centered on his apologizing. For what? Making a living? Seeking success?

Childish though it might be, he had basked in the approval in his mother's eyes as he told about the possibility of getting the Jordan account. But lying there, he knew it wasn't her approval he craved.

It was Meg's.

He turned on his side, studying the curves

of his wife's body, one bared shoulder creamy against the soft green blanket. He raised a hand to trace the indentation of her waist, the rise of her hip, but stopped himself, knowing she would tense under his touch.

He desperately needed to bury himself in her, to leave behind all his macho bluster and immerse himself mindlessly in her love and acceptance. To lose the public Scott Harper in an explosion of pure lust—and intimacy.

But that wasn't going to happen. Hadn't happened in a long time. Meg didn't want him. The sooner he came to grips with that reality, the better. But it hurt. And made him feel more vulnerable than he'd ever thought possible.

BUD JERKED AWAKE, the elbow to his ribs an urgent summons. "What?"

"You're snoring again. Roll over," Marie said, pushing gently against his shoulder.

"Okay," he mumbled, sorry he'd disturbed her, but equally sorry she'd disturbed him. He'd been having a great dream about playing baseball for some high-school team. "Bud, Bud, he's our man," the crowd had chanted. Made him feel good. Young.

But now he was wide awake, while beside

him Marie quickly settled back into the sleep of the dead. She could do that. Fall asleep at the drop of a hat. Didn't seem fair. He'd probably be awake for hours now. Especially since he was unaccustomed to this strange bed.

Around him the house was silent except for the periodic cycling of the air conditioner. Tomorrow they'd be going to watch Justin play soccer in the afternoon, and then to the football game where Hayley was cheering. Good kids, both of 'em. A bit spoiled, though. They hadn't even volunteered to clear the table, much less do the dishes. Maybe they did have homework, as they'd claimed, but while he'd been getting ready for bed, he'd heard Hayley chattering on the phone, and not about school assignments.

After dinner he'd talked with each of the grandkids privately. They'd both assured him they hadn't spilled the beans and that their parents knew nothing about the anniversary surprise. Justin, though, had mentioned something that worried Bud. "Grampa, I don't know if our surprise will help." When Bud pressed him for an explanation, Justin had shuffled his feet and said, "Never mind."

Bud propped himself up on a second pillow to alleviate a touch of heartburn. He replayed his grandson's remark. Not that Scott and Meg wouldn't *like* the surprise but that it wouldn't *help*. Help what?

In the calm of the night, he reflected on their arrival. No Scott. Meg determinedly pleasant. Her careful avoidance of the issue of Scott's lateness. Almost as if she didn't expect him for dinner.

And what about Scott? When he'd finally shown up, he'd been the charming host, asking them all the right questions, entertaining them with his story of wooing the Jordan account.

Bud sat up and burped, relieving some of the pressure in his chest, then lay back down. The missing piece of the puzzle clicked into place. Meg. Scott had touched her rather perfunctorily on his return, but they hadn't addressed any conversation to each other. Certainly, they hadn't exchanged any of those silent, loving glances married couples use as romantic shorthand.

A sense of foreboding caused Bud to roll over on his side and cuddle Marie close. *Not Meg and Scott.* Surely it was just his imagination.

They'd been too polite, too reserved, too distant. What was the word he was searching for? Too unnatural. He tried to relax, tucking

Marie's head into the crook of his neck. Even her nearness failed to ease his worries. He had the strongest sense that something was wrong between Meg and his son.

And whatever the something was, he could only pray that the long-planned anniversary surprise would help. He wished Justin thought so, too.

What did the boy know that he didn't?

CHAPTER THREE

SATURDAYS WERE ALWAYS HECTIC in the Harper household. If Scott didn't have a golf game, he usually spent part of the day working. Justin's athletic schedule frequently underwent last-minute changes and Hayley often came home from a Friday-night sleepover exhausted and moody. Meg longed for that impossible luxury—an entire day free of carpooling, errands and social obligations. But it wasn't happening today. Oh, no, their twentieth anniversary had dawned with Marie's sudden demand for a hair appointment.

Getting her in with Giorgio had not been easy. Now Meg owed him big-time—he'd been appalled that his client actually expected *him,* stylist extraordinaire, to set Marie's hair on rollers. Shortly after returning from the hairdresser's, Meg had heard an anguished cry from Hayley. Upon investigating, she'd discovered her daughter, horrified expression on her face, staring out her bedroom window overlooking the front yard. "See, Mom, I told you it was embarrassing!" Gathered on the lawn were several neighborhood teenage boys examining the motor home. Justin, with the flair of a carnival barker, was pointing out the features of the oversize vehicle.

"Maybe they think it's cool."

Hayley snorted, then grinned. "In some alternate universe."

Unbelievably, Scott had made it to both Justin's soccer game yesterday and Hayley's football game. This morning he'd slipped out of the house for a round of golf with Bud without a mention of their anniversary.

Fresh from a late-afternoon shower, Meg stood in the doorway of her closet studying her choices of party apparel. Darned if she'd wear the black chiffon Scott liked. No, she needed something flamboyant, in-your-face. Something to make a statement about her independence. She pulled out an electric-blue cocktail suit with a magenta silk shell. The short, hip-hugging skirt made her feel halfway sexy, and the color would bring out the blue of her eyes. This could be her last anniversary observance, so she might as well go down with all flags flying.

She'd just finished applying her makeup when she heard Scott return from his game. Fleetingly, she wondered what he was feeling today. Had he spent any time remembering the small college chapel where they'd exchanged vows? The way they couldn't wait to escape the reception in their haste to get to the hotel? Had he recalled how passionate their lovemaking had been? How naively certain they'd been that theirs was a forever-after kind of love?

Scott walked through the door and stripped off his golf shirt. "How much time do I have?"

Like she was his keeper? "We're due at the club at six."

"I showered in the locker room. Is this a sport-coat-and-tie event?"

Meg bit her tongue. Had he even looked at her? Noticed how she was dressed? "Yes," was all she said.

He removed his shoes and socks, then stepped out of his slacks. "Pops managed a couple of birdies today."

"I'm sure he had a good time." Meg groaned inwardly. Talk about a stilted conversation. She was well aware that neither of them had mentioned the anniversary. But what was there to say? *Happy anniversary* would ring false, and they were long past reminiscing about other anniversaries. The big question was whether she cared.

She ducked her head. Despite the brave front she put on, part of her did care. But she wasn't sure there was any way to fix things. Somewhere along the line, their common path had forked, and new paths had led them farther and farther apart, shattering her long-held dream of a happy home, different from the one in which she'd grown up.

She fussed with her hair, then studied her jewelry box before deciding on a pendant necklace and matching earrings. With a stab, she realized Scott had given them to her on their fifteenth anniversary.

"Meg?"

She turned from the mirror to see Scott standing tall and handsome in front of her, his tan suit sharply pressed, his paisley tie matching his shirt nicely. "Am I presentable?"

"You'll do," she said, rising to her feet and, out of habit, straightening his tie. She could smell the fresh tropical scent of his after-shave, sense the wiry tension in his body. She stepped away, determined not to lose herself in his masculine charm. It took more—a lot more—than occasional pangs of sexual need to make a marriage work. Abruptly, she spun around. "We'd better get on with the show."

"Show?" he mused. "Yeah, I guess you're right. All we are is one big act, at least according to you."

His words stung. He made their situation sound so impersonal. "A lot can happen in twenty years, Scott."

"Yeah, more than I ever bargained for." His voice took on an urgent tone. "Are you sure about this, Meg? About the separation?"

For a moment she thought she heard a plea in his question, but when she looked into his eyes, they were stony.

"I don't see that we have a choice. We're both too unhappy. And it's not fair to the kids."

With that, they made their way toward the front hall where the Harpers, Justin and Hayley waited. It was as if the curtain had just gone up and they'd walked onstage, smiles pasted on their faces.

"Happy anniversary," Marie trilled, echoed by the others.

Hayley's skirt was shorter than Meg would've liked and Justin's shirt was sloppily tucked in. Hayley pirouetted, checking herself out in the hall mirror, but Justin stared, first at his father, then at Meg. She couldn't be sure, but she thought she read hesitation and dread in the look he sent them.

"Can we just go?" he asked.

Bud laughed, "Attaboy, son. Let's get this show on the road."

Show? There was that word again. Meg prayed she could get through this evening without ruining it for her in-laws or her children.

INSIDE THE HIGH-CEILINGED lobby of the country club, Scott nodded to the hostess, then, knowing it was expected, put his hand on the small of Meg's back and started toward the main dining room.

"Mr. Harper, this way, please." The hostess redirected them toward a private room.

Bud gave a satisfied chortle. "Nothing but the best for you two."

Just as well, Scott decided, to be out of the public area where it would've been harder to pull off the charade.

Marie joined them. "This is so exciting. I love being able to share such a special occasion with you."

It was special, all right. Short of a miracle, it was probably their last anniversary together. The thought made Scott queasy.

"Here we are, Mr. and Mrs. Harper." The hostess flung open the door, and what she revealed made Scott's stomach even queasier. Beside him he heard Meg's small, sharp intake of breath.

Standing in the room, glasses raised, were friends from the neighborhood, the club, the office. Stunned, Scott barely heard the chorused, "Happy anniversary!" All he could think was that the ante for this evening had just skyrocketed.

Suddenly he felt more tired than he could ever remember. And older. But sure as hell not wiser.

Meg's grip on his arm tightened, and as she caught his eye, a determined smile on her face, he realized what the crowd expected and protocol dictated. He lowered his head and kissed his wife, something he couldn't remember doing for quite some time.

As he drew away, Bud clapped him on the shoulder. "Gotcha, didn't we, boy?"

His mother was hugging Meg. "Did we pull it off? Are you surprised?"

Hayley and Justin stood to one side, observing the scene like proud directors of the drama.

Scott found himself stammering. An intimate family dinner he could've handled. But this?

This called for an Academy Award–winning performance.

JUSTIN HAD SCARFED DOWN three rolls waiting for the main course. That was the trouble with grown-up parties. They stood around boozing it up for ages before they even sat down. Then, all the waiters brought you was a salad with smelly cheese and ruffly greens that looked like his grandmother's doilies. The rolls had saved his life. He hoped to God they'd bring the meat and potatoes soon.

His parents and grandparents were seated at the head table, but he was sitting with the Morrisons from the neighborhood and their kid Trevor, who was palming his roll into pellet-shaped balls.

Hayley looked ridiculous. Holding a champagne glass filled with orange juice, she was acting as if she were twenty-five instead of fifteen. Yet he knew she was as anxious as he was about how their parents would react to what was still to come.

Everyone seemed to be having a good time, especially his grandmother, who'd been working on the guest list and arrangements since last spring. He'd never been able to see what the big deal was about twenty years. What did you expect when you got married? "Till death do us part," right? So what was twenty years?

Lots of kids in his class had divorced parents. In fact, sometimes he thought he was the oddball. Brian, a guy on his softball team, spent a month with his mother and a month with his father. How weird would that be?

Chewing thoughtfully on his fourth roll, Justin studied his parents. His mother was kind of a babe, he guessed. Sleek blond hair, slim figure, blue eyes the color of the Dallas Cowboys' uniforms. She was laughing, but it sounded like glass breaking. And his dad? He had that puffed-up, I'm-a-success look, as if he expected to cinch a huge deal any minute. But they weren't really looking at each other. They'd kissed, yeah, but after that? It seemed like they were more interested in the guests.

He'd thought everybody was supposed to be celebrating love tonight. So why didn't it seem like they were?

Finally. The waiter approached and set a huge slab of pink prime rib in front of him. It came with a side of curlicue-shaped mashed potatoes. Looking at the meat, he was repulsed to find white streaks of fat running through it.

He glanced at the head table once more. His father was bent over his meal as if he'd never seen food before, and his mom had her back to him, flapping her hands as she talked to his grandfather.

Justin stared at his plate and knew he wouldn't be able to eat a bite.

And the worst was yet to come. The party was only the first part of the surprise.

The next one? He was pretty sure it didn't stand a snowball's chance in hell of working.

MEG EXCUSED HERSELF before dessert and sought asylum in the ladies' room. Fielding all the well-meaning comments and fawning expressions of joy had strained the limits of her civility. She and Scott should've been allied in a facade of marital bliss, but he'd become unresponsive, glum. That left her to carry on the pretense that this anniversary was a lovefest.

Fortunately the powder room was empty. She leaned against the counter, studying her reflection in the mirror. The disappointment in her eyes was all too evident. She pulled a lipstick out of her evening bag and carefully redid her lips, knowing that no amount of makeup could mask her rising sense of panic. She dabbed some cold water on the back of her neck, the chill jolting her into awareness.

And just in time. As the door swung open, she could hear Trish Endicott, the wife of one of Scott's colleagues, saying to the woman with her, "She and Scott make an incredible team, don't you think?"

Meg gave a silent laugh. The two of them an incredible team? Then Trish completed her thought. "Brenda and Scott are awesome together. So creative."

Meg swallowed the bile that filled her throat. Creative? She just bet they were.

When Trish caught a glimpse of Meg, she stammered. "You know," she said, blushing, "their work on the department-store account."

Meg put the lipstick in her bag and closed it with a snap. "Yes, they do work well together." She stepped around the women. "If you'll excuse me, I need to get back to the table."

Outside, she leaned against the wall, controlling her breathing. Were Trish's remarks innocent, or was there more to them? Had she merely given voice to Meg's suspicions?

Now, she'd have to go back into the dining room where Brenda was, of course, an invited guest, slap a smile on her face and somehow get through this endless evening.

No sooner had she rejoined Scott and her in-laws, than Bud, a cheery grin on his face, stood up, tapped a spoon against his water glass and called for silence. Beside her, Meg saw Marie straighten, her eyes twinkling as she watched her husband.

Meg's heart sank. Toasts. Please, she pleaded to whatever deity was in charge of graceful exits, just let this be over.

Then Meg saw that Justin and Hayley had joined their grandfather, Hayley preening in her center-stage role and Justin casting uncertain glances at her and Scott.

"The children, Marie and I thank all of you for coming to help us celebrate Meg and Scott's twentieth." He beamed. "And for keeping this party a secret." Raising his champagne glass, he invited the crowd to stand and lift theirs. Then he turned to Scott and Meg, and Meg felt Scott slowly—grudgingly—put his arm around her. "To a bride, still as beautiful as the day she made my son the happiest of men. And to you, Scott, for having such good taste in women. Here's to you both with our wishes for twenty more wonderful years of marriage."

Looking into her father-in-law's loving face, Meg's eyes misted. Then the congratulations of the guests engulfed her.

"Cheers."

"Hear, hear."

"To Meg and Scott."

Scott pivoted her toward him and lifted his glass. She held her breath in anticipation of his obligatory response. "Thank you, Dad, Mother, Hayley, Justin and all of you who gave up your time to be with us tonight." He paused and Meg could feel her husband gathering himself. "And to you, Meg. Thanks for twenty years of—" his hesitation seemed to last an eternity "—togetherness."

That was neutral enough, Meg conceded. Honest. They had been together. Living in the same house. Signing Christmas cards as a couple. Hosting dinner parties. Rearing their children. Earlier she'd acknowledged that physical attraction alone couldn't sustain a marriage, but neither could proximity.

"Thank you," she murmured, averting her head, letting him kiss her cheek. Her gaze fell on the amply endowed, "incredible" Brenda Sampson.

Could this evening get any worse?

The question had just crossed her mind, when the answer came. And not the one she wanted to hear.

"Well, kiddos," Bud went on, "the celebration isn't over quite yet. Marie, the children and I have one last surprise for the two of you."

Meg caught Justin looking at her pleadingly. Her skin prickled. She didn't have a good feeling about this.

"Hope you don't mind, but Marie and I are planning to stay here in Tulsa a little longer than you bargained for." He grinned. "We'll be babysitting."

"What the—" Only she heard Scott's muttered expletive.

Bud gestured toward Marie and the kids. "To celebrate your anniversary, the four of us are sending you on a trip to the Colorado cabin where you spent your honeymoon."

Thunderstruck. That was the only word Meg could come up with to describe her reaction. Opening her mouth to protest, she felt Scott's hand clamp on her forearm.

"Pops, that's very generous and we appreciate it, but it's out of the question."

"Absolutely," Meg murmured.

"We'll talk about this later," Scott added, "but right now it's impossible for me to leave the office."

"Nonsense." Wes, Scott's partner, came to the front of the room. "It's all arranged. Brenda and I have everything covered. You'll join us for the presentation to the Jordan people Monday morning and then take off for Estes Park."

"You were in on this?" Scott's tone carried an edge of accusation.

"Sure. Your mother's been planning this event since last March. You're not indispensable, you know. Brenda and I will take care of business while you play. Any red-blooded man would be thrilled to whisk a wife like Meg off for a second honeymoon."

Scott shook his head, at a loss for words.

Meg cleared her throat. "Some other time maybe. My calendar is full and—"

Hayley stepped forward, a proud smile on her face. "No, it isn't, Mom. I went through your day planner and canceled everything. You have a whole week free."

Was the entire world conspiring against them? How could she and Scott possibly endure seven days cooped up in a cabin that would bring back so many memories, once pleasant, now nothing but painful?

Marie, twining her fingers nervously, said in a plaintive voice, "You won't disappoint us, will you?"

Disappoint you? Wait until you hear about the separation.

Scott went over to embrace his mother. "No, Mom, of course not."

Of course not! Was he out of his mind? Surely he wasn't actually planning to accept this gift. It would be a mighty expensive farce.

Suddenly, Meg became aware of their guests and their slowly dawning bewilderment. Meg knew she had to say something to save face for her in-laws. "You'll have to excuse us, but you really caught us off guard. We're not accustomed to leaving home on such short notice."

"About time you started, then," Bud said as if the matter were closed. Again, he raised his glass. "To Meg and Scott's safe travels."

The guests echoed the words, seemingly reassured that all would go as planned.

Scott leaned over to whisper in Meg's ear. "Don't say anything. We'll talk about this at home."

They'd talk about it, all right. About how to reject this ridiculous gift.

BUD'S FEET HURT. He hadn't danced that much in years. He sat on the side of the bed, massaging his instep.

Smearing night cream on her face, Marie stood in the doorway to the bathroom. "Tired?"

Bud reached for the Tiger Balm on the night table. "It's way past our bedtime, sweetheart." He opened the lid, took a dab and rubbed it on his neck, closing his eyes against the pungent odor.

Marie wiped her hands on a tissue and crossed the room. "Here, let me."

She dug her fingers deep into his coiled muscles, reducing him to a sigh of satisfaction. "You sure know how to make an old guy feel good."

She chuckled. "A far cry from the way I made you feel good when we were younger."

Where had the time gone? Back then, he wouldn't have needed a massage, so eager would he have been to get her into bed and do wonderful things to her. Now? There was no comfort like her hands soothing his aches and pain. "I love you," he found himself saying.

She leaned over and kissed the top of his head. "And I love you, you old coot."

She slipped into bed while he adjusted the drapes and turned off the bedside lamp before joining her. He picked up her hand and entwined his fingers with hers.

Sighing contentedly, Marie began recapping the evening, just as he'd known she would. In her voice he heard how pleased she was that they'd pulled off the party. She raved about the elaborate decorations and gourmet meal, the number of friends who'd come to help celebrate and his job as master of ceremonies.

She snuggled against him. "But you know the best part?"

He kissed the back of her hand. "No. What was that?"

"When we told them about the trip. Did you see their faces?"

Bud tensed, hoping Marie wouldn't notice. He chose his words carefully. "I saw their faces, all right." And they had not looked happy. For Marie's sake, he hoped he was wrong. But he knew love when he saw it, and it had been in short supply tonight between Meg and Scott.

"There was just one odd thing," she said. "I didn't hear anything about Scotty giving Meg an anniversary present."

"Maybe he did it in private."

"I'm sure that's the case." She yawned drowsily and in typical fashion went straight to sleep.

Bud wished he could've had such a welcome release from his thoughts. He knew his son. He had not been himself tonight. Bud hadn't wanted to worry Marie, but, if he had to make a bet, he'd say there had been no exchange of anniversary gifts.

WHEN SCOTT ENTERED the bedroom, Meg was sitting on the chaise longue, a book in her lap, waiting for him. He had loitered in the family room hoping she'd already be asleep, knowing all along that it was a vain attempt to postpone their inevitable discussion. At one time, the prospect of a week together in Colorado would have thrilled them both. The fact that now it most assuredly did not was one more nail in the coffin of their marriage.

Yet he'd seen the delighted look on his mother's face, the kids' smiles, his father's beam of satisfaction. How in hell could he tell them—any of them—that a trip to Estes Park was out of the question? That the marriage was on the rocks? And he doubted that

Ward Jordan would be happy to hear that he was going on vacation for a week.

Meg closed her book. "Do you want to put on your pajamas or talk first?"

He sat on the side of the bed, hands on his knees. "Shoot."

Her eyes pierced his. "You have to tell them."

"What?"

"That we're not going."

"And the reason is…?"

"Work."

He sighed. "You heard Wes. That excuse isn't going to cut it. Much as I'd like it to."

"Then we'll simply have to tell them the truth. We only have tomorrow before we're expected to leave."

Scott hedged. "I'm not sure I can disappoint everyone."

She closed her eyes and let her head loll back. Finally she looked at him and said, "And you think I'm crazy about the idea?"

"Do we have to argue? What would be the harm in going on the trip? It would buy us time to get our story together." He was grasping at straws, but he knew what joy planning this trip had given his folks.

"Are you suggesting we take the trip under false pretenses and then come home with the big separation announcement? That'll thrill everyone."

Damned if he knew what he was suggesting. He only knew that somehow they needed more time before deciding to take such a drastic step. If this trip would give them that time, then he was going. "Meg, here's the deal. Before I move out, I want to be absolutely certain that separation is what's best."

"And you're not?"

He searched his soul. Finally he said, "No, I'm not. What do we have to lose by taking one more week? Maybe being away from here will give us a different perspective. Allow us to figure out exactly why we're separating. If going to Colorado means we let my parents and our kids have a few more days without heartbreak, is that so bad?"

"You're sure you want to go?"

"I'm not happy about being gone from the office, but maybe this is an opportunity you and I need."

She remained silent. Finally she stood, placed her book on the night table and turned to him. "Okay. Have it your way." Then she walked into the bathroom, leaving him with no peace of mind whatsoever.

WHEN MEG OPENED HER EYES the next morning and realized she had another busy day ahead preparing for her absence, she groaned and pulled the covers over her head. Scott was already up, and she wished she never had to leave the protection of her bed. Never had to face Scott's parents, Hayley or Justin—or her broken dreams. Just the idea of a week's stay at the remote cabin with Scott made her restless. But maybe they did need time to decide how they were going to announce their separation.

Faintly, she could hear pots and pans clanging in the kitchen. Marie, the happy homemaker, was probably whipping up her famous apple-cinnamon pancakes. Hayley would still be in bed, but Justin and Scott were undoubtedly perched on kitchen stools applauding Marie's efforts. Would anyone even miss her if she decided not to get out of bed?

That's it. Keep that self-pity rolling.

She sat up, poked her feet into her slippers and headed for the bathroom, eyes puffy, mouth dry. She didn't look forward to the separation. It wasn't an easy choice to make. The fact was, she felt terrified.

But she could no longer endure a sham

marriage. Keeping up appearances for her in-laws' sake had already proved quite a challenge, and she had several more hours to go.

She reached for her toothbrush automatically, wondering how often she'd taken her daily routine for granted. Taken her marriage for granted.

After she washed her face and put on her robe, she wandered back into the bedroom. There on her dresser was an envelope, addressed in Scott's bold handwriting.

She picked it up and held it for several minutes. Finally, she slit the seal and removed one of his monogrammed note cards. She studied the words scrawled there.

I'm sorry, Meg. Yesterday I never wished you a happy anniversary, and I didn't buy you a gift. I guess I thought you'd prefer it that way. Maybe the last few years haven't been so great, but I've never regretted marrying you.

Then he'd signed his name. No "Love." Just his signature. But there was a PS. "Thanks for agreeing to go to Colorado with me."

Meg reread the message. The note was

proof of how far they'd strayed apart. He couldn't even tell her in person how he felt.

Stuffing the card into her robe pocket, she blinked away tears that both betrayed and confused her.

CHAPTER FOUR

MEG GAZED OUT THE PLANE WINDOW at the patchwork of farms and open range thousands of feet below. On the aisle, Scott hunched over his laptop, lost in concentration. Between them was the empty middle seat, a symbolic chasm. Never a confident flier, Meg clenched her fingers in her lap and wished away the headache assaulting her temples.

Somehow she'd survived Sunday's frantic race to wash clothes, pack, write down the kids' schedules and prepare detailed instructions for Bud and Marie—all while wearing the frozen smile of a painted marionette. Had she fooled anyone? Who knew?

Then this morning, Scott had awakened early, totally preoccupied with the Jordan ad-campaign presentation. While he'd dressed, she'd lain curled in a fetal position in their bed, dreading a trip that months ago might have excited her.

Now Scott's heavy sigh interrupted her musings. "What?" she said, that one word representing as much conversation as she felt like offering.

Checking his watch, he shrugged with impatience. "I need to call Brenda before the office closes."

The headache throbbed against Meg's skull. "There's no huge hurry, is there?"

"You've forgotten the switch to mountain time." His patronizing tone grated on her nerves.

"Oh, I'm sure Brenda will be standing by for your call." Standing by? More likely poised like a schoolgirl waiting for an invitation to the prom.

"She'd better be. We have work to do."

So much for the idea of a vacation getaway. But what had she expected? While she read and took long, solitary walks, his work would consume his time. That is, whatever time was left after they finished dissecting their marriage.

She rested her aching head against the seat back and closed her eyes. How had they reached this point? When had their relationship started to unravel?

On paper Scott had fit the profile of her

dream man perfectly—he was good-looking, smart, ambitious, caring. Great husband material. She could just hear her mother's nasal twang followed by her embittered laugh: "Meg, honey, it's just as easy to fall in love with a rich man. Shoulda followed my own advice."

She pictured her childhood home—a two-bedroom house with a sagging front porch in a run-down section of town. Remembered how it had smelled of bacon grease, cats and cloying gardenia air freshener. When she'd been in grade school, she would sit on the front steps in the late-summer afternoons watching fathers come home from work, wondering what it would be like to have a man in the house—a daddy who might hug her and ask about her day and maybe play catch with her out in the yard after dinner. But her father had died when she was three.

In high school, her fantasy had shifted from a daddy to an attentive, loving husband with whom she would live the perfect life. Although she'd never lacked for boyfriends, most fell far short of her ideal, and she saw no point in wasting time on them.

In the spring of Meg's second year in college, her mother was diagnosed with ovarian cancer and had lived only until summer's end, leaving Meg with significant medical bills.

Certainly, no Prince Charming waited in the wings to rescue her.

Given little choice, she'd sold the house, moved into university housing, found an on-campus job and scrimped to fund her final two years of college.

Following graduation, she'd worked as the office manager for a large dental clinic. One day, in a waiting room crowded with mothers and cantankerous children, a construction worker with an excruciating toothache and an old woman nervously awaiting a fitting for new dentures, there appeared a handsome young man with a gorgeous tan and a sexy smile that showed off his white, even teeth—a feature, given her line of work, she couldn't help noticing.

After introducing himself as Scott Harper, an account executive with a small advertising agency, he'd proceeded to tout the benefits of promoting the clinic. "Dentistry is competitive. A practice can't survive on word of mouth alone, if you'll pardon the pun," he'd explained, before launching into the various promotional services his firm could offer.

Never had a media spot sounded so fascinating.

Later, retelling the story of their meeting, Scott would laugh and say, "I didn't sell the dentists on my wares, but I sold myself." Then he would turn that killer grin on her and add, "I got the girl."

He wasn't rich, as her mother would've preferred, but he was all the other things Meg had wanted in a man. She'd always claimed not to believe in love at first sight, but Scott had changed her mind. Dinner that first night, flowers the next day, a weekend trip to the lake. He'd passed every test with flying colors.

Meg opened her eyes and turned to study her husband, poring over computer files. He was still good-looking, smart and ambitious. Emphasis on the ambitious. Just what she'd always thought she wanted.

But caring? Attentive?

Did the lack of those qualities explain the void inside her? The feeling that she was still sitting on that front porch waiting for her daddy to come home?

STANDING AT HIS LOCKER Monday afternoon, scrounging for some notebook paper, Justin suddenly remembered. In all the excitement of the party and his folks' big trip, he'd forgotten about the note from his English teacher. He dug a hand into the black hole of his backpack and finally came up with the envelope addressed to his parents in Mrs. Kelly's perfect cursive. He slumped against the wall. He was totally screwed.

While he watched other kids scurrying down the hall, ducking into classrooms, he stood frozen, debating. He could go into English class, march up to Mrs. Kelly's desk and throw himself on her mercy. Yeah, right. The woman was born without a heart. Or he could hide out in a bathroom stall until the final bell sounded. English was his last class of the day. After that, he could sneak on the bus. If any teachers came into the restroom, he'd tell them he had diarrhea. Yeah, who'd want to question that?

Only a few kids remained in the hall. He glanced at the clock and watched anxiously as the second hand ticked up to the hour. *Do something, idiot,* he urged himself.

When the tardy bell rang, he grabbed his backpack, slammed his locker shut and, with his heart thudding against his rib cage, fled into the boys' bathroom.

It was empty. Quiet. Too quiet. It smelled like pee and disinfectant. Gross paper towels overflowed the trash can and the faucets were slimy with liquid soap.

He slipped into a stall, ready in case "Bozo" Harris, the vice principal, or some other kid showed up.

Okay, he was safe for now. But he needed a plan. Eventually he'd have to show the note to one of his grandparents. They'd find out he'd been "prevaricating." He rolled his eyes. He'd never get used to that word. Maybe Gramma and Grampa would feel sorry for him if they knew he'd been "sick" seventh period and would call the school and excuse his absence. He sure didn't want to serve detention for cutting class.

His stomach cramped. Would Mrs. Kelly still make him read that stupid book?

Just then somebody entered the bathroom. Somebody big. Somebody with suit trousers and old-man shoes.

Perched on the toilet seat, Justin held his breath.

"Harper, you in here?"

Shit. Bozo. How did he know?

"Usually when a fella takes a crap, he'll pull his pants down. Why don't you come out and tell me what you're doing in there when you're supposed to be in Mrs. Kelly's class? She was ticked when you didn't show up."

Ticked? He bet she was. He could just picture her grilling every last kid in the class about him. Probably called him a *miscreant,* another one of her fancy-shmancy words.

"I'm waiting," Bozo barked.

Slowly, Justin stood up, slung his backpack over his shoulder and opened the stall door.

Bozo glared at him. "Follow me, son. We're going to my office for a little chat. I just may have to call your parents."

Jeez, not the chamber of horrors. That was what all the kids called Mr. Harris's office. Nothing good went down there, that was for sure. Justin grasped at his last straw. "My parents are out of town."

Bozo stopped and laid a firm hand on Justin's shoulder. "I doubt they left you all by yourself." He raised an eyebrow as if he could see straight into Justin's brain.

Justin tried a new tack. "No, sir." The "sir" business couldn't hurt.

"Well?" Bozo increased the pressure on Justin's shoulder.

"My grandparents are staying with me and my sister."

Mr. Harris resumed his drill-sergeant march toward the office. "They'll do."

Justin's insides turned to mush. "Do you have to call them?"

Bozo smiled in that smug way of his. "We'll see about that, Harper. But it's a distinct possibility."

BECAUSE OF DENVER TRAFFIC, it was late afternoon by the time Scott and Meg reached the cabin. When Scott stepped out of the rental car, the clean mountain air, redolent of pine, served as a powerful pick-me-up. Overhead, the sun was sinking behind the peaks, and surrounding him was silence, broken only by the gentle tumble of a mountain stream flowing behind the cabin. He drew a deep breath, and for the first time in a long while, felt his muscles relax.

"Are you going to stand there all day?"

He turned toward Meg, who waited by the trunk of the car, her arms folded across her chest. He was inclined to say, "So what if I do?" but thought better of it. Meg had made it abundantly clear that she wasn't happy to be there. At least not alone with him.

He pressed the button on his key chain to open the trunk, then pulled out their bags.

Meg eyed the log cabin with its deep front porch. "Do you think it's the same one?"

"Seems familiar."

"All the cabins look alike. I guess it doesn't matter." She grabbed her overnight bag out of his hand. "I'll take that."

Toting the two larger suitcases, he followed her onto the porch and fumbled in his pocket for the key. When the door swung open, he winced, recalling his insistence twenty years ago that he carry his bride over the threshold. Then another memory swept through him. That day the bags had been left on the porch, forgotten. He'd taken her directly to the bedroom where he'd hurriedly undressed her, shed his own clothes and made love to her beneath the goose-down comforter, not caring that they hadn't turned on the heater. They'd created their own warmth with the delicious friction of skin on skin, with kisses hot and passionate and an abandon born of impatience.

As if she'd entered his fantasy, Meg said, "Can we please get some heat in here?"

Don't I wish, he thought to himself, crossing the living room to adjust the thermostat.

When he turned around, Meg had already disappeared into the bedroom. Scott studied the cabin. Same indestructible knotty-pine furniture and wrought-iron chandelier. Same stone fireplace, blackened with years of smoke. Same small kitchenette spanning one end of the room. "I'll be back," Scott said, returning to the car for the few groceries they'd picked up in town.

The cabin sat near a grove of aspen, its leaves a burnished gold. In the distance, Scott heard the plaintive howl of a coyote. For several minutes he stood there, inhaling fresh air and trying to block out his memories of that unforgettable honeymoon. Finally, he grabbed the grocery sack and his laptop, hoping against hope that the 1950s-vintage lodging would have a dial-up connection for his modem.

Although he didn't expect to hear for a day or two about the Jordan account, there was still plenty to keep him busy—and he figured busy was good in this situation. How long could Meg possibly draw out their inevitable discussion? On the plane, he'd done some preliminary calculations as he considered their financial situation. It made him sick to consider the implications of separation. How much worse would divorce be? Of course he'd end up doing whatever was right, but he didn't want to get screwed in the process.

He'd worked hard to provide for his family, but he liked his creature comforts, too.

Reluctantly, he returned to the cabin. Meg had already unpacked and arranged her toiletries in the bathroom. "Give me those," she said, taking the groceries from him. Opening and closing kitchen cabinets and drawers, she took inventory before beginning to put away the supplies. "Hungry?" she asked.

Hungry? He was starving. He'd had nothing since lunch but airline crackers and cheese. "Yeah. Should we go into town for dinner?" There was a famous steak place he hoped was still in business.

"We're here now," she said, her back to him. "If you wanted to eat in town, you should've said so before we drove out to the cabin."

He groaned. It was only ten minutes to one of the best sirloins in the Rockies. "What've we got?"

"I can whip up some macaroni and cheese. Heat a can of green beans. Then there are those disgusting marshmallow cookies you bought."

Oh, yeah, like mac and cheese would make up for the lack of red meat? But the cookies, far from being disgusting, might make the rest palatable. "Okay, whatever you want."

See? He was as willing to compromise as the next guy, if only she'd figure that out.

While she cooked, he unpacked and changed. Immediately after dinner, Meg picked up her novel and went into the bedroom to read. He pulled on a windbreaker, then carried his coffee to the rocker on the front porch. Bone-weary, he nevertheless knew sleep wouldn't come easily. This morning's presentation had been a bitch. Their AV guy had been late setting up the PowerPoint presentation and Brenda had had to improvise until everything was ready. Ward Jordan and his executives had been impassive throughout, never once letting their poker faces slip. Scott had little idea what they were thinking or how Harper Concepts stacked up against the competition. Their handshakes at the conclusion of the morning had been cordial but noncommittal. Thousands upon thousands of dollars lay in the balance, a fact Scott preferred not to dwell on.

Then, as he'd been throwing papers into his briefcase before dashing off to the airport to meet Meg, Brenda had sidled into his office, her iceberg-blue eyes large and, for once, vulnerable. "Did I blow it?"

"Nonsense. You probably saved our asses.

I doubt the Jordan folks knew we'd ad-libbed part of the presentation."

"You're sweet," she'd said, stepping closer. "How long will you be away?"

"A week, but I'll keep in touch."

"You'd better," she'd whispered, invading his space with her musky fragrance and the warmth of her body. "I'll miss you." Then she'd raised up on her tiptoes to kiss his cheek, lingering just long enough to set off alarm bells.

Scott leaned back in the rocker and sighed heavily. Could Brenda somehow sense the distance between him and Meg? Could she be moving in for...what? Or was she just, by nature, an affectionate woman?

Another disturbing question surfaced: Would he, somewhere down the line, feel like finding out?

In the dark, he heard a rustling. Peering toward the aspen grove, he spotted two does and a fawn, heads up, alert. Sensing danger, they bounded toward the stream.

The sudden quiet washed over him and he sighed again. He and Meg had sat out here almost every night of their honeymoon, wrapped together in a comforter, listening to the sounds of the forest, watching moonlight silver the tips of the pine trees. Holding hands. Cuddling. Making plans. Sharing a dream that was theirs alone.

He scrubbed a hand over his face. Long ago. So very long ago.

BUD KNEW SOMETHING was wrong the minute Justin walked in the door, slammed his back-pack down on the kitchen table, mumbled hello and tore up to his room. It was a beautiful fall day. Up and down the block, kids were riding bikes or shooting hoops. Usually Justin ran with the pack. Yes sirree, something was bothering the boy. Missing his folks maybe? But based on what Bud had seen, that seemed unlikely.

Just as well Marie was off to the store. She'd hover over the young fella, smothering him with questions and pampering.

He switched off the TV and wandered into the kitchen. Food. The kid had to be hungry. Spotting a bag of microwave popcorn in the pantry, he pulled it out and began to nuke it. The aroma ought to entice the boy.

While the corn popped, Bud went upstairs and tapped on Justin's door. "Son, I'm fixin' to have a snack. Why don't you join me? Can't eat that whole bag of popcorn all by myself."

There was no answer, and Bud opted to let the boy decide for himself. Sure enough, as soon as he'd dumped the hot popcorn into a bowl, Justin came down the stairs. "Grab yourself a soda and let's go out on the patio."

Carrying the popcorn, Bud went outside, set the bowl on a table and pulled two chairs together, hoping Justin wouldn't recognize this as a setup for the grandfatherly chat he intended to have. When Justin joined him, Bud waited until he'd taken the edge off his hunger before launching his probe. "Missing your folks?"

Justin gave him a strange look. "No way."

"S'pose they're having a good time?"

The boy shrugged.

Bud tried a different angle. "Everything go all right at school today?"

Justin fidgeted in his seat, then took a swig from his soda can. "I guess." He turned away, avoiding his grandfather's scrutiny.

"Sure?"

Justin hung his head, then let out a big sigh. "They called, didn't they?"

"Who?"

"The school."

Bud eyed him shrewdly. "Not yet. Should they have?"

"Mr. Harris probably will tomorrow. He coaches after school."

Justin shoved the popcorn bowl across the table and wrapped his arms tightly across his stomach. "Uh, Grampa, I'm…well, I'm in trouble."

Easy does it, Bud reminded himself. "How do you figure?"

Justin glanced skyward as if expecting some superhero to sweep down and extricate him from the conversation. "I, uh, I cut class."

"Why was that?"

After a long pause, Justin poured out the story. Bud listened patiently. At the bottom lay the fact that Justin had faked a book report. Why? "Son, you know what you did was wrong, don't you? You tried to fool Mrs. Kelly into thinking you'd read the book, then you failed to give her note to your folks to sign, and cutting class, well, you understand that only made things worse."

Justin nodded, his misery obvious. Finally, he whispered, "I know."

"When the school calls, you can't expect me to cover for you."

"I guess not."

Bud paused, ostensibly enjoying the landscaping, letting Justin stew before he asked the next question. "So…what should we do about that oral book report?"

Justin looked up, startled. "Nothing. I'm not going to read that stupid book."

Bud studied his grandson. "And that will be helpful, how?"

"She can't make me," Justin said stubbornly.

"No, she can't, but there must be a reason you're resisting the idea so strongly."

Justin turned his head away from his grandfather. Finally, he mumbled something unintelligible.

"What is it, son? Spit it out. You'll feel better."

He faced Bud, his face red and mottled. His voice quavered. "Okay, I can't read. Get it? *I can't read.*"

Bud sat there, stunned. He'd expected the boy to say he hated the teacher or that the book was boring, anything but what he'd just heard. Did Scott and Meg know about this? Bud cleared his throat, aware that whatever he said next was critical. "How can I help?"

"I dunno." Justin worried his lip.

"What do you mean you can't read?"

"I *can* read. I mean, I know the words and stuff, and they sometimes make sense. But

I'm slow. Other kids, they read a lot easier and faster. I... I feel stupid."

"So it's better to ignore the problem?"

Another shrug.

"I think tomorrow we make a trip to the school, and after we stop in the office and you apologize to Mr. Harris for cutting class, we talk with Mrs. Kelly, as well."

A horrified expression settled on Justin's face. "No way! I can't do it."

"It'd be tough for you to go by yourself. That's why I'm going with you."

Justin's hunched shoulders relaxed a fraction. "You'd do that?"

"Yep. Not only will I do that, we're going to find out how to get you some help with your reading. It's just like soccer or basketball, a skill that needs lots of practice."

Justin appeared skeptical. Again, Bud gave him some time to think it over. Finally he said, "I guess I don't have much choice, do I?"

"That's my boy." Bud picked up the popcorn and handed it to Justin, who seemed, miraculously to have recovered his appetite. "I'll set up the meetings tomorrow when Mr. Harris calls."

When Marie returned, she smiled at the two of them, still sitting in the yard, now talking football, an empty bowl between them. She brought Justin another soda and left them, mumbling something about rearranging Meg's pantry.

The calm lasted only briefly. Through the screen door, Bud and Justin heard Hayley's noisy arrival from cheerleading practice. "Gramma, Gramma, you'll never guess what! It's happened. I'm so pumped!"

"What's happened?" Marie asked.

"Zach Simon invited me to a party Friday night!" Bud heard the swoon in Hayley's voice. "He's *so* hot!"

Bud could've gone a long time without hearing those words from his granddaughter's lips.

"I can go, can't I, Gramma?"

"Well," Marie hesitated, "I don't know. What kind of party? Would your parents approve?"

Justin strolled to the screen door. "Gramma, ask her if it's a car date."

"Shut up, Justin."

Bud followed his grandson into the family room. Hayley was shooting daggers at her brother. "Is it a car date?" he inquired mildly.

Hayley rolled her eyes. "Of course it is. You don't think a junior's going to have his parents drive, do you?"

"Probably not," Bud said, feeling his way through the minefield. "Are you allowed to date boys who drive?"

She looked at the floor. "Depends."

Justin's face flushed. "She is not!" He moved closer to his grandmother. "Don't let her fool you."

Hayley glared at Justin, then she fell dramatically into the leather recliner. "Fine, everybody. Go ahead. Ruin my life."

"Nobody wants to ruin your life, honey," Bud said. "But we need to know more. What kind of party. Who this young man is." He faced Justin. "From now on, son, this is between your sister and Gramma and me."

Justin shrugged, then mounted the steps toward his room, calling over his shoulder, "As if I care."

Hayley couldn't let the remark pass. "God. Why did Mom and Dad ever decide a second child was a good idea?"

Bud sat on the sofa with Marie beside him. "This Zach must be a special young man for you to be so excited," Marie said.

"I've had a crush on him forever." Hayley sat up. "Gramma, I'm sorry I was mean to Justin, but this date is really important to me."

"Tell you what," Bud offered. "You give us

all the details and we'll call your parents and see what they have to say."

Hayley's body sagged. "They'll say no."

"You don't know that."

"If Dad had his way, I'd wear a chastity belt."

Privately, Bud acknowledged his son had a prudent, if outdated solution. "We'll call them. And, honey, you might be surprised."

Hayley blew out a heavy sigh. "Yeah, in a perfect world."

STILL IN THAT TWILIGHT HAZE between sleeping and waking, Meg tried to figure out what was different. The fragrance of cedar? The softness of the mattress? She opened one eye. Of course. The cabin. The much vaunted "second honeymoon."

She stretched out her arm, encountering nothing. Scott must be up already. She squinted at the clock. Seven-thirty. Taking into account the hour's time difference, she'd actually overslept. She was tempted to sink back under the covers, but sunlight streamed through the window and she could hear the stream gurgling. With or without Scott, she loved Colorado. She hefted herself out of bed. She wouldn't waste time sleeping.

After her shower, she put on jeans, a red

turtleneck and a plaid flannel shirt and stuck her feet into her lamb's wool-lined slippers. When she walked into the living room, Scott brought her a mug of hot coffee. She smiled her thanks, then wrapped her hands around the warmth, savoring the rich aroma.

"You look like a girl," Scott said, eyeing her up and down.

"Must be the no-makeup, fresh-scrubbed look."

"I meant it as a compliment."

"Oh." She'd thought they were way past such pleasantries. She was surprised, too. She doubted the beautiful Brenda ever emerged into the light of day without every hair in place.

Scott studied her. She knew that look— the one that said, "I'll let you have your coffee before the bad news." She obliged, taking a fortifying sip.

"Did you sleep okay?"

She nodded. "Like the dead."

"Then you didn't hear me talking to Mom and Pops?"

She went on instant alert. "When?"

"Last night."

"What's wrong?" They hadn't even been gone twenty-four hours.

"Nothing life-threatening." Scott refilled

his empty mug. "Sit down," he said, gesturing to the small kitchen table. "It's Hayley. We have a decision to make."

"Okay." Meg could humor him. She sank into a chair. Scott stopped at the refrigerator, added milk to his coffee and joined her.

"According to Mom, the man of her dreams has asked our daughter to a party Friday night."

"Must be Zach Simon." She groaned inwardly. The kid wearing the rapper clothes.

"The very one. How'd you know his name?"

She couldn't believe it. If he'd stick around home for any length of time, he, too, would have heard the name in the past week. "I pay attention."

"And I don't?"

She didn't bother to answer his ridiculous question.

"He's a junior."

"I know that, too."

Scott looked steadily at her. "She can't go."

"You've already decided?" she asked, the hairs rising on the back of her neck.

"No, I said I'd talk with you and get back to them." He paused. "Seems this Zach drives."

"Um, yes…" She waited to see what else he would say.

"The party is at a private home. I don't like the sound of it."

Meg pursed her lips. "We knew this time would come. I'm not crazy about the idea of our daughter dating guys who drive, either, but for heaven's sake, Scott, she'll be sixteen in January. We can't lock her in her bedroom and throw away the key."

"What if the parents aren't home and there's drinking?"

"Who's hosting the party?"

"Some kid named Tom DeWilde."

"His mother and I were in the same yoga class. All we have to do is ask Bud or Marie to call her to make sure the party will be chaperoned."

"You're considering letting Hayley go?"

"We could have a worse problem on our hands if we don't demonstrate some trust."

He took a quick swig of coffee. "Lord, Meg, don't you remember what you were doing at that age?"

She stifled a sardonic smile. "I think the more important question is what *you* remember doing at that age."

He pounded the palm of his hand on the table. "Exactly. That's what I'm worried about."

"Get over it," she said, faintly amused at his overprotectiveness. "She's one of the last of her group of friends to have a boyfriend."

"It's too soon." He looked up, then grinned crookedly, almost endearingly. "I sound patriarchal, don't I?"

"Frankly, yes. If you'd hang around your family more, you might get a better idea of what's going on with your daughter. With any of us."

"There's a real vote of confidence to start my morning."

Meg curled her fingers around her mug. "This incident illustrates exactly why our marriage is in trouble. We can't even see eye to eye on a simple matter like who Hayley dates. Or when."

"Hell, I don't even approve of the clothes she wears, but a fat lot of good my opinion does."

"She wears what all the girls wear."

"And that makes it okay?" Scott stared at her incredulously. "I mean, have you looked at her lately—bare midriffs, see-through T-shirts, hip-hugging, skintight jeans? Next thing we know she'll have a tattoo and a nose ring."

"Listen, I'm the one dealing with her on a daily basis, I'm the one showing up at school and figuring out what's going on with the kids, and I'm the one, pardon my French, covering your ass when you have more important things to do than pay attention to your children." She rose to her feet. "So, yes, she can go to the party with Zach. Why? Because I said so." With that, she marched out the door onto the front porch, seething.

How dare he act so high-and-mighty where Hayley and Justin were concerned. She hugged herself against the morning chill, wishing she'd had the presence of mind to bring a blanket, or, at the very least, a fresh cup of coffee.

The splendor of the mountains rising in the distance and the pure air mocked the turmoil within her. She watched a chipmunk scamper across the yard, then pause, his nose twitching, before he resumed his search for food. She'd have to remember to put some nuts out for him. When she and Scott had been here on their honeymoon, they'd taken a blanket outside and lain on their stomachs, tempting the chipmunks with handfuls of peanuts. Finally one had come and eaten out of her hand. She could still remember Scott's delighted laughter.

Shivering, she realized she was too cold to stay on the porch, regardless of her pride.

Reentering the cabin, she saw that Scott had spread some papers out on the table and was setting up his laptop. It figured.

He didn't look up, just said, "Against my better judgment, I called home and told Mom to let Hayley go on the date, as long as she speaks with the DeWilde boy's mother." He plugged a cable into a port. "I hope you're satisfied."

"That was big of you."

"But I'm not happy about it."

"I can see that."

He scowled at the screen. "I have work to do this morning. We can talk this afternoon."

"About what?"

"About *what?* The big issue you can't wait to discuss. Separation."

Meg flinched. She'd waited for him to be ready to discuss it. Now he was.

But, surprisingly, that gave her no satisfaction.

CHAPTER FIVE

AFTER LUNCH, SCOTT CHECKED his e-mail while Meg cleaned up the kitchen. Suddenly, he shut his laptop, glanced at her and said, "Okay."

The resignation in his voice gave Meg pause. Actually talking about how to tell the children they were separating would bring them to the brink. She thought about their life together and all they would be giving up. But also about the pain of tarnished dreams.

Scott stood, spreading his arms in silent appeal. "Your call. Where do we start?"

Meg gazed into his solemn, almost wounded eyes. "Let's go for a walk." Walking would be good. She thought better when she was moving.

He headed toward the bedroom. "I'll grab our jackets."

Meg hugged herself trying to warm up. His businesslike tone and willingness to talk, while welcome, had sent chills racing through her.

When they left the cabin, Scott set off at a brisk pace, and for the first quarter of a mile, they didn't speak. The only sounds audible over the pounding of her heart were the raucous cries of mountain jays and the miniature timpani of aspen leaves. Lengthening her stride to keep up with him, she realized she couldn't remember the last time they'd gone for a walk together, an activity they used to enjoy. Out of the blue came an image of Scott lifting a gurgling Hayley into the baby carrier. He'd called her his little hiking buddy.

Meg clenched her jaw. No use getting sentimental. A lot had changed since then.

Finally, he broke the silence. "I think we should tell Mom and Pops first."

"So they can help deal with the kids' reactions?"

He nodded grimly. "The fallout won't be pretty."

She pictured Hayley's tear-streaked face and Justin's self-protective shrug. "How could it be?"

"So what do we tell them?"

"The truth. That we both love them very much and will always love them but that you and I have been miserable. We need time apart to sort out our priorities."

"Meanwhile, putting the kids in limbo for who knows how long?"

"So what are you suggesting? That we cut right to divorce?"

"One incision. Swift. Neat."

Like hammer blows, his words penetrated her consciousness. Her throat clogged with sudden tears, and she struggled to keep her voice even. "Is that what you want, Scott?"

Head down, he marched another thirty yards, then stopped and whirled to face her. "*Want?* I'll tell you what I want. I want the girl I married."

Anger replaced her shock. "What's that supposed to mean? Am I so awful?"

"You're not awful." His shoulders sagged and he ran a hand tiredly through his hair. "You're just…different."

She stood her ground, staring up at him. "And you're not?"

He took her by the elbow and steered her toward a narrow path through the woods. "I'm not saying that. We're in different places than we were twenty years ago. And what I said back there? About divorce? I don't know whether I meant it or not." He stepped aside to let her lead. "All I know is I don't want to go on the way we have been—you criticizing me all the time about work and being so completely devoted to the kids there's no time left for us."

A branch snapped back and slapped Meg in the face—which was exactly what his words felt like. So that was how he saw her. She'd heard everything now. Not only was she a nag, she was too good a mother. "Well, excuse me for caring."

"Here we go again. Dammit, Meg, we *both* care. We started out with big dreams, and, hey, we've even achieved a lot of them."

"But apparently they didn't buy happiness."

The path widened and he came abreast of her. "That doesn't mean they can't, does it?"

This was what happened every time they tried to have this conversation. They never reached any kind of closure. She stopped walking. "That's up to you."

Placing a hand on her shoulder, he sought her eyes. His voice came out husky. "No, Meg. It takes two of us. The point is, is there anything left between us?"

"That would, indeed, be the point." She raised her hands in surrender. "I wish I knew." She reversed direction and headed back toward the cabin, her vision blurred with confused tears. Somehow instead of forcing the issue, she'd backed away, succumbing to a fragile hope.

He didn't follow her. When she finally looked over her shoulder, he was sitting on a boulder, head down, intently studying the moss and lichen clinging to its surface.

When she spotted the cabin—and, from this angle she could tell it was, in fact, the same one they'd honeymooned in—she realized once again that nothing had been settled. Nothing at all.

JUSTIN KEPT HIS EYES focused straight ahead as he led Bud through the halls toward Mrs. Kelly's classroom. Man, how embarrassing. What kid brought his grandfather to school? And they were hardly invisible. Grampa kept nodding and smiling at kids, like he was their friend or something. It had been bad enough sitting in the vice principal's office and admitting he'd lied about the book report and cut class. Heck, after the lecture Bozo had given him, three days of detention sounded like a vacation.

Some kid deliberately bumped into him, throwing him off balance. Then he heard him mutter, "In trouble, butt-head?" When Justin whirled around, Sam Grider was looking back over his shoulder, smirking. Justin's face flamed. Why wouldn't Grider get off his case?

"Who's that?" Grampa asked.

"Nobody. Just a kid I know."

Grampa nodded, but didn't say anything. It was kinda like he knew about Grider without being told. One of these days, Justin vowed, he'd wipe the grin off that kid's face.

Uh-oh. Room 214. Doomsville. Justin stopped. His throat was dry. "Here."

Mrs. Kelly, dressed in that ugly turquoise dress with the fish on it, sat at her desk, reading glasses perched on her long nose, furiously making red marks on some unlucky kid's test. When Grampa knocked on the door, she looked up, fixing her cold gray eyes on them. "Come in, please," she said in her prissy schoolteacher voice.

She motioned for them to sit down in a couple of desks in the front row. He slid into one, then watched Grampa wedge himself into another. In science they'd learned about how animals establish their territory. That was how this felt. Mrs. Kelly, the alpha dog. He wondered. Did Grampa feel intimidated?

"Justin, are you going to introduce me to your grandfather?"

Oh brother, as if he weren't already feeling

stupid enough. Clearing his throat, he made the introduction. Then Mrs. Kelly folded her hands on her desk and stared straight at him, as if she were waiting for something. Finally, he caved. "I made a mistake."

"Yes, you did. So...?" She continued looking at him.

Embarrassed, he cast around for what he was supposed to say next. "Uh, I'm sorry. I couldn't let on to the other kids that I hadn't read the book."

"So you found it necessary not only to lie but to cut class?"

He hung his head, saliva filling his mouth. Before he could stammer out anything else, his grandfather rescued him.

"What Justin did was wrong. He knows that, don't you, son?"

He nodded miserably.

"But I think there's another problem we need to discuss," Grampa said.

Mrs. Kelly arched her penciled eyebrows.

"Justin is having some reading difficulties. I think if you'd examine his standardized scores, you might find that he could benefit from tutoring. Is there a reading specialist available in the school?"

Crap. Now he'd be one of those dumb kids

who got called out of class for special help. Grider would never let him live that down.

He cringed in his chair while Mrs. Kelly and Grampa discussed stuff like norms and verbal aptitude and comprehension. All he wanted was to get out of there so he could breathe again. "Fine," he heard Mrs. Kelly say. "I'll look into it." She tapped her red pen on her desk. "Before you go, though, we need to discuss Justin's punishment."

Oh, great. Detention wasn't enough. Now he had to face Mrs. Kelly's warped idea of justice. He grasped at a lifeline. "I'll get my oral report done. You can dock me points."

"Yes, but I also want you to write a thousand-word essay on the book."

Beside him, Justin thought he heard a low growl. When he glanced up, he saw his grandfather's hands gripping the desktop, but when he spoke, his voice was reasonable. "Could I offer an alternative suggestion?"

Mrs. Kelly gave him that same judgmental look she gave a student who made a smart-aleck remark. "Such as?"

"It seems to me an essay is not the best way to motivate Justin to want to read. It's, uh, more punitive than productive. What if I spent a few hours on a Saturday with him at the library looking at different kinds of books, trying to find out what interests him, exposing him to all the rich possibilities?" He eyed Justin's teacher over the rims of his glasses, his face open and encouraging.

Justin crossed his fingers under the desk. He'd spend a whole week in the library before he'd sit down and write a thousand words about a book he didn't like or understand.

"Mr. Harper, I believe you're on to something." Her features actually softened a bit. She didn't smile, of course, but that pinched you-kids-give-me-a-pain-in-the-ass look was gone. She hesitated, then eyed Justin. He met her gaze. "Yes. I think that would work."

Only when they were back out in the hall around the corner from Mrs. Kelly's room did Justin turn to his grandfather. "That was so cool!" He gave Grampa a high five. "You rock, dude!"

He and his grandfather had walked into the OK Corral and kicked butt!

FRIDAY AFTERNOON Meg sat in a folding chair behind the cabin, the warmth of the sun soaking into her body and easing the tension between her shoulders. She and Scott had been living in an uneasy truce since their walk on

Tuesday, but despite their problems, she was determined to enjoy this beautiful day. Finding it hard to concentrate on the novel she held in her hands, she set the book on the ground and lay back. The rippling water rushing over and around rocks and boulders created a concert with its own distinct melody. She drew a deep breath and felt her whole body relax.

Scott stood thigh-deep in the stream, fly rod lashing back and forth in preparation for a cast. She followed the arc of the line as it fed out, placing the fly upstream. As if hypnotized, she watched it float with the current, saw Scott, his tanned face intense, lean forward slightly as if willing a trout to lunge for the delicacy he was presenting. On his face was a look of pure contentment.

How she wished this moment could last. No PDAs, no cell phones, no computers. No car pools or meetings. Just endless azure sky and tranquility, their only challenge to land a fish for dinner.

She closed her eyes, a gentle pine-scented breeze cooling her skin. Earlier today they'd gone into town for supplies and Scott's fishing license. Although many businesses were new, others were familiar. The candy shop where Scott had indulged his bride with an entire pound of chocolate-peanut-butter fudge, the western outfitters where she'd insisted on buying the rakish Stetson he'd tried on for fun, the coffee bar where they'd ordered cappuccino and Scott had kissed the creamy foam off her lips.

Now fudge was a forbidden carbohydrate, the cowboy hat gathered dust in the back of their closet and a leisurely morning cappuccino was a dim memory. But she could still taste that kiss and recall the mischievous expression on Scott's face as he'd doffed his new hat and drawled sexily, "What kin ah do fer ya, little lady?" She blushed, remembering exactly what she'd told him he could do for her when they got back to the cabin. The reminiscence evoked a disturbing sexual stirring.

Laughter, carefree and jubilant, snapped her out of her reverie. Scott was wading toward her, holding a net in which a large rainbow trout thrashed. "Got him," he crowed.

She rose to her feet and crouched on the stream bank, admiring the fish. "You haven't lost your touch."

A cloud passed over his features. "At least with some things."

She struggled to recapture the peace of a

few moments ago. "Looks like I'll be cooking tonight." She paused, contemplating her next remark. "Do you think we could spend this one evening without thinking about business, the kids or our problems? Maybe just enjoy being here?" She gestured at the scenery surrounding them. "It's so beautiful."

"Yes," he said, his gaze narrowing on her face, as if memorizing her features. "It is." He pulled a small pair of pliers out of his vest, his eyes never leaving hers. "One night. Yeah. We can try that."

Unexpectedly, she felt shy, nervous. Almost like… a bride.

MEG WAS ALREADY IN BED, reading. Scott unbuttoned his shirt, took it off and put it with the dirty clothes. This day had been strange—in a bittersweet way.

He wanted to believe it was possible. But surely he couldn't be reading Meg's signals correctly. They were too close to a decision. There had been too much bitterness. Yet he could swear she was coming on to him. It would be infinitely easier if he were immune to her.

He wasn't.

She had looked so beautiful—and content—this afternoon by the stream. Her hair, highlighted by the sun, shone like corn silk, and her flawless skin begged to be touched. For a time, he'd almost forgotten their problems, forgotten there was anything or anybody else. Forgotten he didn't measure up to her expectations.

She'd made an entire production of dinner, augmenting the trout almondine with buttered new potatoes, a green salad and a cherry pie they'd bought that morning at the bakery. Over dinner they'd started reminiscing about their honeymoon and early married days. He'd forgotten how much fun she could be. She had a real gift for storytelling. He'd laughed out loud when she'd brought up that ridiculous hat she'd insisted on buying him. The hell of it was, as she talked, he was reminded of how sexy she'd made him feel back then. And then another memory. A naked Meg straddling him, the cowboy hat perched saucily on her head, her fingers lightly massaging his chest, driving him wild with the suggestive movements of her hips.

Great. Stepping out of his jeans, he turned away, hoping she wouldn't notice his erection. He knew better than to throw a pillow at her and jump her bones as he might've done twenty years ago. He couldn't risk another rebuff.

After brushing his teeth and washing up, he'd just about talked himself out of the crazy notion that she might welcome a sexual advance. Unfortunately, his body hadn't listened.

He slid in beside her and lay on his back, studying the ceiling. She smelled good. Like soap and flowers. He sneaked a peak. One strap of her pajama top had slid down her arm, exposing the swell of her breast. He bit his lip and averted his eyes. Her breathing was shallow, as if she were poised, waiting. Oh, God. For what?

He looked again. She hadn't turned the page of her book. He ordered himself to lie still. To remember they were old bedmates, accustomed to each other's sleep habits, not aroused lovers eager for release. What was the matter with him? He'd lived for months without any action. But right now, he was as keyed up as he'd been on his honeymoon. Would she ever put down that damned book?

Finally, she set the book on the table and turned off the lamp. He let her settle. Waited for her breathing to steady. Yet it still had a forced regularity. It felt as if they were both suspended in amber. He rolled onto his side.

He could lie there in agony or he could do something. In a moment of sudden calm, the thought came to him. What did he have to lose?

He raised his hand and tentatively traced his finger along her collarbone, then down the length of her arm. She looked at him, and in the moonlight streaming through the window, her eyes appeared liquid with—could it be?—desire. Somehow he found his voice. "Meggie?"

Was it his imagination or did she move a fraction of an inch closer?

"What?"

He'd planned to say, "Let me make love to you," planned to pull her into his arms and lose himself in her but what came out was "It was a good day."

She rested her hand on his chest. "Yes, the first one in a long time." After a pregnant silence, she whispered, "I wish…" But she never finished her sentence. Instead, she rolled away.

Dread overcame his desire. What did she wish? Whatever it was, she couldn't tell him, and he was afraid to ask.

MEG AWOKE SLOWLY the next morning, the fluffy down comforter a cocoon of warmth.

She wanted to move, but it seemed like such an effort. Last night... She'd thought Scott wanted to make love to her. And for a few unguarded moments, she'd welcomed the idea. Before she came to her senses. Before she realized they didn't need the complication of a marital one-night stand on top of everything else. And yet...

Scott was already up. From the kitchen she heard the sound of the coffeemaker. Would it be too much to hope for another day like yesterday? Or had they deluded themselves—seduced by the warmth of the sun, the beauty of the mountains and the chuckling of a trout stream?

She rolled over on her back, covering her eyes with her forearm, wondering what might have happened last night if she hadn't turned away. Being this vulnerable was dangerous, scary. She'd been so sure she could resist him. But then he'd whispered, "Meggie." He hadn't called her that in years. It was a balm, dissolving barriers and, releasing a surge of sexual need.

If only time could stand still. *Right*. Like a few hours could erase months, even years, of alienation and misunderstanding.

She got out of bed. Scott must've heard her

coming because he was ready with her morning coffee. "Good morning, sleepyhead," he said, with a boyish grin.

The grin combined with the early-morning shadow of his beard and his teasing eyes gave him a roguish look. Despite her best intentions, he was proving disarmingly irresistible. What might another night bring? "Hi, there," she said, taking the cup from him.

He leaned down and pecked her on the cheek. "Ready for another day by the water? Or maybe a hike?"

She couldn't believe her ears. Until yesterday, he'd been glued to his laptop. Was he really trying with her or just softening her up for sex? She didn't dare let herself hope for any permanent change. There'd been too much painful history.

She went to the window and looked out. "It's a beautiful day for a hike. Maybe up to Bear Lake?"

"You're on."

She turned back to him. "Before we go, I need to check in with Marie and Bud. Last night was Hayley's date and I want to be sure Justin's working on his science project and—"

"Can't you let it go?" A flicker of disappointment crossed Scott's face. "They're fine. They can get along without you for a few hours."

What was his problem? They were his kids, too. She bit back the sarcastic *Excuse me* that came to her lips. Okay, she'd wait and phone home while he was in the shower. But this little exchange served, once again, to illustrate the nature of their problem. Why wasn't he as concerned as she was about the children's well-being? Or did he consider the kids as solely her domain?

Over breakfast, she tried to set aside her irritation, to get back in touch with the woman who, in the past few hours, had actually thought there might be a chance of salvaging their relationship. Scott, too, seemed to relax over pancakes and syrup, even joking about the time on their honeymoon when they'd encountered an actual "mountain man" on the Long's Peak trail.

Gradually, Meg's anger dissipated and she found herself looking forward to the hike again. Hoping it might be another tiny step toward bridging the gulf between them.

But that was before the phone call from Wes.

Scott, the attentive husband, disappeared before her eyes, replaced by Scott, the ad executive. It didn't take a genius to figure out from his enormous grin that the agency had landed the Jordan account, a coup that apparently called for immediate action. When he hung up, he relayed the news to her. She could tell he wanted her to congratulate him, and she made a halfhearted effort to comply, but something had gone dead inside her.

A second honeymoon? Not in this lifetime.

Before she'd even finished the breakfast dishes, he'd concluded an excited phone conversation with Brenda and then, even though it was the weekend, gotten right back on his laptop to start sending out e-mails.

Maybe one of these hours he'd remember to shower and dress. Or acknowledge the fact that she fully intended to set out on a solo hike.

SATURDAY, JUSTIN couldn't wait to get to the library with Grampa. Hayley was really bugging him. All she could talk about was Zach this, Zach that. He knew Zach, and he couldn't see what the big deal was. The guy had zits and braces, but all Hayley could talk about were his "dreamy" brown eyes. Girls! And Gramma was almost as bad, asking his sister tons of questions about the stupid party. They sounded like a flock of birds chirping. He could've done a cartwheel when Grampa finished his lunch and said it was time to leave.

His weekend soccer tournament didn't start until five o'clock, so they'd have plenty of time to check out the library. Anything to get Mrs. Kelly off his back. In a way, it was kinda scary. He wasn't crazy about books anymore—not since he got too old for stuff like Curious George and Mike Mulligan. Those were for babies. Now he was supposed to read Harry Potter stories and *Flowers for Algernon.* And next grading period *To Kill a Mockingbird.*

On the drive to the library, he and Grampa talked about the Oklahoma Sooners football team. His father had taken him to Norman for a game, once. He wished they'd go again, but Dad didn't have much time to do things like that with him lately.

"So you like football as well as soccer?" his grandfather asked as they entered the library.

"Yeah. I like lots of sports."

"Good. Let's start over here." Grampa led him past the magazine racks and computer carrels until they found the sports books. "Sit down, son," Grampa said, gesturing to a little stool. "See if you can locate anything interesting."

Justin didn't know exactly how to begin, but finally he pulled out a picture book about Hall of Fame football players and began leafing through it.

"Can you find any O.U. stars?" Grampa asked.

Paul Hornung, Walter Payton, Doak Walker, no… Then there it was—a picture of Steve Owen in a Sooner jersey. He began reading. "Hey, Grampa, did you ever see this guy play? He sounds awesome."

From the sports section, they went to the young-adult biographies where Justin found books about other sports heroes. Even ones about Johnny Bench and Mickey Mantle, both from Oklahoma.

"Come on over here." Grampa walked to the fiction aisle and, squatting, pulled a book off a low shelf and thumbed through it. "Here's one—*The Outsiders*—set in Tulsa."

"Really?"

"Yup. What say we go over there—" he nodded toward a grouping of comfortable-looking couches "—and start this one?"

Justin shrugged. One novel was pretty much the same as another, he figured, but he'd humor his grandfather. They took a seat on one of the sofas and Grampa opened the book and began reading in a low voice. Justin looked around. It would be really embarrassing if anyone saw him being read to. But surely no other middle-school kid would be trapped in the library on a sunny Saturday afternoon.

Before he knew it, he forgot where they were, caught up in the story. After a bit, though, Grampa started stumbling over words, like he was drunk or something. Then he stopped reading altogether, right in the middle of a sentence. Justin figured he was resting maybe or wanted him to take a turn reading.

When he glanced up, his breath caught in his throat. Something was wrong with Grampa's face. He had this weird look. One side was droopy, like a morphing Halloween mask. "Grampa?"

His grandfather tried to speak, but all Justin heard were gurgling noises and funny-sounding words that didn't make any sense. Grampa's eyes rolled wildly like he'd seen a monster, and with his left hand, he kept pointing to his mouth and trying to talk. But no words came out.

An icy chill raced down Justin's spine. "You're joking with me, right, Grampa?"

Another half-choked word that sounded like *Help*.

"Grampa?" Justin knew panic in a way no book could adequately describe. Something was wrong. Terribly wrong. Grabbing Grampa's limp hand, he shattered the silence of the library. "Somebody, help!"

CHAPTER SIX

SCOTT'S MIND WHIRLED with plans, deadlines, things he had to do. This was the big one—the account that would put Harper Concepts on the map. In the midst of all the details, he managed to savor the moment, even briefly imagining himself accepting a Clio Award, his competitors on their feet applauding the success of the Jordan campaign. Brenda had already called two of their graphic artists at home to jump start work on print ads, and the agency media buyer had offered some great ideas on maximizing the Jordan name with the target demographic group. Scott would hit the ground running the minute they landed in Tulsa Monday morning. Just thinking about the challenges ahead gave him an exhilarating surge of adrenaline.

The only sting of disappointment was Meg's lukewarm reaction to the news. Sure, she'd said the right words, but her eyes, had betrayed her. He wanted someone to celebrate with, someone who understood his achievement. *Brenda.*

He sank wearily into a kitchen chair, an uncomfortable tightness in his chest. No way could he entertain that notion. If only Meg would look at him adoringly as she used to and take an interest in the ups and downs of the advertising game. It was a cliché to say it was "a jungle out there," but it was the truth. Why couldn't Meg give him the occasional chance to feel like a hero?

Last night he'd thought maybe they could rekindle what they used to have. Now he wasn't so sure. How could they share a life when neither of them seemed to understand what was important to the other? Like his bafflement that she couldn't trust his folks to handle the kids. Just once when they were together, he'd like her to focus all of her attention on him.

He stared at the numbers on his computer screen, then out the window at a wedge of tree and sky. He'd almost forgotten where he was, why he was here. The second honeymoon he and Meg were supposed to be enjoying. Ironic.

What was she doing in the bedroom? Was she actually planning to go hiking by herself?

He shoved back his chair and stood, just as Meg, dressed in jeans, an oversize sweatshirt and hiking boots, entered the room. She gave him a cursory nod, then grabbed her coat off the hook by the door and started outside.

He ran after her. "Where do you think you're going?"

She stopped, a disgusted expression on her face. "For *our* hike."

"Not by yourself, you're not."

"Oh, really?" Her voice oozed sarcasm.

"Meg, couldn't you at least be a little excited for me? For the agency?"

She put her hands on her hips. "It's not that I don't care about your work, Scott, but for a deluded moment last night I thought this marriage might, just might, have a chance." She shook her head. "But this morning you made it abundantly clear where your priorities lie. You couldn't get on the phone and computer fast enough. Look at you. You're not even dressed, much less ready to go on a hike."

He stepped out on the porch in his bare feet. "It's dangerous to hike alone. Please don't go."

"I need to clear my head. I'll drive to the trailhead and be back later this afternoon. Not to worry, I won't do anything reckless."

He stared at her. The soft yearning he'd seen in her features last night was gone, replaced by a resolute firmness of jaw. "Don't be like this."

Her face flushed. "Me? What about you? Wes, Brenda, Ward Jordan—where exactly do I fit in the pecking order?"

Scott raked a hand through his hair, then sighed. "You're saying I did it again, aren't you?"

"Did what?"

"Put business first."

She glared at him, incredulity sparking from her eyes. "Well, ye-ah. Did yesterday mean nothing to you?"

"You know better than that."

She took a step toward him. "I really thought we'd made some progress. And now?" She shrugged.

Pain filled his chest. "Then I guess we'll have to make some decisions tomorrow before we go home."

"Yes," she said. "We will."

From inside the house he heard his cell phone ringing, a summons impossible to ignore, especially this morning. "I've got a call, Meg."

"Hey, don't let me keep you from anything

that really matters." Then she wheeled around, strode to the car and drove off down the lane.

He'd blown it. Again. The phone rang another time—and twice more before he finally went back inside and picked it up.

When he heard his mother's voice bordering on hysteria, he crumpled into a chair and tried to concentrate on the senseless words she kept repeating. A stroke? His dad was as healthy as a horse. He couldn't quite grasp the thought. "Mom, calm down. I'm right here. Tell me exactly what's going on."

She explained she was with Justin at the hospital where his father had been taken by ambulance following his collapse in the library earlier that afternoon. Indications were that Bud had suffered a major stroke.

A tension headache began to beat against Scott's temples. "We'll drive into Denver right away and catch the earliest flight we can. Could you put Justin on?"

"He's pretty shaken."

"Dad?" The neediness in Justin's voice tore Scott in two.

Like a tidal wave, the story poured out of his son. His panic and helplessness. And worst of all, his fear.

When Scott hung up, he was limp. This couldn't be happening. Outside the sun shone under a cloudless sky. But darkness, unlike any he'd ever known, had taken possession of his soul.

He bent over his knees, trying to concentrate. He needed to plan. Needed to make reservations. He could only pray Meg would return soon. Every sinew in his body called him to action, but he needed his wife. God, where had she gone? Then another thought surfaced: In light of this awful emergency, there would be no opportunity for a discussion of their future.

It had taken care of itself.

EARLY THE NEXT AFTERNOON Meg found herself clutching Scott's hand as a taxi transported them from the Tulsa airport to the hospital. Guilt lay over her like a shroud. Why hadn't she turned on her cell phone yesterday when she left the cabin? Her fit of pique and the resulting long hike had prevented Scott from making immediate reservations, delaying their departure from Denver until this morning. Scott had been too upset to lash out; instead, they had silently gone through the motions of packing.

Eventually, though, crisis had a way of short-circuiting resentment. At least for the moment. Scott adored Bud. Their closeness had been a source of envy for Meg, who'd always keenly felt the absence of her own father. Yet Bud's warm, unconditional acceptance of her had gone a long way toward healing that childhood wound. Marie loved her, too, she realized, but whether it was true or not, her love seemed to be doled out in direct proportion to how well she perceived Meg to be taking care of Scott.

She examined Scott's stony profile. She could only imagine what was running through his mind. He would be expected to be the strong one, the take-charge guy. Marie would probably go to pieces when she saw him.

And poor Justin. She'd talked with him several times on the phone. She was having trouble convincing him he wasn't responsible for Bud's stroke. Though extremely upset, he was trying to be brave. Carrie Morrison had come to the hospital and taken him home with her yesterday, and Hayley was staying with her friend Jill. Thank God for caring neighbors. Meg realized part of her role would be restoring normalcy in the children's lives as soon as possible.

She closed her eyes, exhausted from the impasse with Scott and from rushing to pack and get to Denver in time for the earliest flight they could catch—and from worrying about Bud and what the future would hold for all of them. Would Bud survive? Would he be impaired? How might his condition affect his and Marie's plans? What would be expected of Scott, the kids and her? So many questions.

One thing she knew with certainty. Their lives were forever changed. At the very least, Scott would now have increasing demands to face. Somehow, for the time being, she would have to set aside her frustration with their marriage and be as supportive as possible. Even if it meant sharing Scott in more ways and postponing any decisions about their future. She had no other choice.

Up ahead the hospital loomed, imposing and not in the least bit comforting. She squeezed his hand. "Are you all right?"

He shrugged. "Not really."

She looked into his troubled eyes. "But you'll get through it. You always do."

"Thanks, Meg." He paused as if finding the next words difficult. "I'm glad you're with me. I need you."

Her eyes filled with sudden tears. He hadn't seemed to need her for a long time.

"I'm scared, Meg."

Her confident, competent husband scared? Yet something in her heart leaped. She couldn't think of another person to whom he would've confided such vulnerability.

SOMETHING WRONG. Tongue thick. People. Moving. Strange-looking people. A man with glasses. Leaning close. Too close. "Bud? Bud, can you hear me?"

Shouting. The man's voice was loud. Too loud. *Of course I can hear you. You're shouting in my face.*

"Bud? Blink your eyes if you can hear me."

Blink? Why? Just say it. *I can hear you.*

"Blink your eyes, Bud."

All right, then. I'll blink my eyes. There, are you happy?

"That's better. Do you know where you are, Bud?"

Why did the man keep calling him by name? Did he think he'd forgotten who he was?

"Stay with me, Bud. Where are you?"

Bud moved his eyes. Felt the bed against his back. Saw IV lines. Tried to lift his right hand. Couldn't. Why not? Hospital. Damn.

He was in the hospital. Like a dutiful student, he formed the word. "Hop." No, that wasn't right. "Hop," he said again.

"That's right. You're in the hospital." Strange, he hadn't said *hospital*. For some reason, he'd said *hop*.

"There's someone here who wants to see you."

Who? What was this, a guessing game?

"Bud?" A lady with tight gray curls leaned over him. "It's Marie, honey."

Marie? He knew her. "Mama?"

"No, dear, *Marie*." Then he watched her clutch his right hand. But he couldn't feel anything. Odd. He looked again. Hand in hand. No feeling. Suddenly a cloud of dread suffocated him. The man with the glasses approached again. "We're taking care of you, Bud. You've had a stroke."

Stroke? Golf stroke? Tennis stroke? Something about stroke he knew. Something bad.

"Hop?"

"Stay calm. You should improve in the next few days. Then we'll be able to assess your condition."

Assess? "Ass!"

"Bud? Watch your language."

The Marie lady was scolding him. Had he

been bad? "Mama?" Why had he said that? *Marie,* that was what he should've said. Marie. Nice Marie. He watched her now, kissing his hand. Pretty lady. He liked having her hold his hand.

"I love you, darlin'," he heard the Marie lady say. It sounded nice. His eyes felt heavy. The man with the glasses stepped closer again, lifting one of his eyelids. *Get away.*

Sleep. But before he let himself sink into the vast grayness, he tried one more time, his brain struggling to make his lips and tongue form the word. "Ma… Ma…rie?"

Just before he drifted off, he heard a sobbing sound from the lady holding his hand. Marie. Wife. His Marie.

SCOTT DIDN'T KNOW EXACTLY what he'd expected to find, but what he encountered was far worse than anything he'd imagined. He slumped into the battle-scarred waiting-room chair and hunched over his knees, shielding his eyes with his hands. Meg patted his shoulder, but he couldn't look up. All he could see in his mind was his father's strong body rendered nearly lifeless and his mother's tear-filled eyes as she explained that Bud had some paralysis on the right side and difficulty speaking. The doctor, who had finally arrived had been cautious, adopting an infuriating wait-and-see attitude. Scott wanted to do something, anything, to reverse this awful diagnosis, to wipe the patronizing words from that doctor's vocabulary. "In cases like this," he'd said. Cases like this? What the hell? This wasn't any old case—this was his father they were talking about.

Gradually, he became aware of Meg's hand massaging his back, the manic voices of the Sunday TV sports commentators, the sounds of a vending machine, the rattling of a newspaper. Finally he looked up. "It's bad."

"How's your mother?"

"Devastated, as you'd expect. She'll be out in a minute. She wants to see you."

"I'll wait for her, of course. But then I should go pick up the kids. They're devastated, especially Justin."

"I know."

"Have you called Kay?"

Kay. Yeah, right. As if his older sister would consider coming to help out. Resentment flared in him. His mother had always coddled Kay. Even now, as a grown woman, she was less mature than Hayley by a long shot. She did what she wanted, when she wanted, thanks to an extremely generous divorce settlement from her wealthy ex-husband. He couldn't remember the last time she'd visited their parents in Nashville. They always went to her home in Florida. "Mom called her."

"And?"

Meg could predict as well as he what Kay's reaction had been. Obligatory concern followed by thinly veiled irritation at what would be an inconvenience to her busy social life. Yet Mom, ever blind to Kay's faults, clung to the belief that she'd catch the next flight to Tulsa. "She's standing by for more news before she makes any decisions."

"Probably makes sense."

Maybe. Was he overreacting? Lashing out at his sister because of his own helplessness?

"Before I leave, would you like me to bring you coffee and a sandwich from the cafeteria?"

"Yeah, that would be great. I'll wait here for Mom."

"I'll be right back."

After Meg left, he lolled in the chair, wondering how long it would be before they learned anything more definitive than "wait and see." Memories of his strong, tanned father playing catch with him, shooting hoops out by the garage and teaching him to tie flies flooded his brain. Images of strength and agility, now replaced by the ashen complexion and limp body in a hospital room down the hall.

How could he possibly work on the Jordan campaign in the midst of this? Somehow, though, he had to. Others were counting on him. Compartmentalize. Detach. His stomach roiled. Gut it through. And underlying all of that, was his concern for Meg and the kids and how his dad's situation would impact them. He'd thought things couldn't get any worse. Wrong again.

"Scott?"

He looked up. Brenda, dressed in a form-fitting black dress and killer high heels emphasizing the curves of her legs, made her way across the room, arms outspread, a sympathetic look on her face. "I'm so sorry."

He stood and accepted her hug. "Thanks for coming."

Instead of stepping away, she remained in his embrace, studying his expression. "Are you okay?"

Before he could answer, he heard a sharp gasp, followed by the splat of spilling liquid. Over Brenda's shoulder, framed in the doorway, was Meg, hot coffee pooling at her feet, shock registering in every line of her face.

Worse? Try catastrophic.

WITH A SAVAGE KICK, Justin sent the soccer ball flying toward the left sideline. Out of bounds. He ran to take up his defensive position, trying to block out what his coach had yelled at him: "Keep your head in the game, Harper." Mrs. Morrison had insisted it would be good for him to play this final game of the tournament and get his mind off his troubles. But he didn't even care about winning. All he could concentrate on was what had happened yesterday to Grampa. How he'd been reading along just fine until… Justin's mouth filled with a metallic taste. He didn't want to think about it.

One librarian had rushed over and laid his grandfather on the floor while another had called 911. His stomach tensed every time he thought about Grampa being tended to by the paramedics or about the stunned, fascinated faces of the people in the library and the sickly-sweet way this other librarian had led him into an office to phone his grandmother.

When the ball was inbounded, Justin missed a chance to clear it and start downfield. Crap. His whole life was crap.

What if Grampa died? Justin's heart nearly stopped.

If only he hadn't lied about the oral book report, cut school and caused Grampa so much trouble, they wouldn't even have been at the library yesterday afternoon.

In a daze, he moved toward the opponent's goal, watching the ball carrier as if from underwater. He checked the sideline to see if his mom had come yet and looked back too late, just in time to see the ball bounce past him.

"Harper, heads up!" The coach again. Justin, his face flushed with anger, clenched his fist, fighting tears he knew would make the other guys laugh at him. He wanted to quit. Just throw down his jersey, start walking and never come back.

He'd only been at the Morrisons one night, but it seemed like forever. They acted real hush-hush around him as if he were a guest celebrity or something. He even missed his annoying sister. Go figure. She'd called him a couple of times, all worried about Grampa—and him. He guessed maybe she wasn't so bad.

He wished he and Hayley could go to the hospital. He could tell Grampa how sorry he was. But it was too early, Gramma said.

Brad Ambler tapped him on the shoulder. "You asleep? I'm comin' in for you."

Justin set no speed records getting off the field, and when the coach put an arm around him and tried to tell him how to play his position, he hung his head and stared at the clump of brown grass at his feet. He had no idea what the coach was saying. Big deal. He didn't care, anyway.

He walked along the bench, fumbled for his water bottle, took a swig and sat down. How long were his parents going to be at the hospital? He had this funny empty place in his gut. He wasn't a baby, but he really needed his mom and dad. Maybe then everything would be back to normal.

Then he remembered. *Normal* hadn't been so good, either. Ignoring the game, he picked at his cuticle until he noticed it was bleeding and rubbed his thumb on his soccer shorts, leaving a pinkish trail of blood.

MEG STAYED AT THE HOSPITAL only long enough to get the car keys from Marie, then bolted for the parking lot, barely able to contain the rage and betrayal she'd experienced in the waiting room. The picture of Brenda in Scott's arms had seared an unforgettable image on her brain. Brenda, her platinum hair perfectly coifed, her clinging jersey dress designed to reveal every alluring curve. The mock-innocent look on Scott's face. If the whole scene weren't so tragic, it would have been laughable.

After reaching the car, she sat shaking, her head resting against the steering wheel, nausea rolling in her stomach. The aborted honeymoon had turned into a nightmare. Poor Bud. He was such a gentle and loving man—he didn't deserve this. As for Brenda and Scott? Meg shouldn't have been surprised. It simply confirmed her suspicions, but the timing couldn't have been worse.

Somehow she was supposed to pull herself together, pick up the kids, soothe their worries and keep the home fires burning. Yeah, right.

She started the engine, backed out and made the seemingly endless trip down ramps to the pay booth. Once she was out on the street, the brightness startled her. Long rays of the setting sun highlighted the downtown skyline. The effect could almost be considered picturesque, if she'd been in the mood for something like that. She wasn't.

She felt like a cast-off mongrel, kicked to the curb. If ever she'd entertained thoughts of finding her way back to Scott, today had put an end to that notion. Oh, he'd tried to explain. Brenda was just a friend offering sympathy. Did he think she was born yesterday? She'd heard the hypocrisy in Brenda's voice, seen the possessive way she'd looked at Scott, how her hands fluttered at her cleavage as if to draw attention to her breasts. *"Fool,"* she muttered to herself. How could she ever have thought that one argument-free day in Colorado could turn the tide of their marriage?

She decided to go straight home and get her emotions under control before she saw the kids. They had to be worried about Bud; they didn't need to worry about her, too. And it was nearly dinnertime. She couldn't face going to the supermarket. She'd rummage in the kitchen and see what she had on hand.

Later, of course, loomed the inevitable confrontation with Scott, who would undoubtedly label her reaction to Brenda "ungracious."

Deep down, she knew Scott was exhausted. That he had far more important things on his mind than her jealousy. Now was not the time to throw the whole family even more off balance.

Okay. She'd hang in there, carry on with

the dutiful-wife act, wait out the crisis with Bud, and then she and Scott could settle things once and for all.

Nearing her neighborhood, she called the kids on her cell phone and made arrangements to pick them up in fifteen minutes. When she pulled into the driveway, a wave of nostalgia engulfed her. She loved this house. Loved the dreams she'd had for it.

Inside, the quiet wrapped her in comforting normalcy. The things she treasured—the basket collection on top of the kitchen cabinets, the antique mirror over the breakfast room buffet, a braided rug in varying shades of blue she'd bought in Vermont—represented family gatherings, harmony and love. Not the tense stand-off of the present.

Checking the freezer, she found some chopped sirloin patties and a package of frozen hash browns. That and canned green beans would do for supper. She opened the door of the pantry and reached for the green beans, but instead faced a row of cake and bread mixes. *What the—?*

Anger swept over her. Obviously her mother-in-law had taken it upon herself to reorganize every last shelf.

It was a little thing. Meg knew that. But it

symbolized her own incompetence. Her failure to create the perfect home and family.

Not trusting her eyes, she stared at boxes of cereal, bags of rice, bottles of salad dressing—all in unfamiliar locations—and burst into tears.

CHAPTER SEVEN

AFTER SCOTT HAD CONVINCED his mother there was nothing more they could do at the hospital, she agreed to leave. Once home, he escorted her up to the guest bedroom, then walked back downstairs where he kicked off his shoes, pulled a beer out of the fridge and collapsed into his recliner.

Times like this he missed Buster, the shepherd-Lab mix he and Meg had picked up at the animal shelter when Justin was a toddler. Buster's death last year had hit the whole family hard. A lump formed in his throat. Now Pops's life hung in the balance. It had taken every ounce of willpower not to shake his fist and scream at the situation. But his mother hadn't needed that. Besides, such thinking was counterproductive.

He took a sip of his beer and leaned his head back, remembering Meg's reaction to catching him in Brenda's arms. He brought the cold beer bottle to his temple, as if the chill could obliterate memory. He should drag himself to bed, but his muscles tensed at the thought. Meg would want to have it out with him. Not tonight, not when he was barely holding on emotionally.

Then there was tomorrow. His mind teemed with things to do, questions to ask, people to see. *Get a grip, Harper. You're supposed to be the strong one.* They—all the *theys* in his life—were depending on him. He began mentally prioritizing his to-do list. Hospital. Work. Maybe tomorrow night he'd have to have the unavoidable talk with Meg. Between now and then? He hated walking on eggshells with her, fearful that no matter what he said or how he said it, he still couldn't redeem himself. Especially not after the scene with Brenda.

As he slowly finished the bottle, he was overcome by a deep, abiding sadness for what had been—with Meg, with Pops, with all of them.

Finally, he got up and headed upstairs, driven by a compelling need to check on the kids. Even though he'd spoken to them on the phone, he wanted to *see* them. Pausing to gather himself, he gently pushed open Hayley's bedroom door. There she was, her dark hair a tangle on the pillow, one hand drawn up beside her cheek. A child-woman who had grown up in the blink of an eye. A sudden feeling of love overwhelmed him. Had she ever experienced grief? Well, Buster, of course. But in the human realm? He sighed, thinking of the potential breakup of his marriage. He tiptoed across the carpet, littered with teen magazines, CDs and discarded clothing, and brushed the hair off her forehead, inhaling the fragrance of her lemony shampoo. "Sweet dreams, princess," he whispered.

Turning, he made his way down the hall to Justin's room. The boy lay spread-eagled on his bed, covers twisted around his legs. Scott stood over him, watching his son breathe. In the moonlight streaming through the window, he could just make out the faint line of hair sprouting on Justin's upper lip. Lord, how had that happened? Why hadn't he noticed before? He'd have to remember to have the shaving demonstration with him. Soon. And while he was at it, maybe a refresher session on the birds and bees.

He unraveled the sheet and blanket and covered his son.

"Dad?"

The sleepy murmur stopped Scott in his

tracks. If he didn't say anything, maybe the boy would drift off.

"Dad?" This time Justin opened his eyes, then scooted over, making room for Scott.

He perched on the edge of the bed. "What, son?"

"Will Grampa be all right?"

"We won't know for a while. It's going to take time. The improvement will be gradual."

Biting his lower lip, Justin lowered his head, as if he couldn't bear to look directly at Scott.

"What's bothering you?"

Still without looking at his father, the boy swallowed several times before speaking. "I'm sorry." His voice caught in a hiccup.

"Sorry? What for? None of this is your fault."

"It is, too!"

Justin's vehemence was clear evidence of the degree of his self-imposed guilt, but, for the life of him, Scott couldn't imagine why he'd feel responsible. "The stroke could have happened anytime, anywhere. It had nothing to do with you. In fact, we're proud of how strong you were throughout the whole ordeal."

"But if I hadn't—" The boy strangled on the words.

"Hadn't what?"

Justin rolled onto his side, averting his face. Scott rubbed a hand along his son's back, but his body was as unyielding as stone.

"Can you answer me?"

Justin merely shook his head back and forth.

"Tell me why you think you're somehow responsible for what happened to Grampa."

The boy's words were muffled. "He was only trying to help me."

Scott bent down so he could look into his tear-streaked face. "Help you how?"

"I messed up at school." Then the words spewed out, confessional and self-damning. Heartsick, Scott wondered why Justin hadn't told him and Meg about his difficulty with reading. Had they been too preoccupied to pay attention? Likely. Yet the desperation of their son's cover-up spoke volumes. As the story unfolded, Justin kept moving toward the headboard of his bed, as if retreating from his father's reaction. "So, see, if I hadn't screwed up, Grampa wouldn't have had to come to school with me and he wouldn't have offered to take me to the library, and—"

"He still would've had the stroke." Scott gripped the boy's shoulders. "Listen to me.

This is not your fault. Strokes just happen. Nothing you did caused it."

Before he could say any more, Justin threw himself into Scott's arms. "When you're not here, I really miss you, Dad," he whispered, his warm breath smelling of cheese crackers and toothpaste.

Scott's heart cracked. Did Justin mean he'd missed him while he was in Colorado or, worse, that he'd been missing him generally? Holding Justin tight against his chest, he managed a response. "I missed you, too."

More than his son would ever know.

MEG WOKE EARLY the next morning, knowing the day ahead would tax her organizational and human-relations skills. She stood at the kitchen sink making coffee and mentally compiling her lengthy to-do list. The good news? If she kept busy enough, she wouldn't have to think about Scott—or Brenda.

She'd heard him come in last night, but had apparently fallen asleep before he'd joined her in bed. Just as well. They were both drained from the last two days. If they'd talked, she might've said things she would later regret. This was no time to pour salt on wounds, for either of them.

Nor was it a time to upset the kids more than they already were. Justin had gripped her in a huge hug yesterday when she'd picked him up, and Hayley had been uncharacteristically helpful with dinner, actually volunteering to do the dishes. Their concern for Bud was evident and Meg even believed they'd missed her and Scott.

She was relieved that she'd beaten Marie to the kitchen and took her time, setting the table, pulling bagels from the freezer, slicing grapefruit. When the coffee was ready she poured a cup and wandered out to the patio, trying to put herself in Marie's position. Standing there, looking out at the dew-covered grass, she could almost trick herself into believing this was like any other peaceful dawn.

She couldn't begin to imagine how Marie must feel, her beloved spouse lying helpless in the hospital. The what-ifs must be multiplying in her head. Despite Meg's occasional sense that Marie would've preferred another mate for Scott, she mostly felt she'd come to earn the older woman's acceptance and affection. No doubt Marie would be devastated if she knew her perfect son had been having an affair. But, *had* he?

She fortified herself with another jolt of

caffeine. What if Scott had been telling the truth about Brenda's hospital visit? Maybe as a result of her own insecurities, she was assigning suspicious motives to their embrace. But even if Scott was innocent, it sure looked as though Brenda was making a play for him and he hadn't tried to fight her off. Like it or not, the spark of jealousy that had overcome her yesterday had been a gut-level reaction, and guts didn't lie, did they? If she was truly ready for separation, if she didn't care about Scott, why had the sight of Brenda in his arms upset her so much?

"Meg?" Scott stepped out onto the patio, his khaki suit, blue oxford-cloth shirt and striped tie giving him a totally different look from the relaxed fly fisherman of a few days ago. Her breath quickened. She missed the fisherman.

"Good morning. Are you leaving so early?"

"I want to stop by the hospital on my way to work." He hesitated, then went on. "Can you take Mom later?"

"I'm planning on it."

He shifted his feet. "When the kids get up, you need to know..." He shook his head as if in misery.

She tamped down her impatience. "What?"

"You were right. Justin feels responsible for Pops's situation."

She'd told him as much. Why did men persist in being so dense? "I know."

"He's had some troubles at school. Do you think you could call, find out what's going on?"

"Sure. Isn't that what mothers are for?" He flinched. What was the matter with her? She didn't mean to sound so sharp and vindictive. Maybe it was because they were both being so formal, purposely avoiding the Brenda issue.

Scott touched her arm awkwardly. "We'll talk tonight. We have a lot going on in our lives right now. But, trust me, Brenda isn't a concern." Then he wheeled around and went back inside the house. A short time later, she heard a vehicle backing down the driveway.

Trust me. She'd read somewhere that when people used expressions like *trust me* and *in all honesty,* you could almost guarantee they were lying.

In her heart she admitted she didn't want Scott to be lying. Ever since the beginning of their trip she had felt confused. In some ways he'd been the same maddeningly preoccupied Scott, but in other ways, he'd been thoughtful, fun…sexy. At the cabin, memories had begun to surface—good ones. But they were home now. Would they fall into old routines and patterns?

She watched two mourning doves land on the birdbath, fluttering their wings, cooing softly. Paired. Nature was not without irony.

"Mom!" Hayley bolted out the door in her shorty pajamas. "I can't find my geometry book anywhere. Have you seen it?"

Meg bit back her response. Hayley's room was a disaster area. "No, but you might try making your bed and seeing what you discover."

"I've got to find it. I have a test fourth period."

Meg sent the doves one last glance, then followed her daughter inside where duties—maternal and otherwise—awaited.

MEG CHECKED HER WATCH, then turned onto a side street, hoping to avoid the morning commuter traffic. After dropping the kids off at school, she and Marie were headed for the hospital. Before they'd left home, Scott had called to say he thought there had been a slight improvement in Bud's condition overnight. But hope was a fragile bloom.

In the passenger seat, Marie, her face pale,

stared straight ahead. "I don't know why we didn't buy a little car, you know, to pull behind the motor home. Then you wouldn't be stuck driving me everywhere."

"That's the last thing you should worry about. It's not a problem for me to take you to the hospital."

Marie's voice trembled. "Yes, but for how long?"

"It's hard to know. We need to take it one day at a time."

"But this is so inconvenient for you."

Meg's heart softened. "Family isn't about convenience. We'll all pull together to do whatever we have to."

Marie turned and looked at Meg, her bloodshot eyes watering. "Thank you, dear."

They rode in silence, Meg second-guessing herself. What, exactly, would be required of them if Bud's recovery took a long time? He and Marie couldn't return to Nashville— they'd sold their house. Obviously there was no counting on Kay, who still hadn't made plans to come and visit Bud. Stays in rehabilitation facilities were limited by Medicare and based on continuous improvement. Eventually Bud would be released—to what? A motor home? Her fingers tightened on the steering wheel as the truth she'd tried to avoid surfaced. There was only one home for Bud to return to—hers and Scott's.

A gamut of emotions swept over her, along with a numbing sense of powerlessness. This was not a situation she could micromanage, control or delegate. She and Scott were facing some unavoidable decisions that would affect every single member of the family.

"Will Scott come to the hospital after work?" Marie's voice was tremulous—her take-charge mother-in-law was like a tiny, scared child. Yet Meg knew Marie would pull herself together when she saw Bud.

"Of course he will. I'll stay with you for a while this morning, but I'll have to leave right after lunch."

"I know. You have things to do at home." She sighed. "I need to call Kay again."

Hearing the wistfulness in Marie's voice, Meg bit her lip. Kay. Scott's sister, so involved in her globe-trotting lifestyle, seemed oblivious to family obligations. Always had.

Marie went on, her voice weepy. "I don't know what to do about the motor home. About anything, really."

Meg patted Marie's knee. "Nothing needs

to be decided today. Let's concentrate on Bud right now."

When they entered the hospital and the first draft of antiseptic-laden air hit her, Meg experienced a sinking sensation. Unless Bud had undergone a miraculous recovery, they were in for a long period of caregiving.

THE WORDS. TWO WORDS. He knew them. He cleared his throat. *Motor home?* Why was Marie looking at him so funny? It was a simple question. Ma-rie. He rolled the name around in his head. Wife.

"Take your time, dear. I can't understand you."

Well, doggone it. His brain was perfectly clear. He wanted to know about the motor home. "Two words."

"Two words? What words?"

Bud closed his eyes. He'd tried to say it. *Motor home.* But that wasn't what had come out of his mouth. He tried again. "Two words."

The worry visible in Marie's eyes scared him. Why couldn't his mouth form the words for the thought in his brain? What kind of idiot says "two words" because he can't say what he means? Then he remembered. A stroke. Like in the commercials? *Take an aspirin a day.* That kind?

He gripped the sheet with his left hand. Then he studied his right hand, lying at his side, limp and useless. Fear pinned him to the bed. Was he going to die? Be paralyzed? What?

"What?"

Marie brushed a cool hand over his forehead. "Don't worry, Bud. Please. You've had a stroke. It will take time for you to recover. Patience was never your long suit, but you're going to need some now."

Patience? Patience took time. He didn't have time. He struggled to tell her to get the doctor in here—pronto. Fix him. Fix him. But all he heard coming out of his mouth was a strangled sound, like somebody gargling.

"Do you understand? You've had a stroke, but you'll get better day by day."

He didn't have days. He was on a trip. He screwed up his face. But where was he going? He couldn't remember. Tears pooled in his eyes and he clenched and unclenched his left fist. "Damn!"

"I'LL BE RIGHT OVER." Jannie Farrell's words on the phone had given Meg the first relief she'd felt in forty-eight hours. Now, engulfed in her friend's warm hug, she slowly began to unwind.

"Thanks for coming," she whispered, grateful in a new, more profound way for her friend. Stepping back, she gestured toward the patio. "It's nice out. I fixed us some iced tea."

"Sounds great."

Outside, Meg poured their drinks and then sat back in the wrought-iron patio chair and surveyed the chrysanthemums bordering the back fence—a riot of gold, vermilion and dusky purple. She knew Jannie was waiting for her to speak, but was respecting her need for silence. "It's weird. This feels like a parallel life. Like who I was two weeks ago and who I am today are worlds apart."

"This business with your father-in-law has to be scary."

"It's more than that," Meg said quietly.

Jannie turned toward her. "Oh?"

"It's as if I've been going through the motions for so long I don't know how to live any other way."

"What do you mean?"

Meg ran a finger around the rim of her glass, wondering how to put into words everything she was feeling. "Do you think we suburban moms get so caught up in rushing here and there that we lose who we really are?"

Jannie's eyes narrowed. "No fair. You just answered a question with another question."

"It's like this afternoon. When I looked at my planner and realized how many obligations I'd have to cancel because of this situation with Bud, I had the oddest sense that who I *am* is so tied in with what I *do* that when I take away all those activities, I'm no longer sure who this Meg I'm left with is."

"Are you saying our identities get swallowed up by our roles? Or, worse, that we're defined by them?"

Meg sat forward. "Exactly. I'm Scott's wife, Hayley and Justin's mother, representative to the neighborhood association, pairings chairperson for the ladies' golf association, bookclub vice president, et cetera, et cetera, et cetera, as the King of Siam would say. And I usually function just fine. But strip those roles away, and then what? Who's left?"

"I think you're being too hard on yourself. But in any event, maybe this stroke of Bud's is a kind of blessing in disguise, allowing you to step back and reacquaint yourself with Meg, who, if you ask me, is a pretty spectacular lady."

Meg managed a grudging grin. "What are

friends for, if not to make you feel better?" She wanted desperately to confide in Jannie about her problems with Scott, but she couldn't overcome the sense that it would be disloyal to him. "I have no idea how quickly or in what ways Bud will improve."

"What a huge worry."

"And a huge responsibility. My in-laws will be confined to Tulsa, at least for the next few weeks." Weeks? More likely months. Meg wasn't proud of the twinge of resentment that reality produced.

"I imagine a large chunk of the burden will fall on you. After all, you're the woman."

Jannie had articulated Meg's fear. "We'll get through it somehow, I guess."

Jannie raised her glass in a toast. "If anyone can juggle the demands, it's you."

Meg permitted herself a moment to bask in Jannie's admiration and support. Admiration and support of the kind she craved from Scott—and the same kind of admiration and support he undoubtedly needed from her. Or from somebody. She closed her eyes. *Please God, don't let that somebody be Brenda.*

SCOTT PERCHED ON A STOOL in the art department looking at the sketches Brenda had displayed on the drawing table, representing various ideas for the billboard space they'd be renting for the Jordan ads. Brenda sidled up beside him and draped an arm over his shoulder. "What do you think?"

I think I'm dog tired and don't want to make this decision now. He studied the images, trying to sort through the pluses and minuses of each one, and rubbed a hand through his hair. "Brenda, I'd like to nail this down, but to tell you the truth, product promotion is about the furthest thing from my mind tonight."

"Poor baby," she murmured, and while seemingly still focused on the drawings, she began kneading the base of his neck. He closed his eyes and relaxed for a moment, letting himself slump against her. "Do you want to wait till morning to decide?"

Her fingers were like keys unlocking the bolts of tension in his neck and shoulders. "No." He tried to concentrate on the artwork. "What does Wes think?"

"He prefers the second rendering."

Scott willed himself to study it, to assess any possible drawbacks. He should care about this. But warm, sensuous hands robbed him of his will. "Yeah, it's good." He forced his eyes open. "Number five isn't bad, either." He was aware that everyone else had gone home, except for one account executive at the far end of the hall. The shadows at the fringes of the room created a cocoon of intimacy that Brenda's soothing fingers did nothing to dispel. "What do you think?"

"I agree with you. Those two are my favorites."

"Aren't you going to help me out here?"

She chuckled, a low, throaty sound. "Hey, I thought I was." And her thumbs ratcheted down his back.

She abandoned the massage and moved between him and the drafting table. Close. Very close. He breathed in her musky perfume. He could see the tiny mole on her neck, right where a blood vessel pulsed. Her eyes sparkled with veiled amusement as she leaned back provocatively, bracing her hands on the edge of the table.

She raised one eyebrow questioningly. "Decision time, boss."

At first, he wondered if she was talking about the next step in their relationship. Women were hard to read, but unless he missed his guess, maybe Meg did have justification for her concern. This was awkward.

Brenda Sampson was one of the most sought-after creative directors in the business. He didn't want to compromise their working relationship. But darned if he didn't think she was coming on to him. *Decision time?* He prayed she meant about the ad campaign.

Abruptly he shoved back his stool, stood and straightened his tie. "Number two," he said with all the confidence he could muster. Then he beat a hasty retreat, hoping against hope that her signature fragrance had not left traces on his shirt. It was a hell of an insight into his feelings for Meg when escaping to a grim hospital setting was preferable to the company of an attractive woman.

He needed to watch himself. The scariest part of this little encounter was how very aware he'd been of his own physical reaction to the tiniest bit of female pampering.

BUD WATCHED MARIE. She dozed in one of those hospital chairs that doubled as a commode. She looked tired. All day she'd tried to cheer him up. Once he'd said *Damn* real loud and she'd almost cried. Sometimes, though, she would try to smile. He loved her smiles. When they were real. These today had been fake. Her eyes had been gray hollows of fear. When he'd tried to say, "Tell me the truth," all that had come out was "Telly." She'd assumed he'd wanted to watch television and had turned on some cockamamy show about people whose pets resembled their owners.

He tried to move. Darn sheets were scrunched up and the hospital-issue pillow was worthless. He'd been lying here all day, fidgeting. Why weren't they doing anything to help him get better? The nurses either treated him like a baby—"Do we need to shave, Mr. Harper?"—or had about as much compassion as a Marine drill sergeant. Then there were the vampires with their blood kits.

But the worst was the panic that swept over him every time he tried to perform a function and couldn't. Was he going to be an invalid? He closed his eyes, wondering whether it wouldn't be easier just to give up. He didn't want to become a burden to anyone, but, heck, if he couldn't even talk? Walk? Never mind drive a motor home, dance, have sex.

"Pops?"

He looked toward the door and watched his son cross the room to his bed.

Marie, instantly awake, stood. "Scotty?"

Scott picked up Bud's good hand. "How's it going?"

Crock of shit. That described it perfectly. But all he heard himself say was "Shit."

Marie hovered solicitously. "You need the bedpan?"

Angrily he responded, "No!" Then he almost smiled. For once, thought and word had coincided. Hallelujah!

Scott grinned crookedly. "Mom, I think he means this is a shitty situation, pardon the expression."

Bud grunted in satisfaction. Finally somebody who was on his wavelength.

"I stopped at the nurse's station," his son said. "Tomorrow you're going to start therapy."

Therapy? That was for nutcases. He shook his head violently. "Crazy."

Marie wrung her hands. "It's not a crazy idea, honey. It's part of your treatment."

Bud gritted his teeth. Why couldn't she figure out what he meant? Just once. Please.

"Not that kind of therapy," Scott said. "Speech and physical therapy."

Well, thank God. Once again his son had come to the rescue. Speech therapy. That would be an everlovin' godsend. Maybe then he'd be able to communicate with these idiots around here. Oh, that wasn't nice. He didn't mean Marie. She would understand him fine when she wasn't so worried. But, for now at least, Scott could interpret for him.

Marie. He needed to help her. Make her feel better. Maybe he'd been rude. Just because he'd had a stroke didn't mean he should mistreat her. He sought her eyes. Then he made the effort. "Ma-rie."

She bent over him, smoothing his brow with her soft hand. "What, my darling?"

He stared intently into her eyes, remembering the first time he'd seen her, how his heart had tumbled in pieces around his feet with the sure knowledge she was his forever-girl. He moved his lips, trying to make sure he would get it right. Then he forced the word into the air. "Love." Then the second word. "You."

Tears came to her eyes, but better, a real smile, the kind he hadn't seen all day. Then he felt her warm lips on his. "Oh, Bud, I love you, too."

After a moment, Scott cleared his throat. "Am I disturbing you two lovebirds?"

When Bud looked at his son, he saw another genuine grin. "No." He rested, gathering his concentration before going on. "You. Love. Too."

Bud watched Scott move closer, then give him a thumbs-up. "Dad, you know what? I think you're on the mend. This is great progress for one day."

Great progress. Being able to talk in monosyllables, only occasionally getting his point across?

Suddenly he felt exhausted. Marie and Scott looked as if they were celebrating a Super Bowl championship. Bud groaned. He wanted to be cured. Now. He didn't want to hear any more about patience. About one-day-at-a-time. Especially not about therapy.

And, dammit, he wanted to see his grand-children!

ONE OF THE FEATURES Meg had liked best about the house when they'd bought it five years ago was the alcove sitting room off the master bedroom. She'd loved decorating it as a retreat. On one wall was a built-in entertainment center and bookcase, full of family photos and favorite books; opposite were two swivel rockers. Occupying the third wall was an off-white love seat, over which hung a hazy pastel of an apple orchard in full bloom. Meg had pictured herself curled up there with a good book, having quiet conversations with

Scott and passing on sage advice to her daughter.

None of that had happened. On the contrary, she hardly had time to enjoy what she'd hoped would be her sanctuary. And even when she did manage to escape for some privacy, invariably one of the kids would show up, intruding on her solitude with one request or another. Still, kids weren't there forever. Eventually, her time would come.

Now, dressed in her robe, she sat in one of the rockers, cradling a book in her lap, the soft glow of the reading lamp the only illumination. But she wasn't reading, she was waiting. For Scott.

"We'll talk later," he'd said, brushing her cheek with a light kiss when he and Marie had arrived home from the hospital around eight. She'd kept dinner warming on the stove for them, and after eating, Scott had excused himself to make some phone calls. She could hear him outside now dragging the trash cans to the curb for tomorrow's pickup. Forcing her mind off the topics she knew they'd have to discuss, she turned back to her book, reading and rereading the same paragraph until Scott finally entered the sitting room wearing only flannel boxers and a T-shirt. She tossed him a soft fleece afghan. "Here, your legs will get cold."

He threw her one of those you're-mothering-me-again looks, then settled on the sofa, obediently covering his bare legs. "Where should we start?" The weariness in his voice matched the sadness in his eyes.

"With Justin, I guess." She filled him in on the conversations she'd had, first with Marie and then with the school counselor. "The upshot is he's going to be getting extra help three days a week from the reading specialist."

"I'm glad to hear it. But I'm not happy about the lying."

"I think he's punished himself quite enough."

"I agree. Sounds as if Pops dealt with the situation."

"Probably more effectively than we would've," Meg admitted. "But it disturbs me that we had no clue about his problems, except for his somewhat lower-than-average test scores."

"Maybe we weren't paying enough attention."

Meg bristled. "Are you saying I should've been on top of it?"

"Didn't you hear what I said, Meg? I said

we weren't paying enough attention. Last I knew, *we* included me."

Meg's head ached. This conversation was in danger of spinning out of control. As usual. "I'm sorry. Of course, you're right."

"It's not going to get any easier. With Mom and Pops here, the Jordan account…" He shook his head.

"I know." She swallowed the wedge of fear lodged in her throat. "Realistically, what do you think we're facing?"

He looked directly at her. "They may never be able to go on their trip. At best, I imagine we can anticipate a fairly lengthy recovery period."

She ran her fingers up and down the cover of her book. "Here?" Okay. The question was out.

"Here," he said, leaning over to put a hand on the arm of her chair. "Can you handle it?"

"What happened to that *we* of a few moments ago?"

"You and I both know the brunt of care will fall on you. Of course, I'll do what I can when I can, but the daily routine? You and Mom will be on the front line."

Meg studied the back of his lightly veined hand, the fingers splayed against the plaid fabric. "Is there any other option?"

"No." He looked up at the ceiling. "We can't rely on Kay. Insurance will only cover so much." He hesitated, as if choosing his words with care. "What'll this do to us, Meg?"

She set her book on the lamp table. "I don't know." She considered the question. "It'll either drive us farther apart or bring us closer."

"You could just walk out of this whole bloody situation."

"Bud and Marie are my family, too," she said, realizing the truth of that statement. In fact, they were her only family.

He patted the seat beside him. "C'mere."

She didn't want to be sweet-talked or patronized. Nor did she want to hear about Brenda. This wasn't something that could be solved with a cuddle. Despite her misgivings, though, she moved to the love seat, nestling beside him. His arm went around her shoulders, pulling her against his chest. "About Brenda..." he said.

Her mouth went cottony. "You've already explained. Maybe she's just the demonstrative type." Helpless to stem the spate of words, all intended to keep from hearing the worst, she continued. "You work closely with her. I know that. Of course she wanted to express her sympathy and—" He shut her off with a kiss, gentle, yet probing. A kiss designed to make her tremble. And it succeeded. Finally she surfaced. "But—"

"But?" He cupped her face in his hands. "I'm married to you. I'll grant you Brenda is an attractive woman, and maybe she does come on too strong, but—"

"You're vulnerable."

He rubbed his thumb across her temple. "Yes, Meg, I am." He lowered his forehead to hers. "That's why I'm counting on you."

In an attempt to overcome her girlhood disappointments and to feel good about herself, Meg had spent most of her adult life tending to others, especially her children, and participating in all those community and school activities. Yet now, in her husband's embrace, she realized it was his opinion that mattered most. But after years of feeling ignored and taken for granted, could she do what he needed her to do? *Could* he count on her? Could she count on him?

Only time would tell.

CHAPTER EIGHT

JUSTIN SQUIRMED uncomfortably in his seat. All around him the other kids were busy working on their essays. *A memorable Halloween*. Talk about a lame topic. Did Mrs. Kelly really think he wanted to tell her about when he was a little kid and his sister made him dress up like Prince Charming because she was Cinderella? He could still remember the scratchy purple tights and the old ladies on their street who thought mint patties and coconut creams were treats. Nah, he sure as heck wasn't going to write about that.

He stared out the window. A gusty north wind was blowing the last few leaves off the trees. Great. Now he'd have to spend Saturday morning raking. Nobody else was available to do it. Dad was working all the time, Mom was taking care of Grampa, and Hayley? Forget it. She was too busy being a high-school cheerleading goddess to stick around the house.

He checked the clock. Half an hour till the bell rang. He'd have to write something. He drew a picture of a robot on his brainstorming sheet. Then, when his stomach growled, Mikela Smith swiveled around in her seat and gave him one of her snooty shut-up-can't-you-see-I'm-a-brain looks.

A Halloween memory. Okay. Mrs. Kelly had asked for it. He'd give her one. He tried to remember the goriest scenes from movies like *Nightmare on Elm Street* and *Friday, the 13th*. Yeah, that'd be good. He'd gross her out. He picked up his pen and began: "I was home alone when I heard the wind blow the door open. Then steps on the creeky…" He crossed out *creeky*. He didn't know how to spell it, so he'd find another word.

When the bell rang, he sat back in satisfaction, barely able to control a diabolical chuckle. Other kids had probably written about bobbing for apples and boring stuff like that. Even if his wasn't true, he liked the part about blood oozing from underneath the bathroom door.

"Justin?" His teacher was standing over him. "Are you planning to hand in your essay?"

He glanced around. The classroom had cleared. "Yes, ma'am." He grabbed up his notebook, stuffing the robot picture inside, gave her his paper and headed for the door. He'd almost made it when Mrs. Kelly spoke again. "How is your grandfather?"

He turned around slowly. He didn't want to talk about that. But maybe a miracle had happened and she was actually trying to be nice. "Um, okay, I guess."

"I understand he's recuperating at your home."

Justin focused on the corny cutouts of pumpkins and black cats and leaves on the bulletin board, then gazed out the window to watch school buses pulling into the circle drive. He didn't want to picture the way his parents' bedroom had been transformed into a hospital ward. Didn't want to visualize Grampa's walker, that ugly potty chair or the shower seat. He didn't want to listen to the speech therapist teaching his grandfather to speak again or overhear his parents talking in hushed tones from the small guest bedroom next to his, where they'd moved when Grampa had gotten out of the rehab place.

"Yes, ma'am." He thought maybe he ought to volunteer something more since she'd asked. "He's, uh, been home about a week."

She seemed to be debating whether to say something else, and he edged toward the door.

"Justin, I know that means some adjustments for everyone."

"Yes, ma'am."

"How are the special reading sessions going?"

He felt his face burn. He didn't suppose it would do any good to tell her Sam Grider called him a retard every time he had to leave study hall and go to the reading teacher's room. "Fine."

She scrutinized him like a scientist who'd discovered some new species of insect. Finally, she said, "I'm glad to hear it. Have a good day."

He escaped into the hall and made a beeline for his bus. *Have a good day?* Right. He wouldn't know a "good day" if it bit him in the ass. His whole life was in the toilet. Grampa was like a little baby, needing to be taught to walk and talk all over again. His parents were too busy to pay any attention to him. His sister was being a jerk, and he didn't know if he should tell his parents that she was sneaking around after school with that loser Zach Simon. Riding in his car, even. And Gramma? It was like she was in never-never land, thinking Grampa was doing so well, applauding as though it was a gosh-darned miracle when he did a simple thing like button his shirt left-handed.

Besides that, soccer season was over.

And Sam Grider? Blood rushed to Justin's face. He'd love to pound that kid. Someday he would. A guy could only take so much.

"WHERE'S THE CANDY?" Hayley stood at the pantry door, examining its contents.

Since her daughter claimed to be on a diet, Meg was at a loss. She looked up from the jellied fruit salad she was making.

"What candy?"

With all the scorn of a drama queen, Hayley spun around, her eyes rounded in incredulity. "The trick-or-treat stuff."

No. Not one more thing added to this day from hell. Meg quickly calculated whether she had enough time to run to the store. "I forgot."

"Earth to Mother. Hel-lo. Today is Halloween. The trick-or-treaters will be coming in less than an hour. You don't want our house egged, do you?"

The image of yolks and whites dripping over the brick-and-stone exterior was not comforting. Meg sighed. "I'll call your father. Maybe he can pick up something on his way home."

"If I could drive, you wouldn't have to worry."

Meg couldn't help laughing. "Oh, believe me, if you could drive, I would worry."

Hayley tossed her head. "You don't trust me, is that it?"

"I was joking."

"You're so not funny. I'm sick of being treated like a little kid."

Meg bit back her instinctive response. She lacked the energy for a verbal sparring match. "Nobody's treating you like a little kid."

"Ha! Then explain why you only let me go out with Zach once a week."

"Your father and I have agreed—"

"You are so retro. I'm the only girl I know who has these stupid rules."

Meg fell back on the mother of all clichés. "We're not talking about other people. We're talking about you."

"It's bad enough I'm practically a prisoner in my own home, but then I'm supposed to help with even more chores now that Gramma and Grampa are here and—"

"Hayley, honey, please. We don't mean to make trouble."

Hearing her mother-in-law's voice behind her and seeing the stricken look on her daughter's face, Meg wilted. Just when she'd thought the family dynamic couldn't get worse.

Hayley had the grace to look contrite. "I'm sorry, Gramma, it's not you. Really. It's just—"

"She's frustrated, Marie." At this point Meg sought peace at any price. "We're having a classic clash of overprotective mother and rebellious teenager." She shot Hayley a warning look. "But it will pass."

Thankfully, Hayley picked up on the cue. "I have homework to do," she said and bolted for the stairs.

"I'm sorry you had to hear that, Marie."

"Having Bud and me here is creating problems." As if unaware of her actions, Marie took the spoon from Meg's fingers and continued making the salad.

On visits, her mother-in-law had always puttered about repositioning knickknacks, straightening pictures and putting whatever was amiss in order. Now, though, Meg had noticed Marie's almost manic need to keep busy. When she wasn't with Bud, she was almost always in the kitchen, cooking, cleaning—and, yes—rearranging. Most recently, the pots and pans. It was as if the kitchen were being held hostage by her mother-in-law. "Nonsense. It's just taking us a while to adjust to a new routine."

Marie studied the concoction in the mixing bowl. "Don't you think a bit of diced celery would add some zest to the salad?"

No, she didn't. If she did, she would already have added some. "It might." Meg picked up the phone. "I need to call Scott and have him stop at the store to get some trick-or-treat candy."

Marie stared at her, goggle-eyed. "You don't have anything?"

Her implied accusation rankled. "I forgot."

Marie stayed her hand. "No need to call Scotty. I'll whip up some cookies. Maybe I'll wrap a little card with each one telling who baked them so the parents of the little tykes won't worry."

Meg shrugged. With this new wrinkle, she was unclear just exactly when or how she was going to make dinner for Scott and the kids. Or even if she was still the cook. Having one's house egged was beginning to look like a desirable alternative.

"Run along, dear. But if you would, check on Bud for me."

Meg nodded, then started for the master bedroom. Despite her reassurances to Marie, the household had turned topsy-turvy. It had taken the better part of two days to move all of Scott's and her belongings to the guest bedroom upstairs. Already, sharing the bathroom with Justin and Hayley was an adventure. After years of sleeping in a king-size bed, the double was also proving problematic, since Scott slept in a sprawl, often encroaching on her side. As evidenced by her fraying temper, she hadn't had a good night's sleep since they'd moved upstairs. She barely had time alone with Scott except in bed. Up to his eyeballs in work on the Jordan account, he generally fell asleep within seconds of hitting the pillow. Any conversation was limited to survival issues.

Bud lay propped up against two pillows, his eyes closed, his face lightly stubbled. Although he'd made progress during his three-week stay at the rehab facility, it would be months before the full scope of his recovery could be determined. He was now able to walk with a walker and, following the suggestions of the occupational therapist, to dress and feed himself and to move from his bed to a chair. He was slowly regaining some movement in his right hand and arm. His speech impairment, though, would take longer to address. Meg drove him three times a week for his therapy and Marie tried to work with him at home, but she was easily stymied by his complaints and frustration.

Meg looked longingly toward the cozy sitting room, then eased herself into the bedside rocker, letting her head fall back. The rhythm of Bud's breathing was calming and, oddly, she found comfort in being here. Despite the pain and the difficulties his regimen presented, he was determined to do whatever his therapists advised. "Me. Back soon." This was his repeated rallying cry, as if his stroke were a journey from which he would return fully restored.

Meg worried about Marie's coddling. The social worker had suggested there was a thin line between compassion and tough love. Marie tended to let Bud off the hook with his exercises and seemed reluctant to permit him to try new skills. In short, she hovered. Scott wasn't around enough to help much. By the time he got home from work, Bud was exhausted, so therapy then was out. Several times when Marie was otherwise occupied, Meg had slipped in and worked with Bud on the exercises. In each case, he had seemed almost boyish in his desire to please.

"You."

The word snapped her to attention. Bud's eyes were open and he was managing a twisted smile.

"Yes, Bud. I'm right here."

He reached for her hand with his good one. His skin felt warm and soft against her palm. "You. Good girl."

Meg's eyes filled with tears of gratitude. Somebody had noticed her efforts, and no one—not Hayley or Marie or Scott—was going to rob her of the satisfaction of this moment. She squeezed her father-in-law's hand and smiled at him. "Thanks for noticing, Bud. I needed that."

He nodded knowingly. "I guessed it."

SCOTT PULLED THE CAR into the garage, turned off the ignition and sat in the dim light, summoning the strength to go inside. On the way home along the suburban streets he'd spotted little ghosts, goblins, Shreks and ballerinas. How long ago it seemed that he'd cradled Justin, dressed in his tiny pumpkin suit, and held the hand of "Beauty" Hayley as they traversed the neighborhood. Hayley's lilting toddler voice echoed in his memory. "Twick or tweat?"

He leaned his head back against the seat. He couldn't sit there indefinitely. People were counting on him. But he could hardly bear to witness his once-vigorous father struggle to ask a simple question or feed himself, or to watch his mother wringing her hands from worry. Meg grew more thin-lipped every day, the hollows under her eyes mute testimony to the strain of their situation. Hayley, pulling a classic Greta Garbo act, preferred the solitude of her room—and her cell phone—to their company. And Justin? Like a chameleon, he adapted as necessary to his environment and tried not to make waves. Scott knew he'd go nuts if he had to be home all day, as Meg was. Even the frenetic atmosphere of the agency was preferable. Still, on some level, he knew he was copping out by escaping so totally into his work.

A cinnamon aroma greeted him when he finally made his way into the house. His mother stood in the kitchen, face flushed, spooning dough onto a cookie sheet. Spread on foil on the counter were at least six dozen cookies. "May I?" he asked, picking up a warm snickerdoodle.

Marie smiled as if recalling happier times. "Could I stop you even if I wanted to?"

He kissed her on the cheek. "Probably not." Gesturing at the array, he said, "What's the occasion?"

She shook the spoon at him. "Not you, too. It's Halloween and these are our treats. Meg forgot to buy the candy."

"These are better anyway," he said, stuffing the cookie into his mouth. "Where's Dad?"

"In our room. With Meg."

"I'll go say hello."

Pausing in the bedroom doorway, he observed the two of them, Meg sitting in the rocker holding his father's hand. Something lurched in his chest. She looked so peaceful he hated to disturb them. Then Bud lifted his eyes. "Son."

"Hi, Pops."

Meg glanced up, nodded by way of acknowledgment, then stood. "I'll go see about dinner."

Before she could brush past him, Scott put an arm around her. "Hello," he said.

Her eyes softened briefly before she moved away from his embrace. "I'm glad you're home." He pondered her words. Did she mean she was happy to see him or that he was a welcome reinforcement?

Just then, the doorbell rang. "Here they come," Scott said.

As Meg hurried from the room, Scott heard Justin clattering down the stairs. With any luck, he'd want to cover the front door tonight.

"Coming?" Bud's brow was furrowed.

"Trick-or-treaters, Pops. It's Halloween."

Bud scooted back against the pillows and swung his legs over the edge of the bed. "See."

"See?"

Bud nodded, then pointed to himself. "Me. See."

Scott felt relieved laughter rumbling up from his stomach. "You want to help greet the monsters and witches?"

"Bitches."

He bent down so he was in his father's line of vision and carefully moved his lips to form the word. "Witches, Pops. Witches."

"Wh-wh-wit-chez."

"Bravo." He turned and positioned the walker. "Your chariot awaits."

Laboriously, they made their way to the entry hall. Scott pulled a dining-room chair close to the door and helped Bud into it. Justin, holding a huge basket of wrapped cookies, peered out the side window. "Here come some more, Grampa."

Scott stood back and watched his father's face light up when a three-foot-tall pirate grabbed a cookie, then approached him, and eyeing his jeans and loose-fitting cowboy shirt, said, "I like your cos-toom. You be's a cowboy, right?"

Bud lifted his good hand over his head in a twirling motion. "Hi, ho!"

A grin wreathing his face, Justin caught Scott's eye and patted his grandfather's shoulder. "Ride 'em, cowboy!"

Just then, Marie muscled Scott aside and put a protective arm around Bud. "Darlin', what in the world? You'll catch your death of cold." She turned on Justin and the pirate. "Close the door, please."

Justin gently ushered the boy out, then shut the door. And not a minute too soon. Bud exploded. "Me! See! You—" he waved his hand imperiously at Marie "—you, cook!"

"Now, Bud, sweetheart—"

"Damn, damn, damn!"

"Mom, he's enjoying this," Scott said. "I'll get a jacket and hat for him."

"But if he gets sick—"

"At least he'll have had some fun."

Bud glared triumphantly at his wife. "Treat," he said in a loud voice.

Justin had stepped back, out of the line of fire. Scott put a hand on his mother's arm. "It'll be fine, Mom."

Marie looked from one of them to the other and then, with a sniff, returned to the kitchen.

The victory was evident on Bud's face. "Treat. Me. Ha!"

The bell rang again, and another group of children arrived. Scott watched with a sense of bittersweetness as Justin helped his grandfather distribute the cookies.

There was a time when Bud would've wired his front porch with eerie sound effects, draped cobwebs and skeletons from hooks and greeted trick-or-treaters in his World War I phantom-aviator costume. Now all he could do was utter the one word, *treat*.

The children, interested only in filling their goody bags, didn't seem to care.

But Scott did.

IT WAS AFTER MIDNIGHT when Meg gratefully sank into bed. Between the great cookie challenge, seemingly hundreds of trick-or-treaters, and the silent treatment from Hayley after Meg had insisted she do the dinner dishes, she craved the oblivion of sleep, however short-lived.

She'd just fluffed her pillow, settled into her customary position and closed her eyes when she felt Scott's hand on her shoulder. Surely he didn't think she was in the mood for... Not tonight. Please. She really was too tired.

"Meg? How're you doing?"

Did he really want to know? Actually, did *she?* She'd made up her mind that if she just kept busy and didn't think about the myriad responsibilities and changes in their lives, she could carry on. If she ever stopped to take stock, she might crack. Especially if she took the time to think about Scott and their marriage. Right now she felt as if they were in a holding pattern, one with no apparent possibility of a safe landing. "Okay, I guess," she said.

"That doesn't sound very convincing."

What did he want? A ringing endorsement for the job of manning the home front? "It's...different."

He moved closer and gathered her in his arms, snuggling her against his chest. She could hear the steady beat of his heart, smell the vestiges of his expensive cologne. "We're asking a lot of you."

She couldn't take his sympathy. Tears were too close to the surface. "What choice do we have?"

"None, I guess." He was quiet for a long time, his fingers ruffling her hair. "It's not forever."

"We don't know that."

"You're right, we don't."

"You heard what the doctor said. There will come a time when Bud's made all the improvement he's going to. Then what?"

"But don't you think he's getting better?"

Denial rang in his every word but she cut him some slack. He wasn't around enough to observe the effort it took for Bud to make even the smallest advance. Or to witness his father's frustration when he didn't immediately master a skill. "Yes, but don't get your hopes too high."

"In my business, we have to be results oriented. But with Pops? I guess he's not the only one who'll have to learn patience."

She nodded drowsily, then answered his original question as truthfully as she could. "I'm okay for now."

"What about the kids?"

She honestly didn't know. "They're coping," she said. Justin seemed to relate well with his grandfather, showing sensitivity beyond his years. But was he spending time with Bud because he still felt guilty? And Hayley—it was as if she resented the unpleasantness and the disruptions in her schedule, but maybe she, too, was in denial and unable to express her true feelings.

"I hate this."

"You can't change the fact that it happened, Scott. Hopefully, we'll all learn something from the experience."

He pulled her closer and nuzzled her cheek. "You're a rock, Meggie. I don't know what I'd do without you."

Her heart thudded. Of course he felt that way under these emergency circumstances, but would he feel the same once they returned to life as usual? "Thanks," she said before turning away from him. But he didn't back off. He wrapped her in his arms, like a parent protecting a child against the terrors of the night. She found herself drifting off to sleep, but not before she thought she heard him whisper, "I love you."

In the morning she wondered if she'd dreamed it. It had been so long since she'd heard those words from him. And she needed them too desperately to accept an illusion.

THE FOLLOWING FRIDAY NIGHT, Justin hunched beside Trevor Morrison in the high-school football stands, trying to keep warm. The Tigers were tied with their crosstown rivals with three minutes to go in the fourth quarter. Sitting two rows in front of him was the cute new girl in his science class—Holly or Molly or something like that. She had this long red hair that rippled down her back in copper curls and she was sorta shy, but she'd asked him for help with their assignments a few times. That didn't necessarily mean she liked him or anything—but maybe it could.

Hearing a collective groan from the fans, he looked back at the field. "Did you see that?" Trevor asked. "Sanchez dropped the pass on the five-yard line."

Justin glanced at the scoreboard. Third down and fourteen long yards to go. The team huddled. When they broke to take up their positions, the crowd noise became deafening. Justin had thought about going out for football when he got to high school, but he didn't know whether he'd like getting creamed by some two-hundred-fifty-pound tackle. He studied the players. Sure enough, the defensive line looked like gorillas. He and Trevor stood with the rest of the spectators as the critical play started. The quarterback took the ball, danced around like spit on a skillet, then pumped his arm several times before lofting a high pass into the far corner of the end zone. Sanchez went high in the air. The crowd roared. Touchdown, Tigers.

Justin thought it would be cool to be a hero like Sanchez—girls would drape themselves all over you. But you could be a soccer hero, too, couldn't you? Maybe not in Oklahoma. Football was the really big deal. Way bigger than soccer. Trevor punched him in the arm. "That was awesome, huh?"

"Now if we can just hold them."

The boys watched the seconds tick away until the opponents tried a last-second desperation pass into the end zone, just off the fingertips of the receiver. The Tiger fans went wild.

Justin trailed after Trevor, who had already started hopscotching down the bleachers. Mr. Morrison was picking them up. Naturally, Dad was working late. When he was a little kid, his dad used to take him to some of the games. Not that he'd want to sit with a parent now. That'd be weird. Especially if Holly—or Molly— saw him. Still, it kind of made him sad that he and his father didn't do stuff together anymore.

Walking with Trevor across the parking lot,

Justin imagined that he was in high school. Popular. A big jock. Then he'd have his own car. A girlfriend. Independence.

"Hey, Harper, isn't that your sister?" Trevor had stopped in his tracks and was pointing toward a dark corner of the football field.

Stunned, Justin could only stare at the scene unfolding in front of him. Hayley, dressed in her cheerleader outfit and jacket, was locking lips with Zach right there in front of God and everybody. "Gross," he muttered.

Trevor shot him an incredulous look. "She's hot, man. I wouldn't mind a little of that action."

Justin made a mental note to sock his friend later. Zach was all over his sister. As they watched, he put his arm around Hayley and they started walking. "Where's she going?"

Justin didn't realize he'd spoken aloud until Trevor said, "Beats me. Let's follow them."

There was a weird feeling in the pit of Justin's stomach, but he figured maybe it was his brotherly duty to make sure Hayley was okay. He still hadn't told Mom and Dad he'd seen Hayley out joyriding with Zach lots of times after school. They'd freak out if they knew. But this could be even worse.

As the crowd thinned, the boys wove their

way between the remaining cars, keeping just enough distance to avoid detection. They crouched behind a Jeep and watched as Hayley and Zach got into the front seat of his car. Stealthily, Justin and Trevor approached. Zach didn't seem to be in any hurry to leave the parking lot. And why should he be? He was necking up a storm with Hayley. "She told my parents she was going home with Jill after the game to spend the night there," Justin muttered.

"She's busted, then," his buddy replied. "I already saw Jill and some other girls leave."

Justin's gut twisted. What the hell did his sister think she was doing? He didn't want to watch anymore. Didn't want to see Zach kissing his sister like he was sucking her up through a straw. Or notice the way her fingers toyed with his cheesy platinum-tipped hair.

"Wow." Trevor spoke almost reverentially. "They're really goin' at it."

"Shut up!" Justin could definitely do without his friend's play-by-play. Yet there was something at once disturbing and titillating about the scene. Spellbinding—like not being able to look away from a car accident.

In the distance, Justin could hear the celebratory toots of car horns, the chatter of excited fans and the grinding sound of tires on gravel. The normal post-game noise. But this night didn't feel normal.

"Look," Trevor said.

Zach had pulled apart from Hayley and was reaching over the seat, fumbling for something in the back. "What's he doing?"

"I dunno. Come on, let's get closer."

Justin shivered and followed Trevor. Now there was only an old Buick Skylark between them and the Zachmobile. Transfixed, Justin watched Zach haul a six-pack of beer into the front seat. "Damn," he mouthed. His sister didn't drink, did she?

"Looks like a brewski," Trevor whispered with glee.

Justin nudged around the hood of the Skylark and hunkered beside the fender. Even through the closed window of Zach's car, he could hear the metallic snap of a tab top. Then another. He watched in shock as Zach handed a beer to his sister. Then both of them took a big chug and followed it up with a sloppy kiss. Then another chug. Justin thought he might throw up. He couldn't stand this. Before he could stop himself, he stood, rounded the Skylark and knocked on Zach's window.

He could hear the low growl in Zach's

voice. "What the hell?" He rolled down the window and glared at Justin. "Get outta here, kid. Mind your own business."

"Justin?" It didn't take a genius to figure his appearance had stunned his sister.

Zach looked at Hayley. "You know this jack-off?"

"He's my brother."

Justin should have taken some satisfaction from the fear he saw in his sister's eyes. But he almost felt sorry for her. What was she doing with such a loser? "You're supposed to be with Jill," he sputtered.

Zach glowered. "No shit, Sherlock."

"You gotta get out of that car and come home with me," Justin managed to say in his most authoritative tone.

Hayley shook her head, as if cursing the day her brother was born. "You've got to be kidding. I'm sick of you and Mom and Dad ruining my life."

To Justin's surprise, she got out of the car and came around to face him, her expression menacing. "Listen, Justin, I'm going back to Jill's, but not until I feel like it. I know what I'm doing and it's got nothing to do with you."

Justin stared at Hayley. "But Mom and Dad—"

Her voice lowered to a hiss. "If you say even one word to them about this, you'll be so sorry." Then her expression softened a little. "But you're not going to tell, are you? They have enough problems. You don't need to pile on another one. After all, I'm just having fun." He couldn't be sure in the dim light, but it looked as if there were tears in her eyes. "Like there's been any of *that* lately."

Helpless, Justin searched for words to change her mind, but before he could summon a coherent thought, Zach stepped out of the car and took Hayley's arm. "Come on. We'll be late for Greg's party."

"You're not supposed to go—"

"She's going. Get used to it."

Justin watched as Hayley climbed back in the car, picked up her beer and gave him a halfhearted ta-ta toast. When Zach gunned his car out of the parking space, gravel sprayed over Justin's shoes. But he hardly felt it. He was shaking with anger and confusion.

Then he felt Trevor's hand on his shoulder. "Jeez, Justin, that sucks."

"Yeah." His throat clogged. Everything was so screwed up. His mom and dad were still acting weird around each other, and this deal with his grandfather had affected them all. And now he had to worry about stupid Hayley, too. Still, he wouldn't tell on her. Not yet. But she better watch it.

As he and Trevor hurried across the lot to where they were supposed to meet Mr. Morrison, Justin added a new name to the list of guys he'd like to beat the crap out of. Zach Simon.

CHAPTER NINE

HUNCHED OVER HIS DESK, Scott reviewed media coverage for the San Antonio market, unsure whether they had sufficient exposure in the Hispanic community. Already some ads were running on TV, and Sunday's paper would have a huge spread. With the grand opening less than a month away, it was crunch time. Ward Jordan expected results and Harper Concepts aimed to produce them.

But at what expense?

Scott rose, stretched and walked to the door. Up and down the hall, employees were hard at work, the atmosphere tension-charged in the same way a locker room heats up with pregame jitters. By and large, his group was motivated and committed to making this campaign successful. Scott wished he could get into it more. Here he'd realized a dream, but he didn't have time to savor it. He worked longer hours than ever, sometimes getting home well after midnight. But his heart wasn't in it the way he had anticipated it would be for such a major account.

At the oddest times of the day he would find himself thinking about his father. Was that how it all ended? Work your fingers to the bone, retire and get zapped by a stroke or a heart attack?

Then there was Justin. Something was eating the kid, beyond his grandfather's condition. When Scott had tried to talk to him about the football game, Justin had mumbled the final score and then flipped on the television, effectively forestalling any father-son chat. Maybe he could simply chalk the kid's behavior up to adolescent moodiness, but there was this look about him. Watchful. Wary. Secretive.

Scott worked the kinks out of his neck and shoulders as he returned to his desk, but when he sat down, he ignored the stack of papers and focused instead on the photograph on his desk of Meg and him at some long-ago country-club function. She wore a stunning, low-cut black dress, the material draped gracefully across her breasts. Scott studied the picture—her face turned toward him, one delicate hand resting lovingly on the lapel of his tuxedo. He'd give anything to see that same adoring look again. Had they truly been happier then or was it just a trick of photography? He did remember having the distinct sense that she adored him, earlier in their marriage. And he'd basked in it. From junior high on, girls chased after him, and he'd thrived on the attention. He'd taken for granted that as captain of the basketball team, class president and honor-roll student, he could have his pick of any girl in his class. College was no different. But something had been lacking. He'd never been sure any of them wanted him for him and not for the status he represented.

Meg was different. When he met her in that dental office, she'd had no idea who he was, what accomplishments were listed in his résumé. For the first time, he was pretty sure a woman liked him solely for him. He admired her grit, making something of herself following her mother's death. She had nobody. He'd figured he could protect her, be her everything.

He picked up the photograph to look at it more closely. They'd been so young, then. So carefree. Finally, with a sigh, he set it down. How long had it been since she'd needed him? She was competence personified handling the kids' schedules and activities, running half of the women's clubs in their area, learning to play nearly scratch golf and a decent game of tennis. At times he felt like a plasterboard figure propped in the appropriate place at the appropriate time and labeled Meg's Husband.

Under the current circumstances, though, he didn't know what he'd do without her organizational skills. Just keeping track of all Pops's appointments and medications was a full-time job. His mother, used to being dependent on her husband, was struggling with the whole situation, which put even more of the burden on Meg. She was managing. Just. But for how long?

He stared at the work memos in front of him. What should've been a fulfilling challenge for him held all the excitement of sawdust.

He leaned back in his chair, hands behind his head. How could he be feeling sorry for himself when professionally he had it made? Somehow he'd have to gear himself up for the big push. Win one for the Gipper. But as he mentally recommitted to the campaign, he experienced niggling guilt. He'd basically abdicated the home front to Meg.

"Scott, got a minute?"

He looked up to see Wes peering into his office. "Sure. Have a seat."

"How's your dad this week?"

"Moving better, getting some of the feeling back in his arm and hand. But the speech? It's slow."

"Tough break. I'm sorry he's having to go through this."

Scott sighed. "Me, too." He tilted his chair forward. "How can I help you?"

"It's about San Antonio. The preopening gala for the chamber of commerce, civic leaders, the media. You know the drill. I told you I'd cover it, but something's come up."

Scott bit back a twinge of irritation. What could be more important? "Oh?"

"Susie's hysterectomy got rescheduled for that week. I'll need to be here with her. Help out with the kids." He lifted his hands in resignation.

"Of course, you need to be with your wife and family." Scott held his breath, waiting for the other shoe to drop.

"Can you cover it? Brenda'll be going, too. So will Jim Tate."

The mention of the middle-aged account executive's name did nothing to assuage the sudden apprehension Scott felt. Meg already had her suspicions about Brenda, and even though he'd tried to convince himself that his colleague's affectionate gestures were just part of her personality, he didn't trust Jim Tate to serve as an adequate chaperone.

Nor was he sure he trusted Brenda. Or himself. Could one pleasant day with Meg in Colorado weeks ago fortify him against temptation? "Sure, Wes. Not to worry."

Not to worry? The mere fact that he'd thought about Brenda in that way scared the hell out of him. More than anything he wanted to go home, take Meg to the bedroom, shut the door and find himself again. And maybe in the process find his wife. His marriage.

IF IT WOULDN'T BE PERCEIVED as rude, Meg would've clapped her hands over her ears and closed her eyes to escape sensory overload. The ladies' locker room reverberated with the shrill voices of women with nothing more important to discuss than new shades of nail polish, their winter golfing vacations to Florida or Arizona and the insidiousness of the pin placement on the seventeenth hole. Bright yellow lockers, lime-green walls and the earthy scent of newly mown turf mixed with heavy, floral colognes was a perfect recipe for a headache.

She wouldn't be there today except as pairings chair of the Ladies' Golf Association, she was expected to participate in the golf round and end-of-season luncheon. Once upon a time, the country club had symbolized her arrival, the pinnacle of her and Scott's upward climb in Tulsa society. Today, after weeks of tending to Bud, it screamed superficiality. Or was she merely experiencing sour grapes? She'd had to give up a lot to make room for her new responsibilities. Looking around the locker room, she wondered if any of the other women had the faintest idea how demanding caring for a stroke patient could be.

When the crowd thinned, Meg slipped out of her golfing outfit and headed for the shower. Prickles of hot water soothed her bunched shoulder muscles and she relished the time to herself. Still, she had to make her requisite appearance at the luncheon before going home.

Sighing, she turned off the water, wrapped a hand towel around her wet hair and padded back to her locker. She'd hesitated to leave Bud alone all day with Marie, which was silly, she knew. But what if he wanted to go for a walk? Marie was tiny. Could she support him if he stumbled?

Marie was turning over more of the home therapy to Meg. It seemed she was either in denial that Bud needed help, or she just didn't have the heart to inflict any discomfort on him. She was more content to hole up in the kitchen cooking far more food than was healthy for any of them and let Meg put Bud through his paces.

Two or three ladies remained in the locker room, one of them Candy Stimson, whose daughter was in Hayley's class. Candy was the kind of mother whose parenting decisions more often than not indicated a lack of mature judgment, as if Candy herself were the teenager pursuing the goddess of popularity.

Cradling a soft-drink can, Candy looked over at Meg. "We haven't seen you here for a while."

Meg gave her the shortest answer she could think of. "I've been busy."

"I imagine you've got your hands full with Hayley." The woman practically simpered, her eyes glinting.

Indignation, hot and pure, rose from Meg's toes up, but she didn't want to give Candy the satisfaction of a retort. "Well, that's teenagers for you."

"Maybe, but at least my daughter isn't dating that wild Zach Simon."

Meg fought back panic. What was Candy implying? "Hayley isn't dating much."

"Oh no? How come I see her riding around after school most days in Zach's car?"

Meg drew herself up. She was under the impression that Hayley stayed for cheerleading practice every day. "You must be mistaken."

"Well, choose to believe what makes you happy. But Lori said they were quite an item at Greg Farraday's after-game party last weekend."

Hayley? At a party? She'd gone back to Jill's after the game. Hadn't she? Meg glanced at her watch. "Excuse me, but I need to finish getting dressed. I don't want to miss the luncheon."

Candy knew a brush-off when she heard one. "Never say I didn't warn you." Then, taking the final swig of her drink, she swept out of the locker room.

Meg sank down on a bench. Could there be any truth in what Candy had said? What if Hayley was, indeed, sneaking around with the Simon boy? She didn't even want to think about it.

Nor did she want one more problem to deal with. She found herself yearning for Scott in a way that was immediate and painful. She needed his help. She was tired of being a martyr to the family, tired of once again playing second fiddle to Harper Concepts.

She wasn't going to deal with this one alone. Hayley was Scott's daughter, too. No matter how late he returned home tonight, he wasn't getting off the hook. However difficult it might be, she and Scott needed to present a united front.

Meg finished dressing and left the locker room, only then realizing she'd actually given credence to what Candy had said about Hayley. Yet no matter how hard she tried to come up with alternative explanations, in her heart she knew it was true.

BUD SAT WITH MARIE in the sitting room off the master suite watching one of her favorite television shows. The steady clack of her knitting needles made it hard to concentrate and, anyway, some of the words made no sense to him. Those people on the screen talked too much. He preferred sports. He could follow those with the mute button on.

He clutched the arms of his chair in frustration. Why wouldn't his brain untangle the jumble of words? Something was still wrong. He had the same trouble with reading. Certain words he recognized would pop out at him, but the others might as well have been Swahili. Even his glasses didn't help. What would it be like just to be able to sit and read the newspaper? It wasn't happening. And he wasn't sure it ever would. "Scares me."

He hadn't realized he'd voiced his thoughts aloud until Marie gripped his hand in alarm. "What?"

He nodded in the direction of the set. "Tee, uh, vee."

"Oh, honey, it's all right. The bad man won't kill the heroine."

He grimaced. She'd misunderstood again. She was treating him like a child who didn't know the action on the set wasn't real. The words were what scared him. The words he couldn't process in his brain.

He tried again. "Words. Can't understand."

Marie reached for the remote. "Let me turn up the volume."

"No!" Why couldn't she get it? It was like they were on two different planets with two different languages.

She shook her head sadly. "I'm sorry, I guess I don't know what you mean."

Inexplicably, his eyes filled with tears. He'd never been much of a crier. At least not until this blasted stroke. "Want to be better," he whispered.

"You're getting better every day, Bud. Look how well you're getting around."

Oh, yeah. Using a damn walker. With luck, someday maybe he'd walk with a cane. But it was the words he missed. He sighed, knowing he'd get himself all worked up if he thought about this too long. He stared uncomprehendingly at the screen for a few more minutes. Finally, he patted her knee, and bracing himself on the arms of the chair, hoisted himself to his feet. "Tired," he said by way of explanation.

She stood. "Let me help you."

"No," he said firmly. "Undress myself. You, watch TV."

The simple act of preparing for bed now took him nearly half an hour, but he was getting the hang of it. Not too long after he'd stretched out on the bed, Marie slid in beside him, the almond scent of her hand lotion reminding him of so many nights cuddling her. He'd missed that. He reached out with his good arm and drew her close. "Snuggle?"

As her arm came across his chest, she buried her head in the crook of his neck. "Oh, Bud, you mean so much to me. In sickness and health, remember?"

He shut his eyes tightly. He didn't want to remember. He wanted to be healthy. Manly. Virile. Gently, he stroked her shoulder. He was lucky. She was still here. It felt so good to have her familiar body next to him. He kissed her forehead. "Love you," he whispered. Then he searched for the other word, the important one. Finally it came. "Always."

Together. It was good.

His eyes grew heavy. Beside him, Marie snored softly. Sleep. Good. Very good.

MEG HUDDLED IN THE ARMCHAIR in the family room waiting for Scott. She pulled her bathrobe more snugly around her, wishing Buster were still alive to keep her company. She longed to bury her fingers in his soft fur, to watch him stretch on the floor at her feet, to confide in him the feelings she couldn't express to anyone else.

When the clock chimed ten, she glanced at the copy of *Good Housekeeping* in her lap. She'd read several true-life stories of women triumphing over obstacles in their lives. Hooray for them. At one time she would've described her own life as a success story, too. Even her mother would've been proud of her. And her father...if she'd had one. But she didn't feel that way anymore. Especially not considering the confrontation with Hayley looming ahead.

Both kids were in their rooms doing homework. She'd called Scott to ask that he get home before their bedtime. He was cutting it close. She thumbed through the magazine, wondering what the editorial staff would do with her story. Drudge Loses Sense of Identity? St. Meg of Tulsa? Marriage on Rocks vs. Marriage on Hold?

Finally, she heard the garage door open. When Scott walked into the family room, he'd already shed his sport jacket and was tugging at his tie. "Okay, I'm here. Where's the fire?"

Meg seethed. No *Hello, dear, how are you this evening?* "Sit down." She gestured to his recliner. "We need to deal with Hayley." She filled him in on Candy's report. "I don't know if she's guilty or not, but if she is, we better get to the root of the situation. And there will have to be consequences."

Scott groaned. "Like I need another problem today."

That was his response? Meg wanted to scream, to say, *Excuse me all to hell for trying to involve you in parenting your daughter.* But St. Meg came to the rescue. "You've had a bad day?"

He stripped off his tie. "One of our guys missed the estimate on the cost of newspaper supplements. By a lot."

"I'm sorry." She waited. She'd extended herself as far as she could. Now it was his turn.

"Yeah, me, too." He kicked off his shoes. "So? What do you want to do about Hayley."

"Confront her." She struggled for calm. "Together."

"No time like the present."

They both rose and went upstairs. When Meg knocked on Hayley's door, she heard a muffled "See ya tomorrow" from within. The cell phone. Gee, maybe she and Scott would have more success communicating with their daughter if they just called her on the phone or, easier yet, text-messaged her. "What?"

Meg nudged the door open. "Your father and I would like to talk with you. Downstairs?"

"Now?" Haley's face contorted. "I still have a book report to write for English."

"You should've thought of that before

you spent valuable time on the telephone," Scott said.

"Can't we talk later?" she whined.

"No." Meg turned her back and started down the hall. "Now."

Hayley, dressed in flannel boxers and a gray T-shirt labeled Property of the Football Team, stalked down the stairs followed by Scott, and curled up in the rocker. "So, talk."

Meg launched in. "We're more interested in hearing what *you* have to say about your after-school cheerleading practices."

"What's to say? We practice jumps, holds, catches, the usual stuff."

"Every day?" Scott inquired.

"Well, yeah. I know you guys wanted me to be involved in activities."

Typical, Meg thought. Turn the argument back against the parents. "You're sure you're in the gym every day after school until five?"

Meg detected a flush of pink on her daughter's cheek. "Where else would I be? I mean, don't you trust me?"

"Your mother heard someone say you'd been driving around with Zach Simon."

Hayley flailed her arms. "Someone? Who's 'someone'? So you're going to believe anyone except me, is that it?"

Meg was grateful that Scott remained unflappable. "Answer this simple question, Hayley. Have you been driving around with Zach in violation of our rules?"

"I suppose now I'm grounded." Hayley shook her head as if she were dealing with a clan meeting of village idiots.

"Only if you did something wrong," Scott said.

Hayley got to her feet, her eyes spearing each of them. "You are so not trusting."

Meg knew she had to deliver the coup de grâce. "Where were you after last Friday night's football game?"

Hayley took a step back, her complexion decidedly more pale. "Jill's. Like I said."

"Really?" Scott watched Hayley narrowly. "Then it would be all right for us to call her mother to verify that?"

"You're treating me like a baby!"

"I've been informed you were at a party with Zach after the game."

Hayley beat her fists against her thighs in frustration. "That brat. I'll kill him!"

"Kill who?" Scott asked.

"That jackass brother of mine."

Scott stood up and marched toward Hayley, stopping directly in front of her. "First of all, you will never call your brother that. Do you understand?"

Hayley held his gaze, her lower lip thrust out.

"Furthermore, you just incriminated yourself. Justin hasn't said one word to us about what you've been doing."

For the first time, Hayley's expression wilted and she glanced helplessly from one of them to the other. "He hasn't?"

"No," Meg said. "One of the women at the country club told me today."

"Who?"

"It doesn't matter. What matters, young lady, is what we're going to do about it."

"Until further notice, you are grounded." Scott eyed her quietly. "You asked earlier if we trusted you—the funny thing is, we did. But now that you've abused that trust, you've left us with no choice."

"What about cheerleading practice?"

"I guess you'll have to bring a note from the sponsor each time you're there."

"I'll die! That's so embarrassing. You're both so old-fashioned."

Meg supported Scott. "A note will work well. As for us being so 'old-fashioned,' you brought this on yourself. Decisions have consequences. Your decisions resulted in this grounding."

Scott went to stand beside Meg. "Since you'll be spending much more time here at the house, I'm going to expect you to do something else. Help your mother and grandmother with Grampa's therapy."

"What?" Her jaw dropped. "I can't."

"What do you mean you 'can't'?" Scott asked.

"I love Grampa and want him to get better, but he's like a baby. It's gross."

Meg expected the top to blow off Scott's head. Instead, his voice grew steely. "God help you if you ever get sick. You have a lot to learn about compassion. Fortunately you will now have the time and the opportunity to start." He put his arm around Meg. "Your mother will show you what to do tomorrow. And, Hayley? Until further notice, you are not to see this boy." He paused for effect. "That is not negotiable."

"I hate you!" Hayley screamed as she took off for her room, leaving behind a gust of tension.

Scott started after her, but Meg stopped him. "Let her go. She needed to get in the last word because she knows we're right."

Scott sighed. "I hope so. That was not my idea of fun."

"Welcome to my world," Meg said softly, but for once without a single trace of bitterness.

Tentatively, he laid a warm palm against her cheek. "I had no idea things were that difficult with her."

"Until today, I just thought she was being a typical mouthy teenager." She smiled ruefully. "I never thought I'd have a reason to thank Candy Stimson for anything." The feel of his hand against her skin was like a tonic. She wanted so badly to throw herself into his arms and burrow away from all her troubles. "Thanks for helping me deal with this."

He gazed at her with a look that at one time had started fires in her belly. "It's my job. One I'm afraid I've been neglecting lately."

Memories of times he *had* been neglectful rushed to the surface, but, for once, she didn't want to react defensively. Instead, she savored his support.

The silence between them lengthened. Finally he spoke. "I think I'll peek in on Mom and Pops."

For some reason she didn't want him to leave. "May I come, too?"

He smiled, then nodded. "I'd like that." He circled her waist and together they walked to the door of their old bedroom. Two night-lights burned brightly enough for them to make out the bed.

Meg's breath caught in her chest. Bud slept slightly turned toward Marie. His good arm enfolded her and her head rested on his chest, one hand curled over his weakened right arm. Even in his sleep, a gentle smile played across Bud's face. Meg had once seen a sculpture called *The Embrace*. But it paled in compar-ison to the touching scene before them.

Scott's arm tightened around her. "Meggie, they look so…" his voice faltered "…so…"

"Happy. I know."

And then her big, strong, capable husband clutched her to his chest and began to sob.

CHAPTER TEN

MEG CLUNG TO SCOTT, aware only of his deep, wrenching breaths as he tried to control the emotional torrent racking his body. She had never seen him like this. A watery smile, maybe, when the children had been born, some rapid blinking at funerals, but nothing of this magnitude. Strong men could handle anything. Golden boys didn't have meltdowns. Or so she'd always assumed. Apparently she'd misjudged her husband.

As she held him in her arms, she hoped so. Maybe he cared more than she'd ever given him credit for. About all kinds of things. She thought about Bud and Marie and the bond of love they obviously shared. About the way they lay entwined in peaceful slumber, despite physical limitations. Had they had rough patches in their marriage, too? Could she and Scott learn from their example?

Scott stepped back. "Sorry," he mumbled, swiping a sleeve across his eyes.

Meg raised her fingertips to his mouth. "There's nothing to be sorry for." She paused, struggling to get her own emotions under control, then nodded toward the bed. "It's okay to love them."

He took both her hands in his and bowed his forehead to hers. "I do." He took a shuddering breath. "But it's more than that."

"Do you want to talk about it?"

"Maybe," he said.

"Tonight?"

He consulted his watch. "It's late."

As if she'd narrowly missed the sailing of an important ship, her heart sank.

"But, yeah. There are some things I need to say to you."

A sudden foreboding overwhelmed her. "Okay."

He led her back into the family room and settled her in one corner of the sofa, dropping into the opposite corner. "I don't know where to begin."

She waited, hardly daring to breathe.

He kneaded his forehead. "This thing with Pops," he began. "It's really thrown me."

"How?"

He shook his head. "What's the point? You work your entire life, you do all the right things and then, just when you should be able to enjoy retirement, zap! I mean, think about that hunk of machinery sitting in our driveway. Mom and Pops had talked about this trip for years. Where's the justice?"

She tucked her feet under her and waited, knowing there was no answer to his question.

"Did you see them in there? No matter how bad things are, they still have each other." He rubbed his hand over the sofa back, then looked straight at her. "Do we? Will we?"

The enormity of his question struck her dumb. She knotted fingers, fearing what was to come. She'd been alone before in her life, and it was awful.

"Meggie, look at me."

Slowly she raised her eyes. "I don't know, Scott. I'd like to think so. But we have a long road ahead of us."

"Tonight, with Hayley. I had no idea what things were like for you."

"You've been busy."

"Yeah, I have. And it's not going to get better any time soon. The Jordan account is becoming more and more demanding. But looking at Mom and Pops in there, realizing my own kids are practically strangers and that you…" he struggled to go on "…you're here picking up the pieces for my family…well, I just lost it."

"That's something you seldom do."

He snorted. "Like *never.*"

"Maybe you should. It's a lot more honest than your Mr. In-Control mode."

"Is that how I seem to you? In control?"

"Almost always. You see life as a series of steps on the way to reaching your goals. You're not great about stopping to smell the roses."

His eyes filled with sadness. "You're one of those roses, you know."

"I'd like to think so. As are Hayley and Justin."

"I can't just give up on my business."

"Nobody's asking you to do that. But there is such a thing as balance in life."

"Does that apply to you, too?"

Her hackles rose. "What are you saying?"

"About balance. You're always so busy with the kids and your club activities that—"

"Don't tell me you've felt neglected?" How could he possibly accuse her of the same crime of which he was most guilty?

"Okay, have it your way," Scott said. "Paint me as the bad guy."

Where had this conversation come off track and turned accusatory? She didn't want their evening to end this way. "Nobody's the bad guy. We just have so much going on in our lives right now."

"So what do we do? Wait it out and hope things will take care of themselves?"

"What choice do we have?"

He moved closer and picked up her hand. "I don't know," he said, bringing her palm to his lips and kissing it. "But you are and always have been a rose worth stopping for."

Anger drained away like poison being flushed out of her system. "Thank you." She pulled their clasped hands against her breast and held them there, their combined warmth unraveling the knot in her chest.

"And you know what else, Meggie?"

She looked up into eyes lit by a tiny spark of humor. "What?"

"Consider this. At least now we're talking."

HAYLEY, HER TONE MARKED by an air of false bravado, greeted Bud the next afternoon. Meg hoped she was the only one who could feel the tension in the girl or see the worry in her eyes. When Meg had taken her aside after school to teach her how to use the flash cards designed to help improve Bud's speaking vocabulary, Hayley had confessed she felt inadequate. Now Meg seated Bud at the dining-room table and threw her daughter an encouraging smile. Hayley glanced at the cards as if unsure how to begin.

"I'll help you get started," Meg offered. "Ready, Bud?" She picked up the first card, showed him the picture and slowly said, "Orange."

"Ball," he said, before pounding his fist on the table in frustration. "No."

Meg gentled her voice. "I agree, it looks like a ball. It's round, but it's a fruit. Try again. *Orange.*" On the far side of Bud, Hayley leaned forward. "Watch my lips. O-range."

"O…or…enj." He looked up expectantly.

"That's right. Try it again."

"Orange."

"Good job. Now let's try the next one."

After *apple* and *banana*, Meg handed the deck to Hayley. Hesitantly, she flipped up a card.

"Move closer to your grandfather, so he doesn't have to turn to look at you," Meg suggested.

Hayley did as she was told. "Look, Grampa. What's this?"

He squinted at the card, then cocked his head. "Balls. Lotsa balls."

Hayley darted a puzzled glance at Meg, but then, with a shrug, corrected him. "Grapes. A bunch of grapes." He continued studying the grapes. "Read my lips, Grampa. Grr-apes."

His jaw moved, his lips pursed. Hayley waited with a patience Meg didn't know she possessed. Bud made a guttural sound. "Grr." Hayley sat quietly. "Grapes!"

"Way to go, Grampa!" Hayley said, a delighted grin relaxing her features.

When Bud had also mastered *peach* and *plum* under Hayley's direction, Meg thought it was safe to leave the room. Surprisingly, her daughter seemed to be a natural therapist.

Meg found Marie in the kitchen mixing up a meat loaf. "Would you like a cup of coffee, dear?"

Meg stifled a pang of resentment at being treated like a guest in her own kitchen, but truthfully, she didn't know what she would do without Marie, who freed her from cleaning and cooking chores to work with Bud and take him to his appointments. "That sounds divine."

Marie gave a final pat to the meat loaf, washed her hands, and then served Meg. "Join me, why don't you?" Meg said.

"I'd like that." Marie slid the meat loaf in the oven beside some baked potatoes and poured her own cup. "Let's go into the family room."

Late afternoon sun sent strips of light across the carpet. Marie took the rocker and Meg sat across from her in the armchair. Sipping her coffee, Meg sighed contentedly. "It feels good just to sit."

"You don't get to do much of that," Marie said.

"Neither do you."

"But it's different for me. Bud is my husband. I'd do anything for him. You didn't bargain for this. For us." She paused. "Frankly, though, I don't know how we'd have managed without you and Scott."

"We're happy to help."

"Yes, but I'm not blind. I can tell the toll it's taking on you. On your marriage."

Meg cringed. So it was that obvious. "I'll admit it's hard to juggle everything."

"Even so, your marriage should come first." She must've picked up on Meg's discomfort, because she went on. "Believe me,

I know it's difficult. Scott is working these long hours, just like Bud used to. I remember very clearly resenting his dedication to his work."

"You?" The word was out before Meg could stop herself.

Marie managed a wry smile. "Oh, yes, me. I needed attention. Every wife does. But men don't always understand that. In fact, sometimes I think they're big babies, needing even more pampering than our children do." She took a sip from her cup. "This isn't easy for me to say, Meg, but I may have made a mistake with Scott."

"What do you mean?"

"I spoiled the boy. I still do. Maybe I ruined him for marriage. He thrives on attention. Success. Sometimes he can seem pretty self-serving."

What was her mother-in-law trying to tell her? It didn't feel condemnatory. In fact, it felt a lot like girl talk. "We were discussing that just last night."

"Oh?"

Meg sensed she'd stepped over an invisible boundary and into a new intimacy with Marie. "When does it start, this pattern?" she asked.

"Of neglecting one another?"

Meg nodded.

"When you let other things become more impor-tant. Children, work, friends, hobbies, anything. You know—" she nodded sagely "—things don't last and people move on. In the end, you're left only with each other."

Unless you jump ship, Meg thought, and separate. Or divorce. Meg regarded her mother-in-law with new understanding. "You and Bud seem to have made the best of that scenario."

"Even now," Marie mused. "But it wasn't always easy. It took honest communication and a lot of hard work. Relationships have to be fed. Love requires tender nurturing."

Meg had no answer for her.

Marie broke the silence. "I know having us here is a huge imposition."

Meg started to demur, but Marie inter-rupted her. "It won't be forever. We're very grateful, but soon I need to begin looking at area retirement centers. Do you think you or Scott could take me?"

Meg was dumbfounded. Although her mother-in-law seemed needy at times, she'd clearly found the strength to take a hard look at the future. "Of course." She hesitated, wanting somehow to express her empathy for Marie. "It must be terribly disappointing for you to have to give up your trip, your plans…." At the stricken look on her mother-in-law's face, she faltered. "Oh, Marie, I'm so sorry."

Marie dug in her apron pocket for a tissue and wiped her eyes. "Sometimes life forces you to alter your plans. Adjust your dreams. I try not to think about what might have been. It only makes the present harder to bear. Instead, I force myself to focus on my very great blessing." She sniffled, then smiled through her tears. "I still have my Bud."

Meg crossed the room and gave the older woman a hug. "When I grow up, I want to be just like you," she whispered. "Bud is a lucky man."

The doorbell pealed, and Meg left her mother-in-law to answer it. Passing the dining room, she noticed Hayley had moved from the fruit family to vegetables. Bud was laboriously pronouncing *carrot*.

She opened the door and was surprised to be handed a florist's box by the delivery woman. "What…?" she murmured.

"For Meg Harper."

"Uh, thank you." Meg couldn't remember the last time she'd received flowers. She cradled the box and carried it into the kitchen where her mother-in-law joined her.

"Open them," Marie urged.

Slowly Meg lifted the lid off the box. Nestled against the green of the tissue were a dozen pink roses. She found the card, choking up as she read the message. *I'm sorry I haven't been stopping for you, my sweetest rose. Thanks for everything you do for me and our family. Love, Scott.*

Marie peered at the flowers. "Beautiful," she said. "Who are they from?"

Meg tried to speak, cleared her throat and finally got out Scott's name.

With her forefinger, Marie wiped a tear from Meg's cheek, then chuckled. "I guess I taught that boy a few things about women after all."

BUD LOOKED AT THE CALENDAR hanging on his bedroom wall, with days X-ed off. In one of the empty slots was a turkey. Thanksgiving? Soon? Maybe Kay would come. He needed to be walking by then. Teetering to his feet, he grabbed the bureau and steadied himself. He reached for the cane propped in the corner and took a first cautious step toward the bedroom door. He was sick of having Marie and Meg hover over him. Surely he could make it to the family room by himself. He shut his eyes against the memory of jogging two miles every morning of his adult life, heedless then of the miraculous workings of his body. Now look at him. He would never run again. Never play golf. Bowl. But he could for darned certain toddle down the hall and into the family room. Whoo-ee. One small blow for independence.

Gritting his teeth determinedly, he made his way, one labored step at a time.

Marie hurried toward him from the kitchen. "Bud Harper, what are you thinking?" She eased him into Scott's recliner. "You could've fallen."

Bud gave a triumphant snort. "Didn't," he proclaimed.

"Still, you have to be careful and—"

"Tired of careful." He gave himself a mental high five. He was communicating better. "Not a baby. Man. Me."

Her tone softened. "Indeed, you are, my love."

"Come." He beckoned her over.

When she approached, he reached around her waist and pulled her down to perch beside him on the arm of the chair.

She rested her head on his. "Silly old bear," she whispered.

"Love you," he said. They sat quietly. Meg was picking the kids up from school, Scott was still at work. This was their time. His and Marie's. Time. How much was left? He felt suddenly old. "Turkey?"

"No, you're not a turkey. I called you a bear."

He shook his head in frustration. "Not bear. Turkey." He racked his brain. "Day. Turkey day."

"Oh, Thanksgiving?"

Go to the head of the class. "Yes. Kay?"

He felt Marie stiffen slightly. "Oh, honey, I don't know yet about Kay. She said she'd try to come then."

Try to come? His daughter. "Try?"

"I know, I know," Marie crooned. "She should have come before now." She sighed. "But you know how she is."

If her words hadn't made him sad, he'd have exulted. At least Marie had understood what he was feeling. Disappointed. Hurt.

The clanging of the garage door opening startled them. They heard Meg pull her car in, then the door to the house slam. Justin stomped into the room, his face a thundercloud as he tossed his backpack on the floor.

Hayley followed. She mumbled a hello, threw her brother a look of disdain and disappeared up the stairs. Meg hurried in, arms laden with grocery bags. Justin cast her a furtive glance.

Bud sat forward, eyeing his grandson, whose complexion was beet-red. "Matter?"

Justin wouldn't look at him. "Nothin'."

Marie patted Bud on the shoulder, then discreetly moved into the kitchen to help Meg put away the food. But from the other side of the counter divider, he could tell Meg was paying close attention to his conversation with his grandson. How he wished he could get lots of words out. "Something. Bother." He tried again. "Bothering."

Meg nodded at Justin. "Talk to your grandfather. Maybe it will help. He knows what it's like not to be able to do something he wants to do."

Bud jumped in, agreeing. "Can't talk. Can't drive. Can't..." he made a throwing gesture "...ball."

Justin shrugged. "But you're not dumb!"

Dumb? Grandson? Dumb? "You," he said in a firm voice, "not dumb."

Justin fished around in his backpack, found a sheet of paper, then brought it over and placed it defiantly in his grandfather's hands. "See? I am, too."

Bud studied the print on the page. He could decipher the words *school* and *Harper* and a few other words, but he was at a loss. "What?"

Standing over him, Justin sneered. "A deficiency report, that's what. I can't read, okay? I'm going to that stupid reading class and still I don't get it well enough to satisfy that Kelly bitch."

"Bitch?" Bud was shocked. Teacher? Bitch? "Not nice."

"Language, Justin," Meg admonished quietly.

Bud tried to puzzle out what this meant. "You? Read?"

"Get this? I'm supposed to practice more. Read aloud, even. Like when? On the bench at soccer so the guys on the team can make fun of me?"

Scratching his head, Bud had an idea. "You. Newspaper. Read. Me." He ran through a mental list and finally found the word. "Sports."

Justin screwed up his face. "You want me to read to you?"

Bud nodded vigorously. "You help me."

"And you help me?"

Bud grinned and held out his good hand. "Deal?"

For the first time since he got home, Justin eked out a reluctant grin. "Deal," he said, grabbing his grandfather's hand.

"Thank you, Lord," Bud heard Meg say as she set a bunch of bananas in a bowl on the counter.

Useful. Bud felt a thrill of satisfaction. Finally. He could be useful.

THE PREOPENING GALA in San Antonio for Jordan's new store was supposed to be a celebration, a milepost on Harper Concepts's upward climb. But Scott's head throbbed. The music was intrusive. The lights, too bright. Cocktail chatter and artificial laughter swirled around him.

Surreptitiously, he glanced at his watch. How much longer? He'd been overwhelmed by the lengthy introductions. Sated with southwestern-style hors d'oeuvres and too much champagne.

And weaving her way through the crowd toward him was Brenda, her blond hair swept up in a chignon, her stunning figure enhanced by a sheer beige dress that looked disturbingly more like a nightgown than party wear. She tucked her hand under his elbow. "What do you think, boss? Satisfied?"

He took in the decorations, planned by the local Jordan executives, but sporting the Harper-designed logo. "Pretty classy," he admitted.

She squeezed his arm. "That's exactly what we were going for. An approach that says to the customer, 'You're worth it.'"

When she didn't move away, he searched the room for Jim Tate. "Where's Jim?"

"Off schmoozing with some of the local Jordan boys." She snuggled closer. "So that leaves just the two of us."

For what? Scott immediately censored his thoughts.

"I think we could blow this shindig. It's nearly over." She looked up at him questioningly, her ocean-blue eyes difficult to read.

"Yeah, I'm beat," Scott admitted. The idea of a hot shower and a good night's sleep was infinitely appealing. "As soon as I thank the Jordan folks, let's grab a cab."

"Suits me," she said, squeezing his arm again before finally disengaging herself.

During the cab ride back to the hotel, Brenda gave him her review of the evening, conveying, in particular, the positive reactions of store executives responsible for opening the Oklahoma City and Phoenix locations in the next year. Scott found himself sinking back into the seat of the cab, enjoying a sense of satisfaction in a job well done. Brenda's low, husky voice was soothing, and he found his eyes closing.

"Wake up, we're here" were the next words he heard. Brenda got out of the cab. Groggily, he reached for his billfold and paid the driver.

Again, she hooked her arm with his and led him toward the elevators. "You've simply got to see the view of the River Walk from my room," she said, punching the Up button. "It's fantastic."

Recovering a sense of gallantry, Scott shrugged. "I'll see you to your room, but I can't stay." Why had he inferred that possibility was even part of her agenda? He winced inwardly. Had it been part of his?

Brenda smiled noncommittally. "Whatever."

Her room, lit by the soft glow of one lamp, was furnished in forest-green and peach tones. Her laptop was set up on the table, but otherwise, her things were discreetly packed away. As if she'd been expecting company? Dutifully he made his way to the window.

Below him were the colorful lights of the River Walk. Gondolas filled with tourists slipped languidly over the shimmering surface of the water. Before he knew what was happening, Brenda had reached up and assisted him out of his suit jacket. He froze.

"You're coiled tight," she said, as her magic fingers began massaging the base of his neck, his shoulders. Goose bumps radiated down his back. "Let me help you relax."

He couldn't move. Was this an invitation? Who was in control here anyway? He needed to be, that was for sure. Finally he turned around. "Brenda, I better leave."

She edged closer, placing her hands on his chest in a way that left little doubt as to her intentions. "Not on my account," she whispered throatily.

Scott drew a ragged breath. He was only human, and her heady perfume, the warmth of her palms and the aura of intimacy that hovered around them were all playing havoc with his resolve. Still, thus far, nothing had been said or done that crossed the line. He gathered her hands in both of his and lifted them off his chest. "No, on mine," he said. He glanced around the room, momentarily lingering on the king-size bed. How could he say what needed to be said and, at the same time, allow them both to save face?

Licking her lips in a way that could be interpreted either as nervous or seductive, she waited for him to speak, her eyes fixed challengingly on his.

"Brenda, first I need to tell you what a valuable asset you are to Harper Concepts. I wouldn't want to lose you." He cleared his throat. "You are also an attractive, desirable woman, but I'm not in a position to confuse those two, tempted though I might be. For both our sakes, I need to leave."

She lowered her eyes. "So you're not interested?"

"No red-blooded man could help but be interested. That's not the point," he said as gently as he could. "I have a wife and—"

"But I thought—"

"There was trouble there?"

Mutely, she nodded.

"Meg and I have our ups and downs, but that's not your concern. Your concern is to be the best darned creative director in the business." He reached for the jacket she'd draped over the desk chair. "I hope we can forget this conversation ever happened."

Brenda helped him straighten his lapels.

Then, giving him a motherly pat, she stepped back and with a short laugh, said, "Well, you can't blame a girl for trying." She crossed the room to the door, opened it and stood aside for him to leave. Before he did, though, she added one more comment. "I love my job, Scott. I was wrong to try to mix business and pleasure. It won't happen again."

"That's good enough for me, Brenda. Good night." The door closed behind him. Alone in the lushly carpeted hall, he heaved a sigh of relief and gave himself a mental pat on the back. He'd dodged a bullet. Not only had he dodged it, it felt good, liberating. He walked to the bank of elevators and punched the Down button. As he waited, he admitted an important truth: If he wanted a beautiful woman in his bed, there was only one place to go. Home.

WITH SCOTT IN SAN ANTONIO, Meg felt even more lost. Somehow she hadn't realized that even the few minutes he could spare her for a bedtime debriefing had helped her maintain her sanity. Hayley grew sulkier by the day. In fact, the only time she displayed civility toward any of them was when she was helping Bud with his speech therapy. Justin apparently enjoyed reading the newspaper to Bud, but Meg worried about him, too. He'd lost interest in playing with his friends lately.

Toting the trash bag from room to room, Meg emptied the wastebaskets. With Scott gone, she'd have to move the barrels out to the curb herself for tomorrow's pickup. It seemed as if the work was never done. And now she had to begin planning for Thanksgiving. Kay was actually coming. *High time,* Meg thought bitterly. Fortunately, her sister-in-law was planning to stay in a nearby motel, but Meg knew they'd all be in for a running monologue about Kay's favorite topic—Kay. It was almost pathetic how eager Bud and Marie were for her visit. As if, just this once, they thought their daughter would be transformed into a doting, caring individual. *God, I sound like Cinderella, sitting, soot-covered, by the fireplace brushing away tears of self-pity while the ugly stepsisters get all the attention.*

Justin's trash consisted of an old sports magazine and assorted cookie and chip bags, while Hayley's was full of soiled cotton balls, an empty shampoo bottle and pieces of notebook paper torn into confetti-size pieces. If she had the time and inclination to play detective, Meg wondered what she'd learn by piecing together the scraps of notebook paper.

When she got to the family-room wastebasket, she was stunned by what she discovered. Clippings. Pamphlets. Maps. All referencing places Marie and Bud had planned to go on the first leg of their motorhome journey.

Meg sank to the floor, fighting tears, as she caressed the cover of a tattered guide to the national parks, then picked up a colorful brochure about campsites on the Oregon coast. These weren't mere scraps of paper. They represented the death of a long-held dream. Without comment, Marie had quietly disposed of the future she and Bud had envisioned. Her mother-in-law's words came back to her: *Sometimes life forces you to alter your plans. Adjust your dreams.*

Instinctively, Meg found herself fingering her wedding band. She and Scott had nurtured dreams, too. But with time and attrition, they had neglected those dreams. Exchanged them, in part, for the expectations and demands of an upwardly mobile culture. Was her own disappointment partially a result of misplaced values? What did she really want, anyway?

No easy answers occurred to her as they might've only a few short weeks ago. The only clue lay in the devotion she'd witnessed between Marie and Bud. And in a bouquet of wilting roses.

Life was, indeed, forcing her to alter her plans. Maybe to dream new dreams. With a surprising lightness of heart, she realized that might not be a bad thing.

CHAPTER ELEVEN

ENTERING THE SMALL BISTRO tucked into a corner of the suburban shopping center, Meg felt as if she'd stepped into a magazine-perfect world, one free from the smell of disinfectant and the sight of cans of Ensure. She was greeted by the rich fragrance of Colombian coffee and tables attractively decorated with apple-green cloths and fresh cut flowers. She paused at the hostess station, then spotted Jannie seated by the window. As she made her way to the table, she reveled in the freedom she no longer took for granted. Lunch with a friend. What a refreshing novelty!

"You're a godsend," Meg said, sinking into the tapestried chair. "I feel like you've busted me out of prison."

Jannie smiled. "I'm happy to aid and abet. I just wish we could do this more often."

"Believe me, I'm grateful for any reprieve,

no matter how brief." She picked up the menu. "Happily, I'm starved."

"They serve fantastic quiche here. And the coconut-cream pie is to die for."

"Let's go for broke then, starting with a glass of wine."

"You're on," Jannie said, signaling the waitress.

Meg noticed that Jannie tactfully waited until after the wine and salad to shift the conversation from school gossip to more personal matters. "How are you doing, really?" Jannie asked, concern in her eyes.

"Really?" Meg considered the question. "Even though it's only been a few weeks, I feel as if I'm in a time warp. Sometimes I have trouble remembering what a 'normal' day was like." She threaded her napkin through her fingers. "It's been quite an adjustment for the whole family."

"We've missed you at tennis and book club."

"I haven't played tennis since Bud's stroke. And read a book? Forget it. I'm always too tired."

"Meg, honey, who's taking care of you?"

Jannie's question struck her where she was most vulnerable. The waitress intervened before she could form a response, removing their salad plates and setting before them two servings of steaming quiche garnished with fruit and melon.

Jannie didn't let her off the hook. "Well?"

"Maybe Marie."

Jannie speared a strawberry with her fork. "What's that supposed to mean?"

"She does pretty much all of the cooking and housework."

"And you bear the brunt of taking care of your father-in-law, is that it?"

"I'm younger. Besides, it's hard for Marie to help him with his therapy. She's too emotionally involved."

"What about Scott? Where does he fit into the picture?"

Meg didn't want to go there, but her friend deserved an answer. "He does what he can when he's home."

Jannie was relentless. "And when is that?"

Meg cut into the quiche. "Whenever he's not working." She paused. "He's working a lot."

"So your mother-in-law's in denial, your husband's playing ostrich and you're volunteering for martyrdom?"

Put like that, Meg found herself growing defensive. "It's not quite that bad. Marie and I have settled on a division of chores that works for us, and she's abandoned the idea of ever taking the motor-home trip. Scott does what he can, when he can. Last weekend he took Marie to look at a couple of local retirement centers."

"That has to be hard for her. But it's realistic." Jannie's features softened. "You can't go on the way you have been, Meg. Your friends are worried about you."

Meg stuck a forkful of quiche in her mouth. Jannie's concern and sympathy were bringing her perilously close to the breaking point. After swallowing, she found her voice. "Thanks. I appreciate that. I miss everybody." She wiped her mouth with her napkin, then went on. "At one time or another, life deals most of us a situation like this. At least I'm learning from it."

"For example?"

Meg mentally reviewed the changes in her life. "Before, I kept myself busy with all kinds of obligations outside the home. I was preoccupied with other people's opinions of me. I forgot about the day, the moment. The only time any of us has—the *now*. Bud and Marie thought they had a lot of carefree years ahead of them. But watching Marie gracefully accept the death of their dreams, I'm beginning to understand that clinging to past hurts or thinking negatively about the future paralyzes me." She laughed shakily. "Wow, this is getting heavy. Sorry."

"No apology necessary. In fact, it sounds to me as if you're making lemonade out of the proverbial lemons."

"I won't kid you, Jannie. Caregiving is tough. Even though Bud's improving, it's clear he'll never fully recover. Scott is at a crossroads in his business, so I'm trying to cut him some slack, but it's not easy. Justin's been a help with Bud, but all of this turmoil is affecting his performance at school, and Hayley is…what can I say? A spoiled brat."

Jannie shook her head in understanding. "Teenagers!"

"Exactly. Maybe now that she's come off her grounding her attitude will get better."

"Some days it's hard to remember that they were once the precious, helpless infants we thought would bring us perpetual joy."

Jannie went on, then, about her own family, but by the time their pie came, Meg had started covertly studying her watch. Bud had a three o'clock appointment with the physical therapist.

"What are your Thanksgiving plans?"

The pie turned to putty in Meg's mouth. "You had to ask, didn't you?"

"Uh-oh. Sorry."

"My sister-in-law is coming. Making her imperial highness's first visit to Tulsa to see her father since his stroke."

"But—" Jannie's eyes widened "—it's been almost two months."

Meg pointed her fork at Jannie. "Bingo."

"That's inconceivable."

"Conceive it."

"If I were Bud, that would've really hurt my feelings."

"You'd think. It's heartbreaking to watch Marie and Bud wait for a scrap of her attention. She'll be no help. To put it into her own words, she doesn't 'do' hospitals. And by extension, she doesn't 'do' sick people."

Jannie's face flushed. "Well, too damn bad."

"My sentiments exactly. But what choice do I have? I'll put on a happy face, fume inwardly and count the days until she leaves—which won't tax my brain. She's coming in on Wednesday night and leaving on Saturday morning."

"Oh, Meg, I'm sorry. That makes my Thanksgiving plans sound downright decadent."

Happy to shift the subject away from herself, Meg prompted her friend. "What's up with the Farrells?"

Meg listened politely while Jannie told her about her and Ron's planned trip to Mexico. Before Bud's stroke, Meg would've envied her friend. Pouted when Scott dismissed her repeated suggestions that they take such a trip. Now, she was filled with bittersweet sadness for what never was and, in the face of current reality, with diminished hope for what could be.

AS HE TRIED TO DO EVERY NIGHT after work, Scott spent some time with his father in the small sitting room off the bedroom. In the distance, he could hear the clatter of silverware being loaded into the dishwasher and the pounding bass vibrations from Hayley's stereo overhead. He'd cut it close getting home in time for dinner after a long, contentious meeting with one of their media buyers who seemed incapable of understanding the concept of budget constraints. Scott shifted in his chair. He should tell Hayley to turn down her music. Invite Justin to play a quick game of foosball. But there was something comforting in this quiet male companionship where he felt no need to prove anything to anybody. "How'd your therapy go today?"

Bud made a face, expressing his distaste better than any words could.

"That bad, huh?"

"Hurt."

"You know what they say, Pops, no pain, no gain."

His dad managed a lopsided grin. "Better, though. Me."

Scott's heart sank. The gains were excruciatingly slow, but he knew success inspired more success. "I noticed. You can almost make a fist with your right hand now."

Bud fixed his eyes on Scott. "Meg helps me. Good woman."

Scott nodded, lost in thought. Meg had stepped up to the plate in ways that, frankly, surprised him. Bud wasn't her father, after all. She could've kept her distance. Instead, she worked with him tirelessly on his exercises, monitored his medications, drove him to his appointments, all while offering support to Mom. But Meg had also made it clear to him from the beginning that she would do what was necessary only through the crisis. After that? Scott felt his jaw tense. Things were bound to change with time. Then what?

Would they just take up where they had left off—on the verge of separation?

He didn't want to fail. Not in business, and especially not with Meg. Despite everything, she was still very important to him.

"You? Busy man?"

"Yep, that's me."

His father shook his finger at him. "Don't forget."

"What?"

Bud flexed his impaired hand. "Wife," Bud said.

Suddenly, Scott felt like a small boy being scolded by his teacher. He'd never been able to put much past his father, and apparently he wasn't going to be able to start now. "I'm trying," he said.

The response came in a strong, authoritarian voice. "Try harder."

JUSTIN GOT OFF THE SCHOOL BUS Monday afternoon and trudged, head down, toward the house. He couldn't wait for the Thanksgiving break next week. No school. No Sam Grider calling him a retard, no Mrs. Kelly watching him like a mother hawk, no Bozo slapping him on the shoulder and saying in that fake hearty way, "Keepin' your nose clean, Harper?" Only two good things had happened to him lately. First, the reading specialist had told him she thought they were making progress. He sure hoped so. He wanted that to be over. Second, and best of all, Molly Thatcher had asked him to sit with her at lunch. *Eat your heart out, Grider.* Now if he could just work up the nerve to call her on the phone tonight.

Gramma had cookies and milk waiting for him, just like a gosh-darned commercial. "Grampa is waiting in the sitting room for you to read to him. He keeps asking me about football. What do I know?"

Yeah, Gramma was clueless. She thought the Denver Broncos were rodeo cowboys. "In a minute."

He raced upstairs, past Hayley's room, and threw down his stuff. His sister wasn't home. That was good. He didn't want to have anything more to do with her than necessary because he had one other major problem: Zach Simon. Hayley was sneaking around with him again after school. He should probably tell Mom and Dad. But if he did, his parents would just have another blowout, blaming each other and arguing about everything, his sister would never speak to him again and, worst of all, Zach Simon would probably slam him against that testosteronemobile of his and rearrange his face. No, thank you.

He returned to the family room, picked up the morning paper and went down the hall to the master bedroom. In his best imitation of Monday-night football sportscasters, he hollered, "Grampa, are you ready for some football?"

His grandfather answered him from the sitting room. "Ready."

Grampa sat on the sofa and Justin sprawled on the floor, the newspaper spread out in front of him. "Okay, let me read you about the Cowboys layin' it on the Packers."

Justin began the wrap-up of Sunday's game, stumbling only over the word *concussion*. Then he moved on to a commentary about the recent Oklahoma University winning streak and their superstar running back. Grampa listened okay at first, but then all of a sudden he waved his hand. "No, no," he said.

"What?"

"Tight."

"Tight?"

His grandfather grimaced. "No! Team. Mine. Tight."

Justin scratched his head, searching the

newspaper columns. Finally a lightbulb came on. "Oh, the Titans?"

Grampa nodded emphatically, a satisfied look on his face. Of course. Living in Tennessee, he had followed the Titans. Justin read the entire article about the Titans' rout of the Falcons, including the statistics. When he finished, he sat up and pulled the paper into his lap. "Anything else?"

Grampa looked around as if searching for something. "Marie?"

"Gramma's in the kitchen. You want me to get her?"

"No." He held his finger to his lips. "Shh," he said. Then he gestured to the paper. "Not sports."

Justin got a weird feeling in his stomach. He didn't want to read news stories with big words like *insurgencies* and *constituents*. And the editorials? The only kids he knew who could understand them were the nerds on the debate team. "What, then?"

"Want."

"Yeah, okay. What do you want?"

Grampa fidgeted. "Not want. *Want.*"

Justin hated it when his grandfather couldn't find the right words and became frustrated. It gave him the same helpless feeling he'd had in the library that day. "I'm sorry, Grampa, I don't understand."

Grampa pointed his finger at the paper and said it again. "Want."

When Justin spread his hands in incomprehension, Grampa struggled to his feet. "C'mon," he said, starting in his lumbering way for the window that overlooked the front of the house.

Mystified, Justin followed him. Grampa drew the curtain back. "There," he said.

All Justin could see was the motor home parked in the driveway. "The motor home?"

His grandfather nodded vigorously.

Justin racked his brain. "You want a motor home, is that it? You already have that one, Grampa."

His grandfather ripped the paper from his hands. "Want." His face screwed up in concentration and he spat out another word. "Ads." He shook the paper in Justin's face.

"Wait a minute. You want me to read you something in the want ads?"

Justin was rewarded with an approving smile. "You. Smart boy. C'mon." Grampa led the way back into the sitting room, sat down, looked around again as if making sure they were alone and then said, "Read."

Justin separated the classified section from the rest and looked at it, bewildered. What was he supposed to find here? "What do you wanna know, Grampa?"

"Money. Sell it. How much?"

"Sell it? Sell what?"

Grampa let out a big sigh, as if he were dealing with a genuine dunce. "Home."

"Your motor home?" Justin croaked.

Again Grampa shushed him. "Silence." Then he added, "How much is it?"

"You want to know what used motor homes sell for?"

"Yes."

"Why?"

His grandfather's eyes reddened. "Can't go. Can't drive." He shrugged, mindless of the tear that trickled from the corner of his rheumy eyes. "Sell it."

Justin didn't know what to do, what to say. He almost hated it that he could read, that he would now have to look in the darn newspaper and tell his grandfather the prices. He was just a kid, but in that moment, he recognized he would never forget the day when his grandfather gave up his dream.

THE SATURDAY before Thanksgiving, Scott arranged for both Justin and Hayley to be home to help Marie with Bud. Despite Meg's initial objections, he whisked her off to the country club for a round of golf, followed by dinner in the grill room. "Do you know how long it's been since we've done this?" he asked her over cocktails.

"I haven't exactly been counting, but nothing is coming to mind in recent memory."

"We haven't been taking time for each other."

"And whose fault is that?"

Would he ever manage to punch through the wall of her defensiveness? "Does it have to be anyone's fault?" He focused on the amber depths of his bourbon and water. "Maybe it's not a question of blame, but of taking responsibility." He looked up. "I want us to have more days like this one. I enjoyed our game. I hope to enjoy our dinner."

"Scott, what are you attempting to say? That you're willing to try harder with our marriage?"

"Are you?"

She looked away, then gave a shrug. "I don't know. One bouquet of roses doesn't exactly make up for months of neglect."

He clenched his jaw in the effort not to explode. "What is it going to take for you to understand you're the only woman I want in my life?"

She rolled her eyes. "And what about your lovely colleague?"

"Brenda? That's all she is, Meg, a colleague. And for your information, I made that abundantly clear to her in San Antonio."

Meg's eyes darkened. "And that was necessary because…?"

Hell, in his effort to bridge the gap, he'd tripped into a hole. "Okay, if you must know, she came on to me. But I made it very clear to her that there's only one woman for me." He reached for her hand. "You." He hesitated. "I mean it, Meg."

Meg's sad look haunted him. "I'd like to believe you. But I need more than a some-time-husband."

"You asked me earlier if I was willing to try. I am. That doesn't mean I can turn my back on the agency, but I can certainly make an effort to be more thoughtful of you." He gripped her hand more firmly. "That having been said, I need *you* to be there for *me*. To put me first."

She gradually withdrew her hand. "It's hard for me to believe things can be different."

"Are you that afraid of getting hurt?"

Picking up a swizzle stick, she slowly stirred her drink. Finally she looked up. "Yes, I am. I want it all—a loving husband, happy children, good friends, a comfortable life. But maybe I'm kidding myself."

"Those are great goals, but maybe the only thing we can do is find our stumbling way together and hope for the best. It's the 'together' part that's most important to me."

When her eyes found his, his heart staggered. The defensiveness was gone, replaced by a glimmer of hope. "Help me, then. Help me to believe in us again."

With the solemnity of a wedding vow, he clasped both her hands in his and said, "I promised to love you in good times and bad. We've had some bad times. I want us to make it to the good times."

"I need you to be by my side, Scott."

"I will be," he said, hoping that he could make good on his promise.

Her final comment took some of the wind out of his sails. "We'll see, then."

THAT NIGHT THEY MADE LOVE for the first time in many months. When Scott reached for her, Meg wanted to steel herself, to keep distance between them, to save herself from even deeper hurt. Yet she was helpless. Her body betrayed her mind, and her defenses fell away with the first brush of his fingers across her nipples. Kisses rained on her forehead, her cheek, the tender spot beneath her ear. Then he cradled her against his chest, gently running his hands up and down her back. "Meggie," he whispered over and over, his voice husky with desire.

She curled against him in a tight ball. Could she put any faith in his words? Believe Brenda was not a threat? Trust that he was sincere about working to mend their marriage? If she moved forward with him, would she be exposed to the potential for even greater disappointment? She didn't want to end up a victim.

All her intellectualizing, though, was no match for the fierce thumping of his heart, the soap-clean smell of him and the urgency thrumming through her body. He had always had this effect on her. She'd missed their lovemaking, that erotic suspension of time in which nothing else mattered.

His hands moved lower, cupping her buttocks, as he pulled her to him. She straightened her legs, entangling one foot with his. As if with a will of their own, her arms found their way around his neck. His breath was warm on her face. "Meggie, I need you."

Her skin smoldered as his lips traced a path of pure sensation from her throat, lower and lower, until he found one nipple, already peaked and awaiting him.

She tried, really tried, to maintain her emotional objectivity, to keep from losing control, but when she felt his hand moving up her thigh, shifting her nightgown aside, she conceded to the urgings of her own body.

When he finally thrust into her, it was as if all his energy was directed at satisfying her. Trembling with desire, she gripped his shoulders, arching with a powerful need. *Just for now. Just for this moment. Love me. Love me.*

And then, release. A sweet exhaustion spread through her body, and she sighed in pure satisfaction.

Beside her, Scott was breathing heavily. He picked up her hand and brought it to his lips. "Please, Meggie. Trust me."

She wanted to. Wanted to believe that nothing—not family, not Harper Concepts, not the Brendas of the world—could come between them. But she couldn't go back to that pre-anniversary world where their marriage was a shallow imitation of the real thing.

"I'm trying to." Her words came out haltingly. "I need a husband who loves me." She hesitated. "And I'd like him to be you."

Once more, he gathered her in his arms. "I'm working on it, love."

When she awoke in the middle of the night, she was still snuggled against him, his regular breathing a calming metronome. No, one bouquet of pink roses wasn't enough. Neither was one night of passionate lovemaking. But there had been something different in his voice tonight. In his needfulness.

She slipped from the bed and went to stand by the window, hugging herself against the sudden chill. Moonlight illuminated the lawn. Bare tree limbs rocked in the November wind. She thought about how men were expected to hold it together—to appear strong, competent, confident. To be able to handle almost anything.

Yet in Scott's vulnerability tonight, she'd found a potent aphrodisiac—and, more important, a reason to hope.

JUSTIN OBSERVED his grandfather. The one side of his face didn't droop quite so much anymore, and with his right hand, he steadily squeezed the rubber ball in his fist. Sundays were hard. Grampa wanted to hear about all the college football games. It took him about two hours to read the sports section aloud and now, if no one was around, Grampa wanted to hear the motor-home want ads, too.

Justin looked longingly out the window. Last night's wind had died down and it was a warm, sunny day. No time to be cooped up inside. As if his grampa had read his thoughts, he said, "You. Me. Walking?"

"Where do you want to go?"

Grampa furrowed his brow. Justin had learned to wait while his grandfather searched for the right word. "Stole." He shook his head, then tried again. "Stroll." He pointed at the window. "Walking..." he finished in a rush "...down the street."

The therapist said Grampa needed exercise. A walk? Why not? "Let me get your coat and hat."

"Cane?"

"Oh, yeah." Justin went to the closet and pulled out Grampa's old jacket, the one that smelled like leather and motor oil, and his University of Tennessee ball cap. Then he grabbed Grampa's cane from the corner and together they started for the front door. Justin paused in the entryway to the family room. His mother was on the phone and his dad was working on his laptop, sneaking peeks every now and then at the NFL game on TV. Gramma was in the kitchen making some kind of cranberry goop for Thanksgiving dinner.

"Hey, everybody, Grampa and I are going for a walk."

His dad looked up, his eyes wary. "Be careful. Don't go too far."

Grampa shook his cane toward Dad. "Me. Not a baby." He nodded at Justin. "Careful. Us."

"It's a nice day for a walk. Want me to come with you?"

"No." Grampa held up his index and middle fingers. "Boy. Me. Two."

Dad grinned. "I get it. It's a grandfather-grandson outing."

Justin nearly laughed out loud when his grandfather came up with a new word, at least new for him lately. "Correct."

They sure wouldn't set any speed records, Justin realized, as they ambled slowly down the leaf-covered sidewalk. About every three steps, Grampa would stop to study something—a car passing by, a little kid riding his trike, a plane gliding overhead. Justin didn't mind, though. He felt at home with his grand-father. Even without all the words, they under-stood each other. That was cool. Lots of kids didn't even have grandparents. Or parents.

He kicked a pebble into the street. He used to think maybe he'd be one of those kids whose parents got divorced. He remembered before the anniversary party when his folks had been acting weird. As if they didn't even like each other. But today they'd seemed okay. He'd even seen his dad give Mom a kiss on the cheek this morning before he went out jogging.

"Girls?"

"Huh?" Grampa's question jerked him back to earth.

"You? Girlfriend?"

Cripes, he didn't know if he wanted to talk to anybody yet about Molly. "Uh, not exactly."

Grampa stopped in his tracks, a sly smile on his face. "Yes? Or no?"

Justin ducked his head and thrust his hands into the front pocket of his sweatshirt. "Kinda, I guess."

"Pretty?"

What the heck? Who was Grampa going to tell? "Don't make any big deal about this, but her name's Molly and, yeah, she's pretty."

"She likes you?"

Justin blushed. He didn't want to say anything about the time he'd called her on the phone and they'd talked for half an hour. Or about how she'd hinted she might invite him to her church youth-group dance. "Maybe."

"Nice." Grampa hobbled a few steps forward, then stopped again. "But…careful. You."

Yikes, he didn't need the big sex talk from his grandfather. It was bad enough to hear it from his dad. "Not to worry, Grampa."

They'd reached the corner of the next block and Justin figured maybe it was time to start back. "Let's turn around."

"Okay."

Suddenly, a group of guys wheeled around the corner on their bikes. All but one raced off down the street, but he pulled a wheelie and turned around. "Hey, retard, who's your pal?"

Damn it to hell. Sam Grider stood near the curb, one foot on the ground, the other resting on his bike pedal. A nasty grin revealed his crooked teeth. Justin stepped in front of his grandfather and snarled, "Get lost, Grider."

"It's a free country, dork. Who's the gimp?"

Justin clenched his fists, a volcanic fury rising up from his feet, through his midsection, to his throat. Before he could utter a word, Grampa stepped around him and faced Grider. "Gimp? No! Me. Grandfather."

"You're Harper's grandpa? Whatsa matter," he taunted, "can't you talk good?"

Grampa waved his cane at Grider. "You. Boy. Go!"

"You gonna make me, old man?" Then he sneered at Justin, shaking his head, as if in disbelief. "Jeez, Harper, no wonder you're such a retard. It runs in the family."

Justin's blood boiled. "Don't you call my grandfather a retard!"

"Oh, yeah? What're you gonna do about it, wimp?"

Erupting, Justin launched himself off the curb, knocking the bike aside and throwing Grider to the ground. "Take it back," he said, straddling his nemesis and pummeling his chest with his fists. Blinded by tears, he kept hitting Grider over and over.

"Retard," Grider grunted, levering himself up and rolling over on top of Justin, pinning his shoulders against the gritty cement of the street. Somewhere in the distance, Justin could hear his grandfather yelling for help. Then a pistonlike fist landed in his face, blotting out the sun, the trees, everything. His ears rang. He tasted blood. He couldn't open his eyes. Bike tires hissed on the pavement. He couldn't catch his breath. Nausea blanketed him. His last coherent thought was *Grampa?*

CHAPTER TWELVE

BUD'S CRIES FOR HELP went unanswered.
Powerless, he stood on the curb staring down
at his grandson. *Damn stroke*. His weak leg
trembled. A sudden gust of wind chilled him
to the bone. His breath came in short pants.
Do something. Where only a few minutes
earlier the neighborhood had been bustling
with activity, now no one could be seen. The
boy was lying in the street. *Do something*.

Holding on to a small tree trunk with his
good hand and using his cane for balance, he
eased himself down to the cold sidewalk.
Then he scooted to the curb and lowered himself onto the street. Justin lay with his head
turned, his face a pulpy mess, saliva mixed
with blood oozing from the corner of his
mouth. His nose was crooked. Maybe broken. Bud trembled with rage. *That bully
called us retards. And I couldn't do anything
to stop the fight. Couldn't do anything at all.*

In desperation, he looked up and down the street. *A car. A car would come. It would stop. Wouldn't it?* Just then, Justin's eyelids fluttered and he let out a low moan.

Bud inched closer. "Boy? You, okay. One day. Promise."

Justin tried to sit up, but Bud held him down. "Wait." Then he searched for the word, the one that stymied Justin in his reading. "Con... cush?" That wasn't quite right. He tried again. "Maybe concussion. Still. Lie still."

"Grampa?" The boy clutched his hand. "Is he gone?"

"Bully?"

"Asshole Grider."

Bud nodded. "Punk," he managed to say.

"Yeah." Justin stirred. "Ow, it hurts."

Bud looked around frantically. Someone had to come along. "Stay. Help. Soon."

As if in answer to his prayer, a truck turned the corner and stopped. A large man climbed out from behind the wheel. "What happened here? You need help?"

Bud tried to focus. Words. Words. "Yes. Injury." Then he remembered. His billfold. He dug in his pocket with his left hand. Meg had changed his identification information just the other day. He held out the opened billfold. "Home," he said. "You. Go there."

Another vehicle pulled to the curb and a young woman got out. "What can I do?"

The man showed her the identification card. "That's just down the street in the next block. Can you go notify the family while I call 911?"

"Certainly."

Justin groaned, and Bud patted his shoulder. "Thank you, lady," he said as the young woman hurried back toward her car.

Then the man hunkered down beside Justin, a cell phone in his hand. "How're you doing, son? Just lie still until help comes."

Justin opened his eyes a slit. "Grampa, you are not a retard."

Bud shivered, then dabbed at the blood with his handkerchief. "Not me. Not you."

MEG COULDN'T BELIEVE she and Scott were actually sharing a quiet Sunday afternoon at home. After getting off the phone with Hayley's cheerleader sponsor, who was explaining yet another uniform change, she stretched out on the sofa and, lulled by the cadence of the football commentators, nearly dozed off. Dreamily, she recalled long ago Sunday afternoons when she and Scott had cuddled as they watched his beloved Dallas Cowboys. She drew the afghan up to her chest, savoring this rare peaceful interlude. Hayley was at Jill's, Marie bustled in the kitchen, and Bud and Justin were off on their walk. She sneaked a peek at Scott, his attention divided between his laptop and the TV. The main thing was he was here. Not at the office. Not golfing. Here. Between last night's lovemaking and today's comforting routine, she could almost believe that things were improving.

Her contentment was shattered by the insistent peal of the doorbell, by a strange young woman's urgent message about Justin and by Scott's muttered expletive as he dove for his jacket. *Justin, oh, God, was he all right?* Wrapping the afghan around her shoulders, she ran after Scott.

The next few minutes passed in a blur. When they reached the scene, Meg blanched. Steeling herself, she sank down beside Justin, covering him with the afghan. "Justin, it's Mom." She wiped his forehead. "Are you all right?"

Justin managed a minimal shrug. "It hurts."

Scott thanked the bystander, and knelt

down beside them. "I'm not waiting for the ambulance. I've called Dr. McCoy from across the street. He's coming right over." Then he turned to Bud. "Let me help you, Pops." He grabbed his father under the arms and stood him up. "What happened here?"

Bud shook a fist. "Bad boy. Called me."

Frowning, Scott leaned closer. "Somebody called you a name?"

Bud nodded, then pointed to Justin. "Fight."

Meg and Scott exchanged puzzled glances. Justin might be an athlete, but he was no fighter. Scott crouched down. "Son, you're not going to win any beauty prizes. What's the other guy look like?"

Justin grunted. "You're not mad?"

"What happened?"

"He made fun of Grampa. The way he talks. Called him a retard."

Meg's breath caught in her chest. She glanced up at Bud, whose chin was thrust out in indignation. His eyes flashed fire.

"You were justified in defending him," Scott said quietly. "But I wish there'd been a less physical way of handling the situation. Who was this boy?"

"Grider."

"Bob Grider's son?"

Justin nodded.

Scott sent Meg an it-figures look. Fred McCoy showed up then and Meg moved aside. Bud joined her as the doctor set down his bag and began to examine Justin. "Boy? Okay?" His words lingered in the afternoon air, begging an answer.

Finally, the doctor helped Justin sit up. "I'll cancel the 911 call," he said. He spoke hurriedly into his cell phone, clicked it shut and proceeded to wipe the dried blood from Justin's face with a dampened piece of gauze. "You'll have a black eye and we need to attend to that broken nose at my office, but you'll be back in business in a few days."

Beside her, Bud slumped in relief.

Dr. McCoy turned to Meg. "Watch him for the next twenty-four hours for signs of a concussion, but he should soon be good as new."

Meg took Bud home while Scott accompanied Justin to the physician's office. Only when they were inside the house did she notice Bud was shivering. Marie hustled him off to the shower and then to bed.

Meg looked around the family room—a cozy haven just a short time ago, now eerily empty. She collapsed onto the sofa, exhausted. Yet thankful. Scott had been home. They'd handled the crisis together.

Hayley breezed in ten minutes later, full of demands. "Mom, I forgot to tell you I'm supposed to bring snacks for cheerleader practice tomorrow. And I'm out of notebook paper. So can you take me to the store? Oh, and I've gotta get—"

"Let me stop you right there. You'll have to look in the pantry and figure out something for snacks. As for the notebook paper, your brother probably has some—"

"Yeah, right. He's always borrowing from me. You have to take me." Her daughter stood, arms crossed over her chest, her exasperation evident.

Meg stifled a sigh. "No, I don't. As for your brother, I'm waiting for him and your father to come back from the doctor's office."

"Doctor's? On a Sunday? What'd Justin do? Trip over his big feet?"

"It's more serious than that. Sit down."

She'd finally gotten her daughter's full attention. Hayley pulled her hair back and flopped back in the recliner. "Is he sick?"

"He was in a fight."

"Justin?" Hayley's incredulous tone echoed Meg's first reaction. "That's crazy."

"It may be crazy, but he has a broken nose, a black eye and a possible concussion."

"Mo-om!"

Finally, a concerned reaction. "Dr. McCoy is taking care of him. He assured me Justin will be fine in a few days."

"A fight? I can't believe it. He's such a wuss."

Meg ignored the characterization. "Justin and your grandfather were taking a walk. Some boy in Justin's class called Grampa a retard."

"That's horrible! So Justin hit him?"

"Apparently."

"Wow! Way to go, Justin."

Hayley's opinion of her brother had undergone a miraculous one-eighty. "Fighting isn't the best solution, but I have to say that under the circumstances, I can't blame him," Meg said.

"Me, neither. Grampa tries so hard. And he's making progress with his speech therapy." Her eyes glowed with a sense of accomplishment.

Meg was proud of Hayley's efforts. Despite her initial hesitation, she'd been faithful about working with Bud. And effective. "Do you know Sam Grider?"

"Grider?" Hayley rolled her eyes. "He's a pain in the you-know-what. I'm glad Justin beat him up."

"I'm afraid it was the other way around."

"Jeez, somebody needs to lock that kid up."

"That's a bit drastic. But I know your father intends to speak with his parents."

Hayley's cell phone beeped and she retrieved it from her jeans pocket. Glancing warily at Meg, she stood up and moved out of earshot. So much for a mother-daughter talk. In the teenage pecking order, parents ranked light years below friends. Meg wondered if she had been this inconsiderate and selfconsumed at fifteen. Mostly she remembered her job as a busgirl, her never-ending chores at home and the late nights when she tried to squeeze in schoolwork. As for mother-daughter talks? They didn't happen. Unless her mom was criticizing her. She used to wonder if having a father around would've changed anything, made her life easier, convinced her she was loved.

She glanced at Hayley, perched on top of the kitchen counter, talking in confidential tones. Had she spoiled her? Made her life too comfortable, overcompensating for her own lonely adolescence?

That was one guilt trip she didn't want to embark on. At least not today. There was too much else at stake.

Meg sat up abruptly when she overheard her daughter's whispered goodbye: "Okay, Zach, talk to you later." Hayley clicked off her phone and started toward the stairs.

Zach? Meg catapulted from her chair. "Stop right there, young lady." She crossed the kitchen and took hold of Hayley's arm. "Who were you talking to?"

Hayley jerked away from Meg's grasp. "Just a friend. What's the big deal?"

"A friend named Zach, I believe."

Hayley's face reddened. "And so what if it was? It's not like he's a mass murderer or something."

"We told you not to see him anymore."

"It was just a phone call, for cripes sake. You don't need to make a federal case out of it."

Just a phone call that stirred an anxious gut-level reaction. The evasive look in her daughter's eyes and her defensive tone told Meg she was hiding something. "You know the rules, Hayley. And you know what it was like to be grounded. You're flirting with danger."

"Give me a break. You wouldn't understand about Zach, anyway." She stomped up the stairs. "Just leave me alone, okay?"

Meg decided she'd like nothing better.

The last thing she needed was round two of Hayley in rebel mode.

BUD SNEEZED, THEN SNEEZED again. Meg was afraid he'd caught cold from being out so long on Sunday afternoon. She glanced over the kitchen counter into the family room, where he sat, dressed in soft navy corduroy trousers, a new plaid shirt and a bright red sweater, watching TV while he waited for Scott and Marie to bring Kay home from the airport. She glanced down at the menu list Marie had drawn up. All of the advance preparation for tomorrow's Thanksgiving dinner had been done. Now she was getting out cups for the spiced tea she would serve tonight with the pumpkin bread Marie had baked. One of Kay's favorites, Marie had delightedly pointed out.

Nothing but the best for Kay, Meg thought cynically. Kay, who'd been too busy traveling abroad to attend her brother's wedding, who thought sending extravagant Christmas gifts made up for personal contact, and who was only now, two months after Bud's stroke, paying her father a visit. At least Scott saw through his sister. The mystery was how Marie and Bud could turn a blind eye to her self-absorption. Looking now at Bud, dressed up for the first time since the stroke, she wondered if on some level, he did sense his daughter's neglect, but preferred to ignore it.

Meg thought about Hayley, who, at the moment, certainly wasn't the world's most charming, thoughtful human being. As a parent, it was all too easy to slip into denial, to see what you wanted to see. Maybe in Kay's case, it was less disappointing for Bud and Marie to maintain their illusions about her.

Meg set out the platter of pumpkin bread and the teapot, then went into the family room, where she muted the TV and perched beside Bud on the arm of the sofa. She slipped her arm around his shoulder. "I don't want any more of those sneezles and wheezles. Are you warm enough?"

"Fire." He nodded at the gas log burning in the fireplace. "Nice."

"It's cozy, isn't it?" They watched the flames, rippling with color. "I know much has changed for you and Marie, but I think all of us have a lot to be thankful for this year, don't you?"

"Can't drive. Can't read..." His voice trailed off and he patted her leg. "But family." Bud gathered his words. "You. Son. Children. Blessings." He smiled his lopsided smile, as if pleased he'd located and used a new word. "Blessings."

They'd been given little choice about inviting Marie and Bud to move in with them. But sitting there with him now, Meg couldn't think of any of her volunteer positions that could come close to giving her the gratification of knowing she was a blessing to him. Her eyes stung with the sudden realization that in these last weeks, she and Bud had bonded in ways she couldn't have imagined in those far-off days when she'd longed for the father she knew would never come home.

Caring for Bud, though it involved some unpleasant tasks, was a small price to pay for this deeper relationship. For a new sense of belonging. She leaned over and kissed the top of his balding head. "I love you, Pops."

He looked up at her, his eyes shining. "Love you, too," he said.

They sat quietly, the only sounds the hiss of the gas log and the muffled beat of music from Justin's room. Her son was still not a pretty sight, but he took boyish pride in his battle scars. He hadn't been able to play in Monday's soccer game, but on the sidelines, he'd clearly enjoyed his moment in the spotlight. And maybe, in the process of defending Bud, he'd learned something about compassion.

When Meg heard the garage door open, she pasted a welcoming smile on her lips, then stood and helped Bud to his feet. Side by side, two soldiers at attention. "Kay. See her. Long time."

Yes, it had been a long time, an unconscionably long time. Meg felt her skin crack under the tension of that smile. Then the door opened and Marie hurried in, glowing with excitement. "Bud, she's here. Our Kay's here!"

Kay entered the room, her dark hair fashionably styled in a sleek, shoulder-length pageboy, her angular body chicly clothed in a deep purple tailored suit, amethyst jewelry setting off the color. Meg felt downright dowdy in her pinstripe slacks and gray cashmere pullover.

When Kay first spotted Bud, she gasped involuntarily and took a small step back before rearranging her expression. "Daddy!" She crossed the room and embraced him daintily. "You look wonderful!" Although she gushed optimism, Meg noticed her eyes were watery.

Bud, however, seemed oblivious. "You, here. Turkey day."

Kay gave a nervous titter and looked around the room in bewilderment. "Turkey day? Oh, do you mean Thanksgiving?"

Scott, standing in the doorway, gave a helpless shrug. "Kay, Dad's made amazing progress with his speech, but 'Thanksgiving' is still a bit of a challenge."

"Can't say it," Bud agreed matter-of-factly.

Kay took a deep breath, as if to regain her poise, then waved her fingers in dismissal. "Well, it won't be long until you're good as gold again." Then, taking in Meg for the first time, she said, "Meg, you look fabulous!"

"Thanks." She didn't add that she'd lost ten pounds since Bud's stroke, thanks to her around-the-clock caregiving. "Why don't you sit down with your parents while I get you a drink?"

The three of them moved to the sofa, and Scott followed Meg into the kitchen. "Can I help?"

"Coward," she whispered. "I know a fellow escapee when I see one."

"Guilty as charged." He watched her fill the teapot with hot water. "Kay's having a hard time understanding Dad's condition. I don't know whether she's in denial or what, but nothing I've said so far has seemed to make a dent. If she were staying a few more days, maybe…"

"So long as Bud and Marie are happy, that's all we need to concern ourselves with."

He placed a hand on her forearm, his eyes intense. In a low voice he said, "You're something else, you know that?"

It was a little thing, but his compliment made a trip-hammer of her heart. The moment, fraught with an emotion Meg had nearly forgotten, lasted several seconds. Then Scott picked up the tray with the teapot and cups. "Ready?"

Meg nodded and followed with the bread, cringing when Kay rhapsodized, "Pumpkin bread? My favorite. Mother, you're spoiling me already."

That's really what needed to happen. More spoiling. "Kay, would you pour?" *There, that ought to make her feel like the queen bee.* "And when you hand your father the cup, make sure he grasps it in his left hand."

For the first time, Kay looked down at Bud's limp right hand, and quickly turned away. Meg could only hope Bud hadn't noticed.

"Boy?" Bud pointed toward the staircase.

Scott clapped him on the shoulder. "Justin? Sure, I'll get him."

While Scott went upstairs, Meg, in her best hostess voice, inquired about Kay's flight and was treated to a litany of complaints about the airline, the terminal and her annoying fellow passengers. When Justin walked into the room, relief washed over her. A change of subject.

"Hi, Aunt Kay," he said, his voice cracking on the *a*.

Kay took one look at his black-and-blue eye, his bandaged nose and swollen lip and let out a screech. "Oh, my God, what happened to you?"

Justin ducked his head in false modesty. "I was in a fight."

"A fight?" Kay stared from Meg to Scott and back again to Meg. "How could you let that happen?"

Fury crested within Meg. Kay had no children, which undoubtedly made her an expert. "I didn't 'let' anything happen. Justin was defending your father."

Kay's teacup clattered as she replaced it in the saucer before rising to her feet and glaring at Scott, the new target of her scorn. "Why does Dad need defending?"

Scott moved forward. "Kay, sit down. Let me explain."

"Explain what? How could Dad need defending?"

"Bully," Bud said. "Bad name."

Marie nodded sympathetically. "Some boy called Bud a retard."

Kay did a good imitation of hyperventilating before turning to put an arm around Bud. "God, is it even safe in this neighborhood?"

"Safe," Bud repeated. He winked at Justin. "Good boy."

"Well, I'm here now, Dad. I won't let anything bad happen to you."

Meg closed her eyes briefly. *Oh, boy. Wonder Woman to the rescue.* She checked her watch. Six minutes had passed. Only a few thousand more to go before Saturday morning.

Bud slowly rose to his feet and faced his daughter with dignity. "Meg. Scott. Good care."

Meg glanced at her husband, whose eyes, full of love, were fixed on Bud.

Kay actually appeared flustered. "Well, uh, I know they've been wonderful, and heaven knows, I'd like to have been in a position to do more, but—"

Marie went to Kay's side. "But you're here now. That's what matters."

Apparently for Marie, "better late than

never" had real meaning. Meg picked up the teapot and retreated to the kitchen, where she silently counted to ten before reaching for more tea bags.

And what about her and Scott? Their marriage? Did "better late than never" apply to it, too?

WATCHING HIS MOTHER and sister, Scott found himself growing angry. What had Kay ever done to deserve such adulation? Darned if he knew.

Later, after everyone had gone to bed, he crept downstairs, poured himself a finger of bourbon and retired to his recliner to think. He'd had the same upbringing as Kay. Was he any better, any more considerate, than his sister?

He recalled their modest home on a tree-lined street, his dad working long hours to establish his plumbing business, his mother hunched over the Sunday ad supplements cutting out coupons. The suppers featuring ever more creative ways of preparing ground beef. As a little kid, he hadn't felt deprived in any material sense, but the day had come when an expensive prom dress had taken priority over the new basketball shoes he'd wanted and when a secondhand car for Kay hadn't been too expensive, but a Boy Scout Canadian canoeing trip had been. Nothing had ever been too good for Kay.

Why?

Then when she'd left for college, he'd inherited the spotlight. To his chagrin, Meg had often teasingly referred to him as the family "golden boy." He'd reaped the harvest of his father's business success in ways Kay never had. No secondhand car for him; instead, a sparkling new Pontiac Grand Am. Still, a great deal had been expected of him. After all, he was the son. The man. Competitive by nature, he'd never minded the pressure to succeed. And succeed, he had.

He took a steadying sip from his glass. His athletic and academic ability coupled with his high-profile involvement in school activities had brought him plenty of attention. And no one had been more full of praise than his mother. He'd taken it for granted; hell, even as his due.

Sitting there, listening to the familiar creakings of the house at night, he reached an inevitable and ugly conclusion. He liked attention. Maybe even craved it. Always had and always would. At work, at the club, at home. From business colleagues, from his golf foursome, from Meg.

Meg. He closed his eyes remembering their lives before Pops's stroke. She'd juggled an incredible number of balls. Her monthly appointment calendar had been crammed with meetings and obligations that didn't include him. The number of errands she ran weekly on behalf of the children put miles and miles on the odometer. And miles of distance between the two of them.

Setting his drink down on the chair-side table, he took a good long look at himself—and at his expectations. All along, he'd expected from Meg the same adoring attention she'd given him as a newlywed.

And what did she want from him? Need from a husband?

Important questions. Ones he intended to find answers for. Anything less would be a guaranteed return to the stalemate in their marriage. Or worse, to a potential separation.

He couldn't let that happen.

JUSTIN DROPPED THE CELL PHONE on his bed, cracking a grin wide enough to make his tender nose sorer. Molly Thatcher had just called to wish him a happy Thanksgiving.

Un-freaking-believable! Wow, that almost made getting beaten up by Grider worthwhile. He moved to the dresser mirror and studied his reflection. Eye still puffy and turning yellowish. Big bandage on his honker. Molly must love the wounded-tough-guy look. But would she still like him after he healed?

He flopped on his bed, his stomach growling from the smell of the turkey and pie. He was starving. He'd never been able to figure out why holiday dinners had to be at two or three in the afternoon instead of at noon. A guy could die waiting to eat. He rolled over and sat up. Maybe he'd go read to Grampa or watch some football. Hang out.

Downstairs, the tantalizing aromas caused him to groan. His dad was carving the bird. That was progress. He wandered into the family room. Aunt Kay was sitting in the rocker—where she'd planted her butt from the time she'd first arrived. She was reading some thick magazine. Maybe she didn't cook or something because Mom and Gramma were scurrying about the kitchen, red-faced, filling about a million bowls with food. He studied Aunt Kay again. She looked kind of frozen, like one of those mannequin things in a department store. He knew he was supposed to love her and all, but it was sort of hard when he hardly ever saw her.

He walked on into the dining room where Hayley was setting the table. She looked up. "What?"

"Nothin'. Need any help?"

"You think I'd trust *you* with Mom's good china?"

"Right, like you're so grown-up."

She rolled her eyes. "Older than you."

She'd asked for it. "Old enough to sneak around with that loser Zach Simon?"

"Shut up." She glanced quickly in the direction of the kitchen. "Go, get out of here."

He shrugged. "Just don't ask me to feel sorry for you when you get busted again."

"You better keep your mouth shut, Justin, or so help me—"

"You children can help carry the dishes to the sideboard."

They both whirled around. Gramma stood in the doorway, taking off her apron and folding it neatly.

Justin's stomach rumbled audibly, and Hayley threw him a disgusted look as they headed for the kitchen. "Gross!"

After everyone had food on their plates,

Dad asked them to hold hands for grace. When he finished the prayer, Grampa said "A-men" really loud. Then he looked around the table and added, "Family. Blessing for me." Justin heard his dad clear his throat and noticed his mother's too-shiny eyes.

The food was awesome. He ate two helpings of potatoes and gravy along with four rolls and a bunch of turkey. But he was saving room for Mom's pumpkin pie topped with gobs of whipped cream. The meal would've been perfect except for Aunt Kay. She ate like a bird, using her fork to push the food around. Maybe she thought nobody would notice she wasn't eating much. But the worst was the way she looked at Grampa whenever he spilled food or got gravy on his face. How would she like to try feeding herself left-handed?

When it came time for dessert, Aunt Kay was the only person who didn't take any. She just kept talking about all these la-di-da trips she'd been on. About the "magnificence" of the European cathedrals and the "impeccable" manners of the French. It about made him gag. She could hop on a plane to "delightful" Siena, but she couldn't make it to Tulsa, Oklahoma.

He wasn't paying much attention until he heard her turn to Gramma and ask, "When will you and Dad be resuming your RV trip?"

Resuming their trip? Was the lady blind? Grampa could barely get around with his cane. And no way could he read a map. What was it with her? Didn't she know Grampa would probably never drive again? And Gramma sure wasn't going to climb behind the wheel of that monster bus.

Gramma teared up. "Now, Kay, honey, we're not going to talk about that."

"Pops isn't ready for that discussion yet," Dad said, the vein in his neck throbbing. "That'll be up to the doctors."

Suddenly, Grampa set down his fork and shoved his chair back. "No!"

"Let's not upset him," Gramma whispered to Aunt Kay.

"Me, not stupid," Grampa said in a firm voice.

"Of course not, Dad, I just meant—"

"Sell." He pounded his good fist on the table. "That's final."

"Sell what?" Aunt Kay looked genuinely puzzled.

Grampa nodded at Justin. "You. Tell."

Justin's full stomach revolted. He knew

what his grandfather was talking about. The want ads. He hesitated.

"You, me. Read about it. Sell." His grampa's sharp blue eyes lasered into Justin's.

Everyone turned to look at him. He wanted to sink beneath the table and avoid saying anything. To explain would make Grampa's decision final.

"Son?" Dad urged softly.

Justin licked his lips. "Well, it's like this."

"Tell it," Grampa insisted.

"He wants to sell the motor home."

Aunt Kay rose halfway out of her chair. "Sell the motor home? But that's been his dream ever since I can remember."

Nobody else said anything. Gramma's head was bowed and her eyes were closed.

"Can't drive. Can't read. Sell."

"But, Dad, you'll get better, you'll see."

Grampa held out a hand across the table, and clasped Aunt Kay's. "Better? Maybe. A little. Healthy man?" He shook his head sadly. "Gone."

Aunt Kay sank back into her chair, bringing her napkin up to her eyes. Justin couldn't be sure, but he thought maybe she was crying.

He watched his mother get up, and, as if in slow motion, circle the table to where his grandfather was sitting. Standing behind him, she leaned over and put her arms around his neck, resting her chin on the top of his head. "Maybe you'll never be as strong as you once were, Pops, but you're still a strong, good man. Maybe not healthy enough to take a long RV trip, but plenty healthy enough to give us all great joy."

Justin swallowed hard. Pretty soon everybody was hugging Grampa. Even snooty old Aunt Kay. Sometimes holidays sucked. Other times? Well, they turned out pretty special. Kind of like today.

CHAPTER THIRTEEN

THE MORNING AFTER THANKSGIVING, Meg reared up in bed and stared at Scott, mouth agape. "Surely you're not going to work."

He continued threading his belt through the loops. "It's Friday."

"But it's Thanksgiving weekend. I thought—" She didn't finish her sentence, giving a resigned shrug instead and climbing out of bed. Tousled from sleep, her cheeks flushed, she would've turned him on—except for the sparks flashing from her eyes.

"I do have an ad agency to run," he reminded her.

"And a sister to entertain?" With jerky movements, she put on her robe. "Just who is supposed to take care of that little detail?"

Scott pulled out a tie from the closet. This was no way to start the morning. He knew Meg was worn out, but why would she have assumed he'd stay home from work? She knew how busy he was. "It's all about Kay, isn't it?"

She shot him a look. "I have my hands full with your father. Today's his appointment with the physical therapist."

"Well, she and Mom can stay home and visit."

"That's all you know. Kay is insisting on going with us to the therapy session."

"Might not hurt. She'd at least begin to understand what we're up against."

"I'd hoped you'd be along to help."

Why did she always have to resort to doublespeak? "To help with what?"

"I can handle Bud and your mother, or I can tolerate Kay and keep her entertained. Doing them both at the same time is asking a lot."

He looked at her closely. The lines around her mouth had deepened and her cheekbones were more pronounced. He got it. He was taking her for granted again. "I'm sorry, Meg. You're right. All of us expect a lot of you, and we're wearing you out."

Defiance drained from her body, and she suddenly looked small, diminished. "It's not as if I have a choice."

He hung his head. It was true. Yet, despite

the difficult circumstances, she was dealing with his father with tremendous concern and compassion, as evidenced by her loving words at dinner yesterday. "I'll try to get home early."

"I've heard that before."

Instead of the customary irritation in her voice, he heard weariness. When she started to walk around him to get to the bathroom, he put his hands on her shoulders, stopping her. "None of this has been easy. For any of us." He gathered her into his arms, aware that while she didn't resist, she didn't relax into the embrace, either. "I'll be home early."

She looked up at him. "You mean you'll *try* to be home early."

Her tone reminded him of the many times he'd put business first. This couldn't be one of them. "Meggie, I'll be home early."

Sitting in his office later in the day, he wondered how he could've been so confident. Stacks of files obscured the surface of his desk, along with videotapes for his review. He'd already fielded two urgent calls from the Jordan marketing department, defused another client and participated in an hour-long conference call with a third client. He swung away from his desk, then stood and stared out the window. Below, the Arkansas River—a bare trickle of water this time of year—meandered toward its meeting with the Mississippi. Traffic hummed along the interstate. The Friday after Thanksgiving. Biggest retail sales day of the year. Jordan stockholders were counting on it, and the future of Harper Concepts, in part, depended upon it.

"Scott, busy?" Wes stood in the doorway.

"Does an O.U. fan bleed red?" Scott waved him in. "What's up?"

Wes closed the door, pulled an armchair over to Scott's desk and sat down. "I need to talk to you about a sensitive matter—but it's one we should deal with, sooner rather than later. When we started the firm, we promised we'd shoot straight with each other, right?"

"Sure. What do we need to discuss?"

Scott was ill-prepared for his partner's answer. "You."

"Me?" His expression must have betrayed his bafflement. "What are you getting at?"

Wes held up his hands in a don't-shoot-the-messenger gesture. "You're strung out, buddy. Taking on too much."

"Come on, Wes, you know what I'm dealing with at home with Mom and Pops." He sank into his desk chair.

"I'm not talking about home," Wes said quietly. "I'm talking about here at the agency."

Scott struggled to keep the lid on his temper. He was putting in fifteen-hour days. What did Wes expect? Barely controlling his sarcasm, he said, "Go ahead. Lay it on me."

"Hey, look, buddy, this isn't exactly a walk in the park for me, either. But something's gotta give. You're burning the candle at both ends."

"Meaning what?"

"In a word? Micromanaging."

"You mean I'm on top of things? Hell, yes." He thumped his desk. "The buck stops here."

Wes pointed to himself. "And here."

Scott gave a nearly imperceptible nod of agreement. Knowing Wes had more to say, he leaned forward. "Out with it, then."

"Scott, you've done an incredible job making this agency a force to be dealt with in the area. You've made great contacts and brought in a lot of business."

Scott knew the other shoe was about to drop. "But?"

"You've hired good, savvy people. Talented people. We need to keep them." Wes laid his palms flat on his knees. "So...let them do the jobs they were hired to do."

"And they're not?"

"Of course they are, but you're hamstringing them. Every last detail has to be approved by you. That's not exactly sending our employees a vote of confidence."

Scott frowned, trying to process what Wes was saying, fighting the instinctive urge to defend himself. "Are you telling me we have a morale problem?"

Wes shrugged. "Maybe not yet. But it's brewing. You have to give people like Brenda and Jim Tate room to maneuver. When they screw up, if they do, by all means bring it to their attention. Work with them. Until then, let these folks do their jobs without looking over their shoulders constantly. Trust the people you hired." Wes paused, letting his words sink in. Then he went on. "As your friend, I need to say one more thing. You're spending way too much time here. It's like you're deliberately burying yourself in work. What are you running from?"

Scott fought the instinct to bolt from his chair and pound a fist through the wall. The distressed look on Wes's face stopped him. It couldn't have been easy for his partner to confront him. Wes didn't pull any punches. Never had. He was entitled to be taken seriously. "I need to think about what you've said. While I can't say I like what you're telling me, I appreciate your concern."

Wes rose to his feet and extended his hand. "I know you'll do what's best for the firm. Find a way to do what's best for yourself, too."

After his partner left, Scott sat back in his chair, fingers steepled under his chin. He'd think about the staff and their needs later. Right now, he had to mull over the more immediate question. What *was* he running from? When had he forsaken his family responsibilities in the name of business success? What had he expected from Meg? And, most important, what kind of changes was he prepared to make?

After a long, searching consideration of those questions, he leaned forward and pushed the intercom button. "Hazel, transfer any calls to Wes. I'm taking the rest of the afternoon off."

His normally imperturbable secretary let out an involuntary gasp. "You're doing what?"

"Leaving," he said, amazed by the buoyancy surging through his body.

MEG'S JAW ACHED from the effort to contain a primal scream. Kay had driven her crazy on the drive to the rehabilitation center and was continuing to do so in the waiting room. When she talked to Bud, she either adopted a honeyed, patronizing tone suitable for addressing a three-year-old, or she acted as if he possessed his full capacities, and then became impatient with him when he couldn't respond on that level. Even Marie had picked up on Kay's insensitivity, interrupting her daughter at intervals to remind her that while her father had some difficulty communicating, he wasn't a child.

The final straw was Kay's insistence on accompanying Bud into the therapy room. Marie and Meg trailed behind, but Kay sailed right out to the exercise mat to oversee the therapist as he put Bud through his paces. The first time Bud moaned in pain, Kay wheeled on the therapist. "Can't you see you're hurting him?"

Gripping the arms of her chair on the periphery, Meg stared, stupefied.

Calmly continuing with the leg flexes and extensions, the therapist turned his head to glance at Kay. Patiently he explained the purpose of the exercises, then said, "Ma'am, I'm going to have to ask you to quit interfering here."

"Interfering?" Kay's voice rose in crescendo. "This is my father we're talking about."

"We're doing everything we can to help him regain his strength."

"I know some kind of therapy is necessary, but I don't like seeing Dad in such pain."

Bud, his face red with exertion, groaned. "Hurts me? Good."

Infinitely patient, the therapist stood. "He's working through the pain. That's how we make progress."

"Easy for you to say."

Beside her, Marie had been fidgeting and clucking. Now, though, she got to her feet and walked over to her daughter. "Kay, stop it."

Meg watched in fascination as Kay rounded on her mother. "I'm only trying to help."

Marie, in an uncharacteristic gesture, took her daughter by the arm. "Well, you're not."

From the mat, Bud exploded. "Go."

Kay jerked away from her mother. "Somebody has to take charge here."

"But it isn't going to be you, Kay." As if the dramatic hero had just swept in from the wings, Scott strode across the floor, letting the door to the hallway slam shut behind him. "Please excuse my sister," he said to the therapist, who merely shrugged as if this was not an uncommon experience. "Mom, take Kay out to the waiting room." He turned his back on them to kneel beside his father. Daggers aimed at Scott shot from Kay's eyes, but she allowed Marie to escort her out.

Meg felt trapped in the middle. She didn't really want to join the women in the waiting room, but she wasn't sure she belonged with Bud and Scott, either.

"Pops, you doin' okay?"

Bud grunted. "Better. Now." He waved a hand at the therapist. "Go on. Hurt me."

Scott rose, then approached Meg. "Thank you," she whispered. She had no idea what he was doing there, but she had seldom been so glad to see anyone.

"I'm sorry, Meg. My sister has always been difficult. You shouldn't have had to deal with any of this."

She got up and laced her fingers through his. "It's not my idea of fun, but at least, for today, we're in this together, right?"

A warm current flowed between their joined hands and the affection in his eyes made her feel almost beautiful.

"Dog." Bud's call caused them to break their gaze.

The therapist leaned closer to his patient. "What is it, Mr. Harper?"

"Dog. No!" He shook his head in frustration. "Dah."

Scott squeezed Meg's hand, dropped it and went over to his father. "What are you trying to say, Pops?"

"Dah. Ter. Want. Dahter."

Scott's face was tense as he struggled to understand. "Daughter? You want Kay back here?"

"No!" With the therapist's assistance, Bud sat up. "Other one."

"Other one what?"

"Other dahter."

Scott looked momentarily puzzled, but then his features relaxed in an ear-to-ear grin. "Meg?"

Bud cackled. "Meg."

Meg couldn't breathe for the overflowing of her heart. Bud had just given her a glorious gift. She was loved. She was somebody's daughter. At last.

Tentatively, she approached the mat and knelt beside Bud. "I'm here, Pops," she whispered.

He patted her hand. "You. Good girl. But more." His mouth moved in the effort to form additional words. "You. Dahter."

Scott hunkered beside her, his arm around her shoulder. "Oh, Meggie, when I think I could've been at work..." He lowered his voice. "I wouldn't have missed this for anything."

Meg couldn't tear her eyes from Bud's look of love and approval. He reached up and traced a finger across her cheek. "No crying," he said.

Meg sniffled through her laughter. "Okay," she promised.

Bud lay back down and turned to the therapist. "Now. Hurt me. Again."

Scott helped Meg to her feet and drew her to the side of the room. "That's okay for Pops, but, Meggie, I don't want any more hurt. Any more pain." Unbelievably, his voice cracked when he went on. "I just want my family."

In that instant something important passed between them. An unspoken promise. Maybe, finally, they both wanted the same thing.

AFTER EVERYONE HAD SETTLED IN for the night, Scott turned off the lights in the family room and made his way upstairs. He'd had little time to consider the implications of Wes's remarks, what with the scene with Kay at the rehab center, followed by his mother's attempts throughout dinner to placate his sister, who'd responded by trying to impress everyone with stories of her social life in Florida. Talk about highmaintenance. The woman wore him out. Yet, at the same time, there was something sad about her shallowness and her need to impress. He suspected that underneath it all she was upset about Pops's condition, but was unable to deal with it.

Recalling his sister's attempts to interfere with Pops's therapy, Scott knew he'd done the right thing by leaving the office that afternoon. How often in the past, though, had he ignored Meg's requests for his presence, his time, his involvement? How many moments had he missed like the one today when Pops claimed Meg as his daughter? Was he, like his sister, so wrapped up in himself and his work that he was missing out on what really mattered? Definite food for thought.

He found Meg in the bathroom brushing her teeth. Sidling up behind her, he put his arms around her waist. "Alone at last," he murmured.

She sent him a questioning look in the mirror, then leaned over the sink and rinsed her mouth. When she straightened up, a fleck of toothpaste remained on her lips. He knew exactly what he intended to do about that. He pivoted her in his arms and kissed her, delving delightedly into the minty-fresh crevices of her mouth.

"Mmm," she crooned in his ear. With her hands linked behind his neck, she cocked her head and studied him. "I'm trying not to raise my hopes unrealistically, but I have to tell you—seeing you walk into that exercise room today was one of the best things that's happened to me in a long, long time."

"Out of character for me, huh?"

"Your words, not mine. But, yeah." She stepped back and poured lotion into her hands. "To what do you attribute this behavior?"

"A wake-up call from Wes."

Her eyes widened. "Wes?"

Scott kneaded her shoulders with his fingers. "I want to tell you about it, Meggie." He unbuttoned his shirt. "You go on to bed. I'll be there in a few minutes. Can you stay awake?"

"With a cliff-hanger like that? Of course."

Meg deserved to know what Wes had said,

but Scott had reservations, too. He didn't want her to expect things to be totally different. And he didn't need to hear any I-told-you-sos. Wes's remarks would take time to process, and he'd be kidding himself if he didn't admit his partner's judgment had hurt. Still, in his gut, he recognized the truth of it. What was he running from? Failure. Pure and simple. At the agency. At home. The ultimate irony? The more he ran, the more he failed.

In bed, he cradled Meg in his arms and told her in painstaking detail about his conversation with Wes and about his own soul-searching. To her credit she listened until he'd exhausted the issue. Then she said something quite surprising.

"You are not your sister."

He did a double take. She'd identified one of his fears—that he was a selfish bastard who thought only of himself. "Maybe not, but I've considered myself pretty darned important."

"Because you are. To the agency. To me. To the children. To your parents. But, Scott, unlike Kay, you know how to love."

For some reason, she was being more than generous. He grunted. "A quality I haven't always exhibited."

"Agreed." She ran a hand over his chest. "But one you sure demonstrated today." She hesitated, as if picking her words, before going on. "This afternoon? Well, I felt such love from you."

The wistfulness in her voice tore him apart. Had he been so busy taking her for granted that he'd forgotten to cherish her? "Those feelings have always been there. I've just locked them away from you." He kissed her temple. "No more."

"But honestly, Scott, I don't always expect you to put me or the family ahead of business. That would be unrealistic. But there are times—"

"When I need to listen and act. Like today."

"Right," she said. "And while we're on the subject of confessions, I have one, too."

"What's that?"

"Something important happened this afternoon."

"When Pops called you his other daughter? That had to be special for you."

"Yes." She snuggled closer. "You, of all people, know how I've always missed having a father. When I was a child, I guess I thought that all my troubles would disappear if only Super Dad would rescue me, brush away my tears, ease my loneliness, make everything perfect for me."

He held his breath, aching with love for the sad little girl and for the woman who felt she was somehow incomplete. What she told him next, about sitting on the stoop wishing she had a dad like other girls did, ate at him. She'd only rarely talked about her father's death, and obviously he'd never fully appreciated the depths of her longing. "Oh, Meggie," he whispered, brushing her hair back off her forehead.

"Wait, there's more."

"I'm listening."

She wove her fingers through his. "I've thought about it all day. Ever since your dad said that magic word, *daughter.* He's the only father I'll ever have, and I'm so grateful. But Scott, I realized something else. I haven't been fair to you. Maybe I've tried to make you a father replacement."

"What do you mean?"

"Think about it. You've been the only man in my life. I expected everything from you. Craved it—*everything*. Attention, approval, and, most important, love. But not *just* love— I expected you, all by yourself, to fill the well of my loneliness. It was too much to expect, and I'm so sorry. There was no way on earth you alone could ever have given me enough emotionally."

He thought about her words and came to an inescapable conclusion. "I failed you."

"No, that's just it. You didn't. I set an impossible standard for you."

"And I'm used to leaping every hurdle put in front of me."

They lay quietly, lost in thought. Once, he'd wanted to give her everything—be her everything. Was that just a naive notion? Had years of diapers, heaps of plastic toys, mounting bills and social and business pressures diminished his desire to complete her? He hoped not. But he would have to start paying more attention. Working at it. Beside him, Meg made a little noise that sounded remarkably like laughter.

"What's so funny?"

"The root of our problems is pretty obvious," she said. "Golden Boy meets Poor Little Match Girl. It's a recipe for disaster."

He smiled to himself. She'd nailed it. "Unless…"

"Unless what?"

"Golden Boy wants to light Little Match Girl's fire."

"Now?"

The seductive edge in her voice coupled with his physical reaction settled the issue. "Now," he said decisively.

JUSTIN STIRRED A SPOON through the remnants of his cereal. Dust motes danced in the sunlight streaming in the kitchen window and the smell of stale coffee lingered in the air. Dad and Gramma had just left to take Aunt Kay to the airport, and Mom was helping Grampa with his exercises. Hayley, big surprise, was still sleeping. He picked up his cereal bowl and drained the last of the milk. Two hours to go before the televised football games started. Two hours to rake leaves.

He slid off the kitchen stool, put his bowl in the sink and grabbed an old O.U. sweatshirt off the peg in the utility room. Here was the thing: Why didn't his stupid sister ever have to rake leaves? Wouldn't it be just too bad if she broke her fingernails or got her hair dirty? He went into the garage, took the rake off the hook on the wall and headed outside. A stiff breeze scattered the fallen leaves. He cursed under his breath. No sooner would he rake them into piles than they'd fly all over the place with the first gust of wind. He fingered his nose, still tender from the fight. Dad would not be pleased if he didn't at least go through the motions. Starting in the corner near the fence, he raked toward the driveway where he could easily bag the leaves.

Something weird was going on with his family, but he didn't have a clue what. Aunt Kay had hardly spoken to anyone at dinner last night. Even Gramma had been quieter than usual, and she didn't fuss over Aunt Kay like she usually did. When they were eating dessert, Aunt Kay had started in about Grampa's therapy, like she was some expert. But almost before she'd begun, Grampa had pointed his finger at her and said, "Stop!" Dad had changed the subject then, and afterward, it had been as though Gramma were trying to make it up to Aunt Kay in case her feelings had been hurt. And Mom? She hadn't said much at all, which wasn't like her. He didn't get it. But then, he was just a kid. What was he supposed to know?

He wrestled the big green trash bag open and scooped up the leaves. He kind of liked the smell—like old gym socks and sun and dirt. After he filled the bag, he grabbed his shirttail and wiped the sweat from his face, careful not to put any pressure on his black eye or nose. He never would admit it, but he'd be glad when school started again. It was boring hanging around adults all the time. One thing he'd noticed, though—his mom and dad weren't arguing as much. He didn't want to get his hopes up too high, but it sort of looked to him like maybe they liked each other again. That funny feeling he'd had a couple of months ago crept back into his stomach, reminding him how scared he'd been then.

"Hey, dude, havin' fun?"

He'd know that voice anywhere. He took his time tying the trash bag before he looked up. "What's it look like?"

Sam Grider, one foot on the ground, rested on his bike at the foot of the driveway. "Nice face," Grider said, studying him.

"You, too," Justin said, pointing to the cut on Sam's chin.

Grider hopped off his bike and walked it closer. "So," he said, "what's the story with your grandpa?"

Justin leaned on his rake, never taking his eyes off the enemy. "He had a stroke. It affected his body and his speech. Know anything about that?" Justin couldn't be certain, but he thought Grider hung his head—not much, but a little.

"My mom tried to explain it to me. And, hey, look, I'm sorry, man. I shouldn't have said your grandpa was a retard."

"Maybe next time you should think before you open your big mouth."

Grider's shoulders tensed, but he didn't charge. "Yeah, that's what my mom told me." He nodded toward the rake. "When'll you be finished?"

"What's it to you?"

"I dunno, I thought we could get some more guys and go down to the park. Play touch football. Then afterward, maybe I could come home with you." This time he actually did hang his head. "You know, apologize to your grandfather."

Justin eyed the other boy, considering his offer. He still wasn't Grider's number-one fan, but playing football beat the heck out of being called a retard or having your face mashed in. And Grampa sure deserved an apology. "Okay," he said with what he hoped was a John Wayne shoulder shrug. "Let me fill another bag first."

Grider threw a leg over his bike. "See you at the park," he said, before pedaling off down the street.

SATURDAY NIGHT MEG SHOVED the last of the sheets into the dryer, hit the switch and slumped against the utility-room counter. The steady hum of the dryer motor and the warm, fabric-softener-scented air created a welcoming cocoon. She used to think of laundry as a chore; now it provided her with an excuse to hide away, at least for a little while.

To Meg's delight, Marie had accepted an invitation from Jannie's mother to play bridge. This was the first time her mother-in-law had agreed to leave Bud for an evening. A change of scenery would do her a world of good. Justin was parked in his bedroom watching a movie on TV, Hayley had gone to a party with Jill, and Scott had taken his laptop into the sitting room, working there and keeping Bud company. Despite the ironing piled in the basket, Meg welcomed this rare time to herself.

Today had been the best day she could remember in months. Last night, sharing their deepest vulnerabilities, she and Scott had been more honest with each other than she could ever remember. She'd found herself wanting to comfort him and make up for those many lost opportunities to give something to him. Even now, thinking about it, their lovemaking had been extraordinarily poignant—and passionate. With every word and gesture, he'd made her feel desirable and cherished. The depth of her emotions had both delighted and frightened her. Love was such a fragile gift.

She'd held the memory close throughout the day, clinging to the hope that their marriage was entering a new phase. Maybe with Kay's departure, things would settle down and she and Scott would have time to build from last night's revelations.

Kay's visit had been exhausting for all of them. The woman exuded negative energy. It broke Meg's heart to recall the puppy-dog eagerness with which Marie, in particular, had greeted her daughter. Whatever hopes she'd nurtured that Kay would pitch in and help with Bud had vanished within the first few hours of her visit. Watching Bud and Marie gamely make the best of the situation had given Meg pause for thought. She mentally fast-forwarded thirty years. What kind of adults would Hayley and Justin be?

As she set up the ironing board to press the Thanksgiving tablecloth and napkins, she thought about her children. Had she made life too easy for them, never denying them anything? She'd indulged their every desire—from the new gotta-have-it toy to the latest in clothing fads. Why? Was it easier than saying no? Or was it her own insatiable need to compensate for a childhood of penny-pinching?

She tested the bottom of the iron with a wet finger, satisfied with the quick hiss. She had believed she was doing the right thing by making their lives comfortable.

Is that what Marie had thought about Kay?

Absorbed in the question, she nearly scorched the linen napkin beneath the iron. Hayley. Self-consumed, moody. Was it a teenage phase—or something worse?

With a vengeance Meg attacked a stubborn wrinkle. Scott had often accused her of indulging their children—a mild indictment compared to his suggestion that she'd sacrificed him and their marriage on the altar of perfect motherhood.

And yet?

She ironed a sharp crease into the folded napkin and reached for another. A vivid image popped into her head. Her father-in-law's defeated expression when Kay had seemed unable to face the reality of his condition. Her blind insistence that he would soon be "good as gold again."

Is that what she and Scott had to look forward to? A daughter incapable of compassion or empathy? A son who thought success would arrive on a silver platter?

Smoothing another wrinkled napkin on the ironing board, she realized she was selling both kids short. After all, Hayley was working patiently now with Bud on his speech therapy. In fact, she seemed to enjoy those one-on-one times with her grandfather. Justin had spent most of the morning raking leaves, and they'd both expressed to her their bewilderment at Kay's behavior.

Still, like it or not, she couldn't excuse herself from her role in spoiling them.

Or from focusing all her attention on her children instead of her husband.

BUD TRIED NOT TO STIR in bed. He didn't want to disturb Marie. In his mind he snared the word for his problem. *Insomnia.* He hated it. Lying here staring at the ceiling. At the nightlight in the bathroom. Listening to Marie saw logs. Hearing the occasional car drive past the house. In the old days, he'd have gotten out of bed, gone into the family room and read or watched TV until he grew drowsy. Now he had to hoard his energy for his twice-nightly trips to the bathroom. A fine kettle of fish.

Kay. They'd said goodbye this morning. He remembered now what she was like. Disappointment. Whose fault? No matter. Too late. She was back in Florida. A relief. Sad, but true.

Not like Meg. That daughter loved him. God shuts a door. Opens a window.

Scott? That boy needed to shape up. All work? Not good. Family, wife. Yep, shape up.

Then his thoughts drifted to the motor home. In his mind, he saw himself breezing down the highway, the open road before him, the beauty of nature filling his soul, Marie at his side. Never again.

Careful not to wake Marie, he rolled over on his side. Okay. He'd tried not to think about it. Had refused to look at the brochure. He didn't want to think about it now, either. But he couldn't stop. He squeezed his eyes shut in the effort to blot out the mental image. The cover with all those color photos of the building with its fountains and rosebushes and picnic benches. Of rooms decorated to resemble a four-star hotel. Of the idiotic, happy-looking old people who smiled as if they'd just discovered a combined cure for hemorrhoids, acid reflux and arthritis.

Sunrise Manor. "An adult community."

Hell. Call a spade a spade. An old folks' home. Ancient geezers shuffling to dinner in their house slippers. Blue-haired ladies waiting to bat their mascaraed eyes at any man still breathing. Not for him.

Motor home.

He clenched and unclenched his fist. Not for him, either.

Scott's house? Bile worked its way up his esophagus. No.

Sunrise Manor? Marie called it a nice facility.

Facility? Tomb.

But staying at Scott's house? No good choices.

Sunrise Manor. Okay. Visit. Look and see.

He lay awake for a long time wondering how his life had arrived at this conclusion. Coming into this world with nothing, accumulating possessions, then watching them shrink back to very little. No longer a boy. An old man. So quickly.

He must've dozed off, because the next thing he knew, he heard a car pull into the driveway. He looked at the clock. Hard to read it exactly, but late. Very late. He lay still, listening. He heard the front door ease open. Granddaughter?

A muffled sob or hiccup. Then the car backed down the driveway, and through the bedroom window, he watched the lights fade as the vehicle disappeared down the street. He listened for his granddaughter's tread on the stairs. One step. A stumble. Two steps. Three. Four.

Then, with a sickening thud, the sound of a body thumping, falling, followed by a moan and silence. His heart raced. He sat up, swung his legs over the side of the bed and grappled for his walker.

By the time he managed to lever himself up and start for the hall, someone had flipped on the stairwell light. He arrived just as Scott thundered down the stairs.

As if awakening from a bad dream, Bud gaped. Heaped on the hallway floor was his granddaughter, her makeup smeared, her hair disheveled. Scott hunkered beside her, cupping her face in his hands. "Hayley, can you hear me?"

Meg tore down the stairs, and behind him, he felt Marie's hands steadying him. Scott and Meg exchanged a look that stopped Bud's breath. "She passed out," Scott said.

"Oh, my God!" Meg crumpled beside her daughter. "She must be sick."

Scott gathered Hayley in his arms and rose to his feet. "Not sick, Meg. Drunk."

Drunk? Bud tried to figure out the word. The child? Drunk?

Scott cradled his daughter protectively. "She reeks of beer."

Hayley's head lolled against Scott's shoulder and she moaned again. Her eyes fluttered. "Daddy?" Bud could barely hear her.

"What is it?"

"I'm so dizzy."

Scott glanced at Meg, then nodded toward the stairs. "Let's get her to bed."

"No," Hayley said. "Bathroom. I think I'm gonna be sick."

Meg and Scott hustled Hayley up the stairs. Bud couldn't move. This didn't make sense.

Marie linked an arm through his. "Oh, poor Hayley."

Poor Hayley. Yes. But poor Scott. Poor Meg. A problem.

He allowed Marie to lead him back to the bedroom. Problems. Lots of them. Him. Stroke. Marie. Houseguests. Another problem.

He crumpled into bed. One choice. Sunrise Manor.

End of the line.

CHAPTER FOURTEEN

MEG HADN'T SLEPT A WINK. She was alternately furious and concerned. Crying one minute and feeling guilt-ridden the next. Blaming herself. Blaming Jill, Zach or whatever slick, pseudo-sophisticated teenager had talked Hayley into drinking. Blaming the laxness of modern society. Blaming the world.

And feeling like an utter failure as a parent.

She dunked her tea bag into the hot water and huddled on a kitchen stool, holding the warm cup, wishing she could draw comfort from the simple act of drinking tea. The clock on the microwave read 4:15 a.m. Hayley had, indeed, been sick. By the time Meg had tucked her into bed an hour ago with a cool compress on her head, Scott, in the inimitable fashion of men who can roll over in the midst of a thunderstorm and immediately fall asleep, was snoring. Frowning, she faced the inevitable. In the morning they would have to confront Hayley, but she and Scott hadn't had the opportunity to agree on a strategy. They would need to play this one carefully. The important thing was to discover why Hayley had gotten drunk.

And to make sure it never happened again.

On the other hand, it could be counterproductive to come down too hard on her. Meg hoped Scott would give Hayley time to tell her side of the story before lowering the boom. That was his way, though. Strict, swift punishment as a deterrent.

But how much of Hayley's rebellion was a result of everything that had gone on in the last few months? She'd undoubtedly picked up on the tension between her parents. And the change in the family dynamic with Bud and Marie living here couldn't have been easy for the kids, accustomed to having their own way.

Meg set the tea bag on a saucer. How much of Hayley's unacceptable behavior could she attribute to teenage angst? How much could be excused? *Listen to yourself. You can rationalize all night long. It won't change a thing. Your daughter has problems.*

Digging in the pocket of her robe, Meg blinked furiously, then drew out a tissue and wiped her nose. When she'd given birth, she'd never expected to spend a sleepless night imagining a wild party. Picturing Hayley chugging from a beer can. Or listening to the leaden thump of an inebriated body and holding back her daughter's long hair as she bent over the toilet and emptied the contents of her stomach.

Meg stood and walked to the patio door. The cloudy night obscured the moon and stars. Except for a neighbor's yard light, it was inky black out. Mockingly, the familiar saying echoed in her mind: *It's always darkest before the dawn.*

This time she wasn't so sure. When the dawn came, she and Scott would be entering murky, uncharted territory: they'd have to deal with their hungover daughter.

SCOTT PUT ON HIS GOLF SHIRT and pants, knowing full well he might never make it to the country club this morning for his regular game. Part of him longed to escape, to avoid the upcoming confrontation with Hayley, but he was kidding himself. It had to be done.

He could throttle the punk who'd supplied her with beer. And what had she been thinking? She knew better. Was there any hell worse than being the father of a teenage daughter? Watching horny young guys ogle her? Pour booze down her throat?

He caught himself. He was descending into a dangerous frame of mind. Outrage wouldn't solve anything. He needed to be calm. Firm.

Sitting on the side of the bed, he pulled on his socks, then his loafers. What had happened to the exuberant, carefree little girl who'd loved to sit on his lap while he read her the comics? Reviewing the past few months, he came to a regrettable conclusion. It had been a while since Hayley had been that adorable creature who could wind him around her little finger. More often than not, she was sulky, withdrawn. Even belligerent.

And he'd been too busy to address his daughter's behavior. He'd left that to Meg.

No wonder his wife upbraided him. Some kind of father he was.

He couldn't avoid a difficult question: How much of Hayley's unhappiness and rebellion was a result of the tension she'd sensed in his and Meg's marriage?

He rose to his feet, squared his shoulders and set off down the stairs. Hayley wouldn't be the only one facing the music today.

He would be, too.

TWICE MEG HAD PEEKED IN on Hayley. Twice she'd tiptoed away, satisfied she was still sleeping. She tried to put herself in Hayley's shoes. Waking up, dry-mouthed, furry-tongued, disoriented. Wondering what reaction she would get from her parents for coming home drunk. Wanting nothing more than to burrow under the covers and never emerge.

Leaving Hayley, Meg cracked Justin's door. He, too, was still asleep. Back downstairs, Meg noticed Bud and Marie had quietly finished breakfast. No one had raised the ugly subject of last night and the Harpers had discreetly withdrawn to the master bedroom. Scott sat in the recliner reading the Sunday paper. Meg felt the long, sleepless night catching up with her. Her eyes burned and her throat was scratchy. Pouring a second cup of coffee, she moved into the family room and curled up in a corner of the sofa. "Are we going to talk about it?" she asked.

"We have to, I guess. Pretty soon she'll be awake." He took his time putting aside the sports section. "This is not a conversation I'm looking forward to."

"I think first we need to listen to what she has to say."

Scott's expression darkened. "Listen?

What's to listen to? She knows how we feel about teenage drinking. She knows our rules. This has to be nipped in the bud."

Meg's stomach roiled. "You sound like a drill sergeant or a prison guard."

"That may be just what that daughter of ours needs."

"Scott, we won't get anywhere if you get yourself all worked up."

"So what's your solution? A gentle pat on the fanny and she's forgiven?"

"Here we go again."

"What do you mean 'here we go again'?"

"Your ideas on parenting went out with the Victorians."

Scott stood and paced to the window before turning around and glaring at her. "Well, I sure as hell am not an advocate of the laissez-faire discipline practiced by suburban soccer moms."

She flew off the couch. "Just a darned minute—"

"Meg, this isn't the time for hand-holding."

His condescension struck a nerve. "Who suddenly appointed you child psychologist?"

He spread his arms in frustration. "For once, can't we get our act together?"

"Oho! And what, pray tell, would that be like?"

He crowded her space. "Answer me one question. You're her mother. How could you not know what she was up to?"

"Her mother? Hell, yes, I'm her mother. But she has two parents last time I looked. Where were you when—"

"Stop it! Both of you!"

Meg wheeled around. Justin stood across the room, hands clapped over his ears, face pale, eyes rounded. "Justin, we—"

"Son—"

"I should've known better. Stupid me. I thought you two were actually getting along again."

"Again?" Scott took a step toward his son. "What do you mean?"

"I'm not stupid, you know. Ever since last summer, whenever you've both been at home, all you've done is rag on each other. But most of the time only one of you was even at home." His fingers played nervously over the buttons of his pajamas. "You want a big laugh? I really thought maybe that second honeymoon would help. Like maybe you wouldn't get a divorce... That maybe things would get better."

Meg reached for the sofa back to steady

herself. Any minute she thought her legs might fail her. In a tinny echo, she heard Scott say, "Divorce?"

Justin shrugged. "It happens. All the time. Lots of kids I know have divorced parents. It's no big deal. I figured it was just a matter of when."

Meg's voice came out as a whisper. "You really thought that? You've been worrying about us?"

"Duh. Me and Hayley never exactly talked about it, but we've both been scared."

Scott stared at his son. "It's a very big deal. Why didn't you say anything?"

"So what if I had? Would it have made any difference? You guys were gonna do what you were gonna do."

"We never—"

"Tell him the truth, Meg." Scott drilled her with his eyes.

How dare he put her in this position? As if their problems were her fault. "And just what is the truth?"

"We weren't getting along." Scott turned to Justin. "Your instincts were right on target."

The bones in Justin's face stood in sharp relief. "So when's the divorce going to happen?"

"Divorce!" Walking into the room, Hayley

took up her post beside her brother, her yellowish green complexion and shaking hands mute testimony to her condition. "What do you mean 'divorce'?" The word seemed to reverberate off every surface. Meg thought she might be sick.

"Everybody calm down here." Scott stood ramrod straight, his face a mask.

"Calm down?" Hayley said. "How am I supposed to calm down?"

"Because I say so," Scott snapped. "Not only are you going to calm down, you're going to do some explaining, young lady."

Justin gave his sister a sideways glance. "You look like dog crap."

She sent him a withering stare. "Shut up, you little twerp."

Meg felt as if she were caught in the grip of a powerful undertow. "Stop it!"

Scott moved toward the children. "Sit down, both of you."

They eyed him for a moment, and Meg wasn't sure they would obey, but finally they perched on the edge of the sofa.

"There isn't going to be a divorce," Scott said.

"What then?" Justin's expression was dubious.

Scott waved the question aside. "More about that later. Right now we're going to hear from Hayley." Meg watched the tic in his jaw, knowing he was churning inside. "And it better be good."

Justin inched down the sofa and turned to look at his sister. "What'd you do?"

Hayley held her head in her hands. "I don't feel so good."

"You have no right to feel good," Scott said. "That's one of the little consequences you pay for getting drunk."

"Drunk?" Justin's expression conveyed shock, a grudging awe and revulsion. "Great. I've got a lush for a sister and a mom and dad who fight all the time. Next thing you know, we'll be guests on one of those morning talk shows."

"Justin—" Meg managed the reproach.

"I want to go back and talk about the divorce," Hayley whined.

"I'll bet you do," Scott said. "That would take the spotlight off you."

Hayley tossed her head. "What's the big deal? So I had a few beers. All the kids do it. Did you think I was one of those straight-arrow kids who have no friends?" She gathered her hair in a hank. "Besides, it was better than hanging around here listening to the two of you go at it."

Scott's face was crimson. "We're not talking a few beers. We're talking crawling-on-your-knees drunk. And you will pay the price."

Meg wanted to intervene. Wanted to erase the tape of the past few minutes. To start over again. She scrambled for a way to shift the focus. To calm Scott down. To reassure Justin. Before she could say a word, though, Hayley rose to her feet, her body rigid, hands clenched by her sides. "You're ruining my life," she screamed. "I hate you!"

"Hate? Not good. Love. Everybody. Love."

Meg's chest deflated in one huge, mournful sigh. Bud, balanced on the walker, stood in the doorway, his face wet with tears.

JUSTIN FELT HIS GUT TWIST in a knot. Grampa looked shaky. Haggard. Old. He knew the feeling. He felt shaky, too, like in one of those sci-fi movies where you suddenly find yourself in a strange universe where you don't know what to do next.

His sister stood stock-still, her mouth an *O* of surprise. The shocked looks on his parents' faces were weird. Kind of like they were the little kids and had disappointed Grampa. Nobody said anything. The silence made him uncomfortable. He didn't know where to look. What to say. It was as if they'd all been playing Statues and were frozen in position.

"Love," Grampa repeated. "Always." Then he pulled this big, wrinkled white handkerchief out of his pocket and blew his nose.

Gramma had come up beside him. She patted his shoulder, then looked around the room, focusing on each of them in turn. "I try not to interfere in family matters. But I'm breaking my rule this morning. Everybody needs to step back before you say anything else you'll regret. Time out," she said. "Now."

Justin's jaw dropped. This was a new gramma, one he'd never seen before. Usually she was pretty easygoing. But looking at her, he knew she meant business.

His dad was the first to recover. "You're right, Mom." He glanced around at his family. "Things were getting hot. We still need to discuss this, but we should proceed calmly." He consulted his watch. "Come back here at noon. Everybody. I think it's time we had a family meeting."

Hayley escaped first, running up the stairs. Gramma started fussing in the kitchen, Dad accompanied Grampa down the hall to the master bedroom and Mom disappeared into the utility room. The only sounds were the distant pealing of church bells and an upstairs toilet flushing. Justin felt creepy, unsettled. Like something huge was about to happen, but he didn't know what.

Slowly he trudged up to his bedroom, shoving the door shut and sprawling on his bed. He'd never figure grown-ups out. Just when he'd thought his life was getting better. Grider and him were sorta getting along, he'd see Molly tomorrow at school, Grampa was improving and he'd noticed his parents had been acting more lovey-dovey lately. Now this.

He glanced at the open book on his bed. *To Kill a Mockingbird.* Mrs. Kelly would have a cow if she knew how much he liked the story. How he wished there were other books out there like this one. Atticus Finch was a really neat guy. Justin picked up the book, rolled on his side and started reading. Losing himself in this imaginary world beat the heck out of wondering what was going to happen next in the real one.

MEG BARELY MADE IT to the utility room before the tears came. She closed the door, and then, like a rag doll, slid to the tile floor where she sat, arms hugging her knees, letting convulsive sobs run their course. She felt raw, exposed, stripped of pretensions. What had happened in there? What should have been a calm discussion of ways to deal with Hayley had escalated into full-scale conflict. Scott had pressed all her old buttons. His father-knows-best attitude coupled with his not-so-subtle attacks on her parenting style infuriated her.

But knowing Hayley and Justin had been aware of their marital difficulties all along made her cover her face in shame. What kind of parents were they anyway? Scott was right. Meg had a more laissez-faire attitude than he did. To him, she probably seemed too soft. And his take-charge, nip-it-in-the-bud approach to discipline seemed overly harsh and unyielding to her. Somewhere between those two extremes had to be middle ground. At one time, she would have shrugged and given up, seeing separation as the only viable answer. Now, she knew that wouldn't work. Because the bottom line was she loved Scott and couldn't imagine life without him. But compromise wouldn't be easy.

If they could present a united front when

dealing with Kay, how much more important would it be to do the same when dealing with their kids?

She stood and absently began removing towels from the dryer, their softness and sunshine-fresh smell comforting. Would Scott meet her halfway? A last involuntary sob escaped her.

He had to.

She would go find him. Talk to him before the family meeting. She wiped her face on a hand towel, threw it back in with the dirty clothes and headed for the master bedroom.

"POPS, I'VE SCREWED UP. With Meg, with my kids. Everywhere."

Meg paused in the doorway, out of sight of the sitting room, but able to hear. The anguish in Scott's voice echoed her own. She knew she shouldn't eavesdrop, and yet...

"I love Meg, but somewhere along the line, I stopped paying attention to our marriage. This morning was a nightmare."

"What's important? To you?"

Though Bud sometimes chafed under the burden of his impaired speech, at other times, his terse, direct insights were more eloquent than the finest speaker's. Meg held her breath, straining to hear Scott's answer. The silence lengthened. Finally she heard Scott clear his throat.

"My wife and my family," he said simply.

"Advertising? Business?"

"Of course doing what I love excites me. I thrive on the challenges and I hope my work makes me a better man. But I've let it rule my life lately."

"Not good."

"I've taken Meg for granted."

"Not good, either."

"So, Pops, what do I do now?"

"Money. Mouth."

Meg couldn't help smiling.

"Huh?"

"Money. Mouth."

It was all she could do not to volunteer to translate: *Put your money where your mouth is.*

"Oh, I get it. Quit talking about putting my wife first and do it."

"Roger," Bud said.

"Any suggestions about where to start?"

Meg could've applauded when she heard Bud's reply. "Listen. Listen. Listen."

"Anything else?"

"Two people. Partnership. Not you. Not

Meg. But together. A partnership. No matter what."

"Good advice."

"Now. Talk to her. Listen."

Scott chuckled. "Sounds like I'm being dismissed."

"Time. Don't waste."

Scott's voice thickened, and Meg could imagine him wrapping Bud in a bear hug. "Thanks, Pops. I love you."

Meg darted down the hall and into the kitchen where Marie was busy fussing with the fridge. When she moved aside, Meg nearly laughed out loud. Her mother-in-law had rearranged all the refrigerator magnets, photos and artwork.

"I hope you don't mind," Marie said, sizing up Meg's reaction.

"Mind? It looks much better." And it did. What weeks earlier Meg would've interpreted as interference, she amazingly now welcomed as help.

When the phone rang, Meg picked it up, but heard male voices. Scott had already answered. "No, Kevin, I'm not going to make our game this morning.... Yeah, something's come up. Family." In his voice was pride, not resentment. Carefully, Meg placed the phone back in its cradle. For the first time that day, her spirits lifted. A partnership. Maybe, just maybe, that was possible.

Scott walked into the kitchen, appealing to her with his eyes. "Meggie, get your coat. Let's go for a walk."

She nodded and turned to Marie. "We'll be back soon."

Marie, her expression full of understanding, looked from one of them to the other. "I know." Then under her breath she said one more thing. "Forever and always."

THEY WALKED THE LENGTH of a block without speaking. It was a bright winter day. The sun shone through the bare branches, and a brisk wind stirred the dead leaves. Scott hesitated to speak, knowing a great deal depended on this conversation. Beside him, Meg kept pace, hands plunged deep into her coat pockets. He couldn't help remembering the walk they took into the Colorado forest, intent on settling the details of a separation. Yet, that hadn't happened. Recriminations, yes. Accusations, yes. But no decision. He reflected on the past few months. Something stronger than their own egos had kept them together. "The park okay? We can find a bench. Talk."

"Fine."

Another block, another five minutes, and they'd be there. Settling the future once and for all. Her blond hair, lifted by the wind, shone in the brittle sunlight, and her skin was rosy with cold and exertion. But the deep caverns of her eyes betrayed her restless night. And the misery of that morning's confrontation.

"Over here?" He gestured to a bench shielded from the wind by a tall hedge.

"Okay."

They sat huddled together, he with his folded hands dangling between his knees. "I'll start," he said. "That was miserable this morning. Did you listen to us? What were we doing? To ourselves? To our family? It was insane."

Meg appeared to be studying the ball field off in the distance.

"I never talked with you about how we should handle Hayley," he confessed.

"No, you didn't."

"Am I always like that?"

She looked at him, and, for a brief second, he thought he saw the hint of a smile on her lips. "Pretty much." Then the smile faded. "For the most part, you've left the parenting to me, but then you sweep in and second-guess my decisions. I understand that at work you're used to being in charge. But we've been sending our kids mixed messages. We need to see eye to eye on things."

"Be a partnership?"

Again, the hint of a smile. "Yes."

He reached down, picked up a stone, then arched it high over the sidewalk. "Justin blew me away today."

"You mean about the divorce?"

"Yeah, I mean, where would he have gotten that idea?"

"Kids are intuitive. And we haven't exactly been modeling a happy relationship."

"Until the past few days."

"Agreed. But this morning we were back to our same old pattern."

"I don't like it," he said.

"What?"

"The pattern. I get controlling, you either light into me or clam up and then we each go off in our separate directions."

"Not a prescription for happiness."

"And you're right. I don't spend enough time at home."

"And I'm not as supportive of your work as I should be."

He turned toward her. "So what now?" His

eyes searched hers. "There's no more stalling. Whatever we say in the family meeting today has to be the truth."

"What is the truth, Scott?"

He gripped her hand, knowing he was making a pledge that this time he would honor. No matter what. "I love you, Meggie. You are the most important thing in my life. You come first. I won't ever forget that again. I'll do whatever it takes to make you happy."

Meg lowered her eyes and took a deep breath. On a nearby tree limb, squirrels chattered, then chased each other to a different tree. Scott waited, his heart beating a tattoo. When she finally looked up, tears glistened on her lashes. "I love you, too. More than anything. I've smothered you with my expectations. Today, I want to set you free."

What did she mean? Did she *want* a separation after all? "Free?" His voice cracked just like Justin's.

"I fell in love with a talented, ambitious man. Then, out of my own needs, I tried to turn you into someone else. It wasn't fair."

"What are you saying?" He struggled to his feet, pulling her up with him. "I don't want to leave. I can't leave."

"Leave?" Her arms went around his neck

and her laughter echoed in the wintry air. "Leave? I certainly hope not. What I mean is that I'm going to put you first and give you the freedom to become the best darned ad exec in the world."

"And the best husband, I hope." He lifted her into his arms, burying his head in her neck. "You had me scared there."

She giggled in his ear. "Good. I don't ever want you to get complacent." Then she slid down his chest to the ground again, and with a voice so sexy it nearly made him hard, said, "I'll do my best to keep you off guard."

"I can't wait." He looked around them. "Too bad there's not a convenient grove of lilacs."

She laughed. "In your dreams."

Then he sobered. "Meggie, it really is going to be all right, isn't it?"

She picked up his hands and brought them up against her chest. "Yes, Scott, it is. You know why? Because it's up to us. And I trust us. Now."

He nodded in agreement, feeling as if the weight of the world had been removed from his shoulders. "What about the kids?"

"We owe them the truth."

"And Hayley?"

"Let's hear her out. We don't have to make any snap judgments."

Now, he felt a grin breaking across his own face. "You mean I should listen?"

She pretended to be considering the idea. "Listen? Hmm. Yes, I think that would be a wise course of action."

"But something of a novelty for me, right?"

She stood on tiptoes and kissed his cheek. "Yes, but a talent you'll master with time."

He chuckled. "If I know what's good for me."

She corrected him. "Good for us, Scott. Good for us."

Arm in arm they walked back toward the house. Together. He liked the sound of it. The feel of it. A partnership.

WHEN THE GRANDFATHER CLOCK struck twelve, Justin's stomach turned to jelly. He hadn't been able to concentrate on his book because he'd kept looking at his watch. The family meeting loomed. He didn't have a good feeling about it. All of this was his fault. Why had he ever said the word *divorce* out loud? Now his mom and dad would feel free to talk about it. To tell him and Hayley news he didn't want to hear. Never wanted to hear.

Who would he live with? Would they have to move? Would he have to change schools? He shut his eyes tight. He couldn't imagine any of it. Wouldn't let himself think about it. It was too scary.

Then came the tap on his door and his dad's voice. "Justin, come on downstairs now."

He hugged his pillow. He didn't want to leave his bedroom. As long as he stayed there, maybe nothing would change. He would be safe. He heard Hayley come out of her room and start down the stairs. Whoa. What if he and Hayley had to split up? He'd heard of that. One kid lives with the father, one with the mother. That would suck. Hayley was a pain, but she was the only sister he had. He guessed she really wasn't too bad.

"Justin?" His mother called him from downstairs.

He climbed off the bed and then took one last look around the room. His model airplanes and soccer trophies, the O.U. Sooners' poster on the wall, the terrarium on his dresser. He knew he was being stupid. But it felt like he wouldn't see these things again. Or if he did, they'd never look the same to him.

"Justin? We're waiting."

Okay, he wouldn't chicken out. He turned

the doorknob, walked into the hall and, with a big sigh, ran down the stairs.

The rest of them were already there. His sister had combed her hair and put on some lipstick. She looked like maybe she just might live. He joined her on the sofa. Gramma sat in the rocker beside Grampa who was stretched out in the recliner. His folks had pulled in stools from the kitchen. His mom sat on one, but his dad stood behind her, his hands resting on her shoulders. Funny thing. She didn't look mad. In fact, while he watched, she reached up and took hold of his dad's hand. Weird.

"Let's start again," his dad said. "Our last discussion got out of hand."

"No kidding," Hayley muttered under her breath.

Justin poked her. Something was different about Dad. He didn't want Hayley messing it up with her sarcasm. "Shh."

"It's time, I think, that we got some things out in the open." He turned to look at Justin. "Son, you mentioned divorce. Obviously you'd picked up on the fact that your mother and I weren't getting along."

Justin concentrated on sitting still instead of fidgeting.

"That must've worried you."

Justin lowered his eyes, then nodded his head.

Dad turned to Hayley next. "What about you? Were you worried, too?"

She nodded. "You acted like you didn't even like each other. It really hurt to see you like that. I hoped the trip to Colorado would help. But I was so afraid when it didn't."

Mom dropped her hand to her lap. "Is that why you've been spending so much time in your room?"

"Well, yeah. Who wants to hang around and listen to their parents fight? Or worse than that, ignore each other?"

Hayley's face was turning red. Justin was afraid she was going to cry. He knotted his hands in his lap.

"This isn't going to be easy," his mother continued, "but we owe you the truth. Before our anniversary we were considering a separation."

Justin felt as if he'd been socked in the stomach. "What happened?" A tiny spark of hope lit the dark place inside him. "Why didn't you separate?"

Grampa spoke up. "Me. Sick person. Stroke."

The spark of hope flickered. "So you just postponed it to take care of Grampa?"

"At first," his father said carefully. "But lots of things have changed."

Hayley sat forward. "Like what?"

Mom looked at Gramma and Grampa. "Having your grandparents here, seeing how they've handled this situation, all of us working together to help, it's taught us a lot about what's important."

"Love," Grampa said in a loud voice.

"Yes, love," Dad agreed. "When you boil it down, all we have is each other. Jobs and houses come and go. But family is forever." He leaned over and kissed the top of Mom's head. "There isn't going to be any divorce. No separation. I love your mother. That's what's important."

Justin hadn't realized he'd been sitting there with his fingers crossed. He let out a big sigh of relief and uncrossed them.

His mother went on. "We love you kids, too." She glanced at his grandparents. "And you, Bud and Marie. You two have taught Scott and me that nothing is as important as a solid marriage, especially during difficult times. I hope it's a lesson we can model for Hayley and Justin."

"Partners," his grandfather grunted with satisfaction.

There was a long silence. Then Hayley spoke in a soft voice. "I screwed up."

"Tell us why you did it," Dad said. And he didn't even look ticked.

"I know better. I was just so mad. You guys were acting so prickly. I just wanted to stay away from home as much as I could so I wouldn't have to watch."

His mother raised her eyebrows. "Zach Simon?"

"Yeah." She hung her head. "At first I thought he was really cool. But then..." her voice trailed off "...then he was like all over me. I hated my life, so I started drinking with him. For a little while it made me forget."

"You mean forget what was going on at home?" Dad sounded tired.

"Yeah. I kept thinking you guys would stop me."

For once, Justin could understand how his sister felt. Scared to death. The same way he'd felt in English class when he couldn't read. The way he'd been afraid of Sam Grider. Hoping his parents could somehow rescue him.

Dad choked on his words. "And we didn't."

"Only today," Hayley whispered.

Dad crossed the room in two steps and pulled Hayley into his arms. "I'm so sorry, honey."

"A new day," Grampa said.

Mom had this funny, kind of mushy expression on her face. She smiled at Grampa. "You're right, Bud. Today is a new day. I propose that we let bygones be bygones and start fresh from right now." She walked over to Hayley and Dad. "Hey, you two, can anyone join this group hug?"

Hayley sniffled and embraced their mother. "You bet," Dad said, kissing Mom's cheek. "And I think Hayley would agree we can forget the past. Somehow I think, along with the rest of us, she's learned her lesson."

Justin wasn't much for hugging, but he was so relieved there wasn't going to be any divorce that when his father looked at him over his sister's shoulder and beckoned to him, Justin let himself be drawn in. The strange thing was, it felt sort of good.

Out of the corner of his eye, he saw Gramma get up out of her chair and go give Grampa a kiss. He'd always thought old people kissing would be gross. But it wasn't. In fact, it was really nice. Who'd have guessed?

His grandparents were still in love. He thought about his family. They weren't perfect, none of them. But everything was going to be all right.

And just in case he doubted it, he stepped back and watched his father lay a big kiss on his mother. They were still in love, too.

It didn't get much better than that.

MEG WAITED IN THE LOBBY just outside the Sunrise Manor dining room, while Scott parked the car. Cutouts of cupids and hearts adorned the walls, red-and-white crepe-paper streamers crisscrossed the ceiling and on each table were lacy Valentine doilies and tiny paper cups filled with heart candies. Love was alive and well among the geriatric set. Meg suppressed a smile. Just last week Marie had told her about a widower and a widow who were conducting a courtship under the eagle eyes of their fellow residents.

After Scott joined her, he peered into the dining room. "Looks like we're a bit early for the festivities."

"Maybe not." She nodded toward the study where several gray-haired ladies dolled up in their finest sat expectantly on the edge of tapestried chairs. "Should we go up to the apartment?"

"No, Mom and Pops said they'd meet us here."

Behind them the elevator doors opened and began discharging passengers, all making a beeline for the dining room except for one tiny lady dressed in a red velvet skirt and frilly white blouse who approached them. "Excuse me, but aren't you Bud and Marie's family?"

"Yes, we are," Scott said.

"They've been a lovely addition to the manor. Marie has already joined our bridge foursome, and they're both looking forward to our bus trip next month to Branson."

"They've settled in better than we thought," Meg said.

"Well, it's not exactly where any of us wants to end up, but the point is to make the best of the situation." She laid a heavily veined, diamond-encrusted hand on Scott's lapel and smiled reassuringly. "And they are. Don't you worry."

Scott picked up her hand and gently squeezed it. "Thank you."

Don't you worry. Meg had worried. A lot. And she knew Scott had, as well. Once Bud had made up his mind to move into the retirement center, there had been no holding him back. Still, as she and Scott had sorted through the details of selling the motor home, getting furnishings out of storage, decorating the apartment and moving them, Meg couldn't help wondering if they shouldn't have asked Bud and Marie to live permanently with them. But she had to admit to a sense of relief at having more free time, getting her home back, seeing her children happy and coming to new understandings with Scott.

"Party. Ready?" Bud stepped off the second elevator, his eyes twinkling. From somewhere, he had resurrected a bright red polyester sport jacket. He no longer needed the walker and, instead, sported a fancy cane. Quite the dapper cupid.

Marie, wearing the same lavender evening gown she'd worn to Meg and Scott's anniversary party, smiled in greeting. "He doesn't want to miss the first dance."

Giving a headwaiter bow, Scott let them go ahead. "Lead on, then."

After they reached their table, they were served fruit punch and a heart-shaped tart. A deejay played tunes from the forties and fifties, and several residents took to the center of the room swaying to the music. When Bud stood and led Marie to the dance floor, Scott clasped Meg's hand under the table. Marie melted into her husband's arms, and although Bud could only shuffle in place, partially supported by Marie, it was a tender moment.

"They're beautiful, aren't they?" Meg whispered.

Scott's eyes watered. "I never thought—" He couldn't finish.

"I know. That it could possibly turn out this well."

As if by way of convincing himself, he said, "They do seem happy, don't you think?"

She rested her head on his shoulder. "Look at them." Marie was kissing her husband's cheek. "They have each other."

Scott's arm went around her shoulder. "And I have you. When I think how close I came to losing you—"

"And I you."

He nuzzled her neck. "I'm glad you wore that sexy black dress I like. Just wait till I get you to bed."

"Ahem. Interrupting? Us?" Bud had a Cheshire-cat grin on his face. The music had stopped.

"Just whispering sweet nothings in my Valentine's ear, Pops."

"Good," Bud said, holding the chair for Marie. "You take care. Daughter."

Scott looked deep into Meg's eyes. "I intend to."

The activities director took the microphone then, and while he made a series of announcements, Meg nibbled on the tart. When he finished, Marie spoke. "Will Hayley and Justin be coming here Sunday afternoon as usual?"

Justin enjoyed reading the sports page to Bud and, to Meg's amazement, Hayley had taken an interest in helping a few of the other residents with their therapy. At a recent career day at the high school, she'd picked up some brochures about opportunities in physical and speech therapy. Thankfully, Zach Simon was a thing of the past. And best of all, Hayley had confided that drinking wasn't that cool.

The party ended after an hour. When Meg suggested they go up to the apartment for a cup of decaf coffee, Marie and Bud exchanged a mischievous look. "Not tonight, dear," Marie said.

Scott held out Meg's coat. "No, I have other plans for you."

"You do?" She remembered his remark about getting her into bed.

He winked at his parents. "A surprise."

"Valentine's Day. Happy," Bud said.

Meg gave him a quick kiss on the cheek. "Happy Valentine's Day to you, too, Pops." She hugged Marie. "And to you."

"Love." Bud nodded his head. "It's good."

It was better than good, Meg thought, as her handsome husband escorted her to the car and opened the door for her. He was so much more relaxed now that the Jordan ad campaign was going well. In fact, he'd handed over a portion of the responsibilities to others in the firm, having finally admitted that delegating was a pretty sound concept.

Several blocks later, Meg became concerned. "This isn't the way home. Where are you going?"

"*We* are going someplace special to celebrate Valentine's Day."

"We are?" She couldn't believe it. A romantic gesture? That wasn't exactly Scott's forte.

He drew up in front of a lovely Victorian home near the downtown area. "Here we are," he said, pointing to the sign. "Homestead House: An Urban Inn."

"But…but…the children?"

"All taken care of. You thought they were visiting friends, but believe it or not, they were already at Sunrise Manor this evening. In the guest suite. I thought you'd prefer that to leaving them alone overnight. Which means, my sweet, that you and I have hours and hours to ourselves in the big four-poster, king-size bed waiting for us inside."

He looked so pleased with himself that she almost laughed. Except she couldn't. Her heart was beating too fast, her breath coming too rapidly, her insides quivering too shakily. "I can't wait," she whispered before being engulfed in his arms.

Later, sated from making love in front of the gas fire and dazed from the way he made her feel as if she were the only woman in the world, she laid her head on his chest and smiled to herself.

"Happy?" he murmured.

"Ecstatic."

"I have one other surprise."

"Ooh, I don't know how much more of this pampering I can take."

"It'll never be enough."

When had her husband mastered the art of pillow talk?

He turned on the lamp and opened the bedsidetable drawer. "Here."

He handed her a thick white envelope.

She sat up in bed, pulling the blanket over her breasts. "What's this?"

"Remember that second honeymoon?"

"Yes."

"We never completed it."

She opened the envelope and pulled out the contents. Looking at what she held in her hands, she gasped. The itinerary for a June Alaskan cruise. She looked up, baffled. "How? What...?"

"Jannie helped me. She and Ron said this was the best trip they ever took." He played with her hair. "Nothing but the finest for my wife."

She couldn't get her hopes up. Face disappointment. Better settle it now. "We can't get away for this long. The agency... And the kids—"

"All arranged. Wes will cover the office. And the kids are staying with Mom and Pops in the guest suite at the manor."

"They'd do that?"

"It was their idea. Believe it or not, my folks have even talked Kay into coming to help with the kids' errands, et cetera. She didn't even put up an argument. Maybe she's finally developing a conscience."

"But—"

He stopped her with his mouth, kissing her most expertly and thoroughly. "A second honeymoon. A real one this time."

He had actually planned this, down to every detail. At last, they were going on a trip. Just the two of them. Suddenly, though, that didn't matter nearly as much as the fact that their marriage was solid, and that, more than ever, they were in love with each other. Forever and always, as Marie had said.

Meg drew his face close to hers. "Moving back into our own bedroom with the man I love was enough honeymoon for me." Then she added with an impish smile, "But I'll take the trip, too."

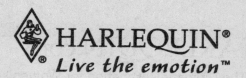
HARLEQUIN®
Live the emotion™

Upbeat,
All-American Romances

 flipside
Romantic Comedy

 Harlequin Historicals®
Historical,
Romantic Adventure

 INTRIGUE®
Romantic Suspense

HARLEQUIN®
HARLEQUIN ROMANCE®
The essence of
modern romance

Seduction and passion
guaranteed

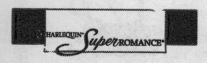
Emotional,
Exciting, Unexpected

Sassy, Sexy, Seductive!

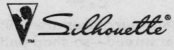